WITH
DRIVE
OPPORTUNITY

WITH
DRIVE
OPPORTUNITY

A journey into protest, told as a series of lifts

PETE GRUGEON

SCORPIUS BOOKS

First published in 2025 by Scorpius Books Ltd

ISBN: 978 1 9193139 2 4

A CIP catalogue record for this book is available from the British Library.

Printed and bound in Great Britain by CMP Books.

Scorpius Books have made a commitment to reducing their environmental footprint and being good stewards of the planet.

www.scorpiusbooks.com

In memory of Bee Tilney
1970 – 2023
She was incredibly cool

I would like to thank:
My partner Anna, without whom this book
would have been impossible to write and
whom I love more than all the stuff in the
Universe(s).

My sister Elf, who read the first draft, which
I thought just needed proof reading, broke
it to me that it needed a lot more work and
helped me to improve it.

Alice, Ellen, Clare and all my other friends,
who read the manuscript and made
comments which have made it a much better
book.

Tom, who read it whilst laughing out loud
and told me to get on and publish it.

Introduction

The first time I ever hitched a lift I was nine years old.

We lived in the middle of nowhere on a winding road, a road which was normally only used by ourselves and our neighbours. There were exceptions. Sometimes, in the early hours of the morning, knowing that the road would be empty, people would race around the country lanes in cars and on motorbikes.

Very occasionally, a driver would find themselves there, having got very lost. If you were at one end of the lane and wanted to get to the other end, it was quicker to use the straighter roads to go around than it was to drive down it.

To get our milk, we used to walk down the road to a dairy farm and dip two small churns in the milk tank. As kids, we all used to take turns to get the milk as part of our chores. It was when collecting milk that I decided to try hitching. I'd seen a man in a film hitching. I'd seen him put his thumb out and a car pulled up and gave him a lift.

This seemed to a very young me, to be a great way of getting around, but I'd seen a lot of stuff on films and I knew not all of it was true.

I was walking back with, what were to me, two very heavy churns of milk, when our neighbours, the Farkases, drove down the road towards me. As I have said, not many people used our road. I recognised the Farkas' Range Rover and as they came closer, I could see their wrinkly old faces. I put my thumb out and waited to see if they would recognise the signal and give me a lift.

I was chuffed when they pulled up next to me. Not only had I saved myself from carrying the heavy churns, which have thin wire handles which are uncomfortable on your hands, I had also discovered a method of transport which didn't require me to get a vehicle or a licence.

When Mrs Farkas lent out of the window to speak to me, the lecture began.

'You shouldn't hitchhike, Jason. You don't know who's going to pick you up.'

This made no sense at all. I knew exactly who was going to pick me up. I had seen their wrinkly old faces. It was completely unrealistic to imagine that they were going to magically change into other people, and I'd find myself getting a lift with strangers.

It's difficult when you're a child and adults come out with complete twaddle like this. If you point out, with a good basis in fact, that they're acting like idiots, you're told off for being cheeky. I was only too aware of this the age of nine, which didn't always stop me, but on this occasion it did.

I exchanged a lift in their car for my silence during the journey and my acceptance of the lecture. The only break in the lecture was when Mr Farkas interrupted it to lecture me on not spilling any milk in their car. By the time we'd reached our house, a journey which took less than two minutes, my ears were ringing from the ongoing drone of their scaremongering nonsense.

I got out of the car, thinking that although this had been an unpleasant lift, I had learnt something about hitching and something about the stupidity of my neighbours. To my great surprise, Mr and Mrs Farkas also got out of the car. They went to my house and then I got a repeat of the lecture as they told my mum how dangerously I had acted and how she should make sure I don't repeat this irresponsible act.

'There are dangerous people out there,' Mrs Farkas declared.

'And idiots,' I thought.

I could never have imagined at that young age how much my life would be influenced by the lifts I'd get. These lifts would go far beyond getting me from A to B. The conversations and experiences that I'd have due to lifts I was given by others would influence my thoughts, my values and my approach to life itself.

Reliving them now, running through them in my mind allows me an otherwise unachievable freedom.

It's ironic really that my form of escapism is to relive the experiences which led me here, to this prison cell.

Madcap

Sometimes people appear in your life through random coincidence and change its direction completely. Like this warm day in the spring of 1995...

I've been watching the hill opposite for a number of hours now, or at least I think it's been a number of hours.

It was still dark when I came and sat here and started staring at the hill and now the sun sits just above it in the distance. It's starting its next journey across the sky before settling back down below the horizon.

This party will carry on through that cycle and beyond, but it'll carry on without me. I have a new job lined up and I need to wake up tomorrow, back in Ashford, ready to start.

It's not far from here to the M5 and from there the hitch back to Ashford should be fairly easy. I have my magic sign in my bag, which Josh and Jess made me last night. It just said M5 on it originally, but they decorated it with stickers and glitter and wrote good luck notes all over it.

They made me promise I'd use it. I'm aware that because of all the extra décor it really isn't that clear to read from a distance, but it'll be fine so long as I've got a reasonable hitching spot, where the traffic is slow enough for the drivers to get a good look.

As I stand up to get going, I realise how much my legs ache from dancing.

I grin to myself; it's been an amazing party and I do question whether I should leave yet, but if I sit down again, I doubt I'll be able to get back up. I can see the road off in the distance and luckily for me, it's downhill all the way from here.

I swing my leg out and let gravity do its thing, landing my weight hard as my foot hits the ground. I then repeat the trick with the next leg. The result is a walk that probably looks from a distance like my legs are in splints.

From my point of view, the track below with cars parked up on either side looks to be swishing around like a hyperactive snake. I decide to walk normally after a few steps because, although I find this walk quite funny, my knees are starting to hurt. The track below is now gently swaying back and forth in the morning haze.

As I reach the track, some funky tune starts up on the nearest sound-system and I'm strutting along enjoying every last minute of this party whilst it's still in earshot.

Strolling past a van which is painted with hundreds of stencilled handprints in different shades of green and brown, all overlapping each other to create a camouflage effect, I notice a strong smell of doughnuts.

This makes me consider whether some sort of breakfast would be a good idea. I can see where this little track into the hills reaches the road that goes to the M5. It looks like it's a long way off, but it's a lovely morning and I don't mind starting it with a little ramble in the countryside.

What I don't see is the legs sticking out from under the van. Having tripped over them, tried and failed to regain my balance, I'm now face down in a big puddle of terracotta-coloured mud.

Turning around, I see a woman in a boiler suit with various colourful items hanging from her long black dreadlocked hair, pulling herself out from under the van. I try to apologise, but just succeed in swallowing and choking on the mud which is dripping down my face.

Clearly, she's not too hurt, because she's now laughing at me. She stands up and offers me a hand to help me to my feet.

When I'm stood up, I try to apologise again, but again I swallow mud, although mercifully less this time.

Again, she laughs.

Finally, I manage to splutter an apology and start walking away. She asks where I'm going and if I need a lift.

I tell her I'm going to Kent and if she could get me to the M5 I'd be very grateful.

She says that she can do better than that as she's going to a protest camp in Kent.

Thank you, Josh and Jess; it seems that your hitching sign has worked its magic without even being taken out of my bag.

The van is actually an old ambulance, or to be more accurate it's an extremely old ambulance, and both the woman whom I have just met and the bloke in the driving seat seem relieved when it starts.

Inside, every square inch is covered in one sort of decoration or another. Some of it has an Indian theme, but also there are photos of past adventures, protest stickers, flyers, posters and all sorts of psychedelic patterns.

In my present post-party state it looks amazing!

The woman's name is Kath, and her partner is Dave.

Dave has a grin on his face and eyes the size of saucers. His hair looks like it was once light brown, but is now mainly grey and is very thin except for tufts around his ears, which seem to have survived the balding process.

He puts the van into gear and carefully drives it from the verge onto the road and then off the road again on the other side and into a rock which is sticking out of the ground. Then putting it into reverse, backs onto the road, suddenly jamming the brakes on, stopping just inches off the car behind us.

After a few attempts, Dave manages to engage first gear and we're off down the road. His grin has remained completely static through the whole operation.

I'm not entirely sure he's in a fit state to drive.

The van's suspension is super-light, creating the sensation that the body of the van is floating above its wheels. This should make for a luxurious ride, but there seems to be something wrong with the steering, causing the wheels to move in an erratic manner with constant oversteering and corrections, and the body seems to be spending the whole time trying to catch up with the latest change of direction.

As we move on to a better, straighter road and from there on to the M5, this becomes less of an issue and I'm feeling slightly less nervous.

I can see from the stickers, flyers and posters that Kath and Dave have been heavily involved with the Criminal Justice Bill protests. I make some comment about it being surprising that any democracy would want to ban parties and protests.

Dave looks at me with what looks like astonishment, but it might just be due to his excessively wide eyes.

'We're not in a democracy. Far from it. We're subjects ruled over by a monarch and an establishment with limited democratic concessions. They allow us to vote periodically to create the illusion of democracy, but the system is designed to reduce interference by the plebs to an absolute minimum.'

My comment about democracy and banning parties and protests was just a throwaway comment. It was intended as an attempt at making conversation. I didn't think it would be in any way controversial. I've been up all night and my brain isn't functioning at full capacity, so I don't know how well I can follow anything right now.

I'm interested in what he has to say though. Anyway, him and Kath are giving me a lift all the way to Kent, so I'm along for the ride. I might as well sit back and enjoy it.

'Our electoral system allows one party to rule without consulting anyone outside the party. Within the party, power is concentrated, solely in the prime minister. He or she has more power than any western president. If you raise the subject of getting rid of the monarch, someone will almost certainly bring up the repugnant concept of President Thatcher.'

As Dave concentrates more on what he's saying, he concentrates less on the road and starts to drift into the next lane. I try to say something, but can't get a word in edgeways.

When he's about halfway between lanes, he suddenly realises and swerves back. The flow of his rant isn't interrupted at all.

'Of course, absolutely no sane person relishes the idea of President Thatcher, but it's much more palatable than having Thatcher as a prime minister was.'

I'm looking at Dave in complete disbelief. Every indication of his views, from the décor of his van to his personal appearance, is at odds with him advocating that Thatcher should have been president rather than prime minister, yet that seems to be his position.

'As a prime minister, she determined which MPs got ministerial positions and by controlling their promotion prospects, she could manipulate them to do her bidding.

'If that didn't elicit the desired response, the whips would subjugate them using blackmail and bribery. Whips know all about MPs private lives and can completely destroy an MP that steps out of line. Along with her use of the royal prerogative, this gave Thatcher almost unlimited power over the executive and the legislature, something that presidents can only dream of.

'It suits the establishment to concentrate power in the hands of an individual, because it's much easier for them to control one person than a whole chamber.'

Dave hasn't paused for breath and seems to be picking up pace as this rant goes on. He's started punctuating his speech by hitting the steering wheel as he makes significant points, which isn't doing his ability to steer properly any favours at all.

He's managing to stay mainly in one lane though, which is comforting.

'She completely dominated the executive and the Commons and to some extent, control over the judiciary through the Lord Chancellor.

'Then, of course, we have the second chamber, the House of Lords. How do you obtain a seat in the second chamber? You can suck up to the royal family, become a bishop or a top judge, fund a political party, be friends with or have something over a party leader or you could be there because some ancestor of yours provided sanctuary for the bastard son of a monarch or did a monarch some other favour, centuries ago. This is all far-removed from democracy.'

For the first time since I got in the van, the fixed grin has gone from Dave's face and has been replaced with an expression of frustration as he spits these words out in anger. I almost regret my comment about democracy, but I'm interested in what he has to say and it's clear that he's got a point to make and he's going to make it.

'It's a crazy little mix of aristocracy, theocracy, oligarchy and kritocracy, with a little bit of plutocracy, kleptocracy and nepotism thrown in for good measure.

'One thing you can be certain of is that absolutely none of them represent you or anything like you. Almost exclusively, they represent sections of society which are already over-represented.

'They're seen as a necessary check on the House of Commons by otherwise discerning people, because the Commons is designed to be so utterly corrupt and top heavy. They're the representatives of the establishment, there to ensure the section of the political system which is influenced by the plebs doesn't infringe upon the interests of the establishment.'

He's getting quite red in the face, but thankfully managing to stay fairly well in the middle of the lane we're in, which I appreciate.

'This brings us to the monarch themselves, who we are told is a steadying figure over parliament and simultaneously, apolitical. Well, I'm very bloody sorry, but you can't be both. She's not apolitical at all. She's exploited the Queens Consent rules to conceal her investments, exempt herself from equality laws and who knows what else. Us plebs are not allowed to know anything about the power she has or see the papers which document how previous monarchs have used their powers. Going to the library to look up *Queens Consent* would be fruitless. There won't be anything there explaining it, that's how covert these powers are.'

It seems unreal that there's part of our constitution where the Queen can change laws in secret. It sounds a bit like a conspiracy theory. He seems convinced that it's true though.

"She has immense influence through her connections, within and outside the country. Why would she hold a private meeting with the prime minister on a weekly basis, if she wasn't influencing policy? They hardly meet up weekly to discuss the bloody weather! In fact, we're told she has a right, nay a duty to counsel, encourage and warn the prime minister. That's lobbying to you and me.'

At this point, Kath starts climbing out of her seat into the back of the van, saying: 'Enough listening to your rant, I'm going to sleep'.

'Do you not agree with him?' I ask.

'Oh, no, to be fair, it's entirely true. I've just heard this one before,' she responds and then closes the curtain.

Dave continues to tell me all about his political

views. He explains how the state has slowly evolved from an absolute monarchy to the mishmash of a system that we have today, through the monarch and then lower levels of established power walking the tightrope of retaining as much power as they can, whilst avoiding a revolution.

He believes the threat of revolution, or at least severe disruption, is always required to persuade the establishment to allow change that assists the lower classes.

Everything he says makes sense. I'm aware I'm tired and still a bit spangly from the party, so not in the best position to judge how true all this is. He speaks in a very persuasive tone, which, I'm aware makes it all the more convincing.

Even though I've never heard anyone discuss the political system like this, it fits in with what little I know about the subject, other than that bit about the queen secretly changing laws.

'The suffragists,' he says, 'politely petitioned Parliament from the 1870s onwards, asking them if they'd be so kind as to allow women to vote. Then the suffragettes started carrying out militant actions in the early part of the twentieth century, including arson and bombings, and within a few years the first women were allowed to vote. This was at the same time as non-property-owning men returning from the first world war were given the vote.

'It's not that the establishment discussed it and thought that extending the franchise was probably the morally appropriate course of action. The powers that be were faced with a simple choice. Either give these people the vote, or expect the men who had been taught to kill and desensitised to killing through war to turn their anger on the establishment, whilst the suffragettes increase their militancy and go beyond burning buildings down.

'You have to bear in mind that this followed the 1917 revolution in Russia when the King's cousin and other members of the Russian branch of the European Royal Family had been killed. The King and the establishment had everything to lose and were terrified. Therefore they had no option but to support the expansion of the franchise.'

The A303 sign appears. I would have taken motorways back to Ashford, but Dave and Kath have chosen the more scenic route. Dave pulls off the motorway and the issues with the van's steering become apparent again as it sways around, seemingly out of control.

He changes out of fourth gear. He tries to engage third but fails. The gearstick is now moving freely, seemingly attached to nothing.

Dave loses his concentration and the van wobbles around even more, as if he's entirely forgotten to steer. With a look of determination on his face, he pulls over on to the side of the road. The gearstick has now flopped down towards me, far further than it should be able to go.

Kath is gently snoring in the back.

'Oh dear,' he says quietly. He then climbs into the back to wake Kath up. 'Kath. Kath, there's something wrong with the van.'

Soon she's back under the van, with her legs sticking out like they were when I tripped over them. I make a point of not tripping over them this time.

She emerges to announce that the universal joint on the gear linkage is broken. From the look on his face, I can see this means nothing more to Dave than it does to me.

He puts the kettle on whilst Kath searches the van for something.

After some rummaging, she steps out of the van with a toolbox, two forks and a happy look on her face. She bends some of the prongs on the forks over with a pair of pliers and crawls back under the van.

Dave steps out and hands me a cup of tea. I dig out some biscuits and samosas from my bag. The biscuits at one end of the packet are just crumbs now.

I hitched to Devon with them, and they spent the duration of the party in my bag.

I open the packet at the other end where they're

just slightly broken. I bought the samosas in the early hours of this morning in the mistaken belief I was hungry. They're only a little squashed.

Dave gets out some cake and other snacks and by the time Kath has fixed the "universal joint", we're already enjoying our breakfast by the side of the road.

Kath drives for the next stretch of the journey and Dave is asleep in the back. I soon realise there's nothing wrong with the steering on the van; with Kath driving it seems fine.

She puts a cassette of the Tofu Love Frogs on. They're supposed to be playing tonight at the party I just left. This is the third time I've nearly seen them play, but missed them for one reason or another.

We chat about protest and parties and politics. She tells me about the protest camp they're going to. Apparently, they're building a new road right through an ancient woodland. It'll shave ten minutes off people's journeys by destroying a rich ecosystem which has taken thousands of years to evolve.

It doesn't sound like a great idea, but I'm not convinced that they're going to stop building it just because some hippies set up camp there.

I ask Kath if she thinks the protest will be successful, and she asks me to define success. In this case it seems pretty obvious what success would look like. If they gave up on the road and left the woods alone, that would be the mark of a successful protest.

Kath laughs when I say this and says that by that definition, the protest will not be successful.

I ask her how she would define success.

'It could take many forms, to be fair,' Kath says. 'If you look on protests as divided neatly into success and failure, with success being that the protest achieves all of its objectives, and failure being any other outcome, you'll give up after your first few protests. You have to look at it more as chipping away at the system that you're fighting. If you can chip away just a little, or at least prevent its advance, you're doing well. When you're protesting against a road, success may come in the form of another similarly badly thought through road not being built, or even being moved to a less damaging route, to be fair.'

I ask her if she feels there's a reasonable prospect of that happening as a result of this protest. As I do so, we come up behind an estate car with a roof-rack, crawling along at 30 miles per hour.

'For fucks sake,' Kath mutters at the car whilst gesturing with one hand. 'If you don't want to go anywhere, just pull off the fucking road and park up.'

Then glancing briefly towards me and smiling, she says, 'I don't know, but to be fair, the reason they build roads through woodland is because the land has a low monetary value, so it's cheap to build a road through it. We're going to make it bloody expensive to build through this bit of woodland, so maybe that will make them think.'

At this point, Dave clambers over into the front and declares, 'We're almost at The Farm, I see.'

They then explain they have to fill up the van and pick up some post and a few bits at a farm along the way. They make me promise not to accept any food whilst we're there. They tell me that if we do, we'll be there for ages and like me, they need to get to Kent.

My gut is telling me it's lunchtime, but I do really need to get back to Ashford, so I agree not to accept any food at all. They emphasise this as if they expect my resolve to be heavily tested.

When we arrive at "The Farm", it is exactly that; a farm. They tell me that they went there on a working holiday in the seventies and it's been their official address ever since.

'It's in a marginal seat,' says Dave.

'And it's a great place to be when you just need to escape from the world, to be fair,' says Kath.

We drive into the farmyard and are greeted by a herd of cattle which are walking in the opposite direction. Kath stops and turns off the engine whilst they pass. At the back, there's a woman who must be in her seventies if not her eighties. She's wearing overalls and leaning heavily on a long stick.

'Hello, strangers,' she says with a smile. 'I'll be back at the house in a minute. You're just in time for lunch.'

'We'd love to stop for lunch, Mary, but we really can't,' says Kath. 'We're going to pick some things up and go. We'll come back in a couple of weeks for a proper visit.'

'I'll just get the gates shut and I'll see you inside,' is the response, and Mary follows behind her cows and heads away from the van.

'Bill... Bill,' calls Kath as we enter the house.

It's an old stone farmhouse with walls that must be two foot thick. The big solid front door is mainly black, but where the black has been worn away, layers of paint are revealed, showing the different colours it's been painted over the years.

Inside the farmhouse, the walls are an off-white; not the kind of off-white you buy in a DIY shop, but the kind you get by rarely painting the walls and often having an open fire. The furniture is old and battered, but comfortable-looking and timeless in its state of semi-dereliction.

Sat in an armchair, having clearly just woken up, is Bill.

He's a short, slightly rotund man, definitely in his eighties rather than his seventies. He's wearing black trousers and a shirt. These clothes could once have looked smart and may have, back in time, been his Sunday best, but are now only really suitable for farm work.

'I won't get up,' says Bill, 'on account of my knees.'

'You just sit there,' says Dave, picking up a pile of letters from the sideboard. 'Don't get up on our account, we're only passing through.'

The front door swings open again and Mary walks in. 'You're a new one,' she says. 'What's your name?'

'Hello,' I say, putting on my politest voice. 'I'm Jason.'

'You look like you could do with a good meal, Jason. I'll rustle something up.'

I go to open my mouth to turn down the offer as politely as I can, but Dave gets in before me. 'We really can't stop, Mary. I'm sorry, but we have to go.'

'Look at the poor boy, he's starving. It won't take long to get some food together.'

'No, really, we can't…' Kath starts to say, but Mary interrupts.

'You can at least stop for a cup of tea.' Mary looks at me for a reaction.

I am under strict instructions not to accept food, but no one has told me if I'm allowed to accept drinks, so in trying to work out what I'm allowed to say, based both on my instructions and the normal rules of politeness, I probably look a bit lost and confused.

'A cup of tea would be lovely,' says Dave. 'But then we must be off.'

'We really can't stay for long, to be fair,' adds Kath.

I'm extremely relieved, not because I'm particularly desperate for a cuppa, but because I didn't slip up and accept food and Dave accepted the tea, so that is not in any way my fault.

Mary disappears into the kitchen and there's the sound of a kettle going on the hob and general clattering.

After a bit, she returns with a pot of tea on a tray, five cups on saucers and a small plate of biscuits. She pours the tea and hands us each a cup with a biscuit on the side. She then takes the empty teapot and the tray back into the kitchen as we eat our biscuits and drink our tea.

She returns with an already sliced cake and hands me a piece without asking if I want it or not.

What can I do? Politeness requires I take the cake.

The cake is a delicious moist fruitcake, which tastes just slightly alcoholic. It has a layer of marzipan under a thin layer of crisp white icing.

* * *

We're just leaving The Farm now. I'm so stuffed I can hardly move. They were possibly the best dumplings I've ever had and I'm still trying to work out how much of the feast we've just eaten was already made and how much was rustled up whilst we were there.

It would have taken them a week to get through that lot on their own and there's still cake and some apple crumble left, which Mary was trying to get us to eat as we left.

I fully understand the warning about not accepting food now. I'm hoping for a quick lift from Canterbury to Ashford, otherwise I'm not getting a proper night's sleep before work tomorrow.

Kath drives out of the farmyard, goes to change gear and, I assume, the universal joint has gone again. She lets go of the gearstick and it flops down to the side.

This is not looking promising!

'Oh well,' says Kath. 'To be fair, at least there are tools here.'

Bill, who had insisted on coming out to wave us off against the advice of Kath and Dave, seems to take on a new lease of life when he hears the van needs a repair.

He and Kath head off to get some tools from the barn, whilst Mary ushers Dave and me inside to try to get us to eat some more cake, still insisting that we "must be hungry". I have never been so far from hungry in my life.

I say that I really can't eat anything more, but accept a cup of tea, which, of course, comes with a biscuit on the side.

Dave asks Mary how Bill's doing. It's clear to see it's quite a struggle for him to stand up and move around.

'Well,' says Mary. 'I used to be a farmer's wife, but now I'm the wife of someone who just grumbles about his knees, and I do all the farm work.'

Dave points out that she always did a lot of farm work and Mary agrees, adding, 'Maybe he was the farmer's husband all along.'

She looks sad and lost in thought and says, 'He gets very bored, you know. You really should come and see him more often. He perks up when he sees you.'

After more tea and some cake, Bill walks in, followed by Kath. He lowers himself into his chair, looking as if he's using all of his remaining strength to fight gravity and control his descent.

Kath and Dave insist that he stays sitting as we leave and he doesn't put up an argument this time. He makes some joke to Kath about forks and jubilee clips which I don't get, and wishes us a safe journey from the comfort of his excessively well-worn armchair.

It's pretty obvious that I'm getting home late, but at least the van works now. Kath changes up through the gears with confidence and soon we're back on the road.

All that food has made me feel sleepy and I'm starting to drift off.

My head hits the window as we turn a corner, causing me to wake up with a jolt. I pull my jumper up onto my shoulder to use as a pillow against the window.

I wake up again as we get to a roundabout. I'm not sure where we are but it's now dark.

Kath and Dave have said they'll wake me up where I have to get out and hitch, so I figure I can sleep for a bit.

I can feel a cool breeze on my face and something shaking me, but then it stops, so I ignore it and enjoy my slumber.

The sun is hot on my face and there's a flyer directly above my head which says:

You can picture a scene in your mind if it's clearly defined,

But to see how long something takes it has to be timed.

A team with one dream can make a machine,
but like a swimming pool of paddling turtles
why walk in straight lines when you can run around

in circles?

I read it again and it makes no more sense.

I'm trying to remember where I am when the van door right next to my head swings open and a face appears.

From my angle it seems to be upside down, but that's by far not the most unusual feature of this face. The bloke looking down at me has a bright-red mohican and the letters ACAB tattooed on his forehead.

Before I can even attempt to work out what's going on, he starts speaking.

'Who's this sleeping in Madcap's van then?' He has a heavy northern accent and a big smile on his face, like a small child who's discovered a new game.

'Madcap?' I say. Nothing more eloquent comes to mind and I truly don't have a clue what's going on.

'You must know who Madcap is. You're in her van.'

'Hey Prof,' I hear someone shouting. 'Your lodger's woken up.'

Then, as I sit up, Dave comes over with his big grin and his eyes as wide as saucers.

'Good morning,' he says. 'We did try to wake you, but you were out like a light.'

'No worries, Dave. Thanks for the lift.'

'You should call me Prof while we're here. Nom de guerre and all that.' His grin widens further.

'Nom de what?'

'Fake name to confuse the police and security.'

I have no clue what's going on; I'm trying to work out who is who and where I am and I have that poem about turtles running around in my head, confusing further what would anyway be a confusing situation.

'And you are fucking sketchy,' the guy with the mohican and the tattoo declares, laughing.

My moment of confusion is interrupted as the whole place suddenly goes crazy, with people shouting something about a digger, whistling and making strange animalistic noises.

'Come on, Sketchy,' the tattooed bloke shouts in my ear as he grabs my arm. 'Let's jump on a fucking digger!'

Without thinking, or even having time to think, I stumble out of the van.

We're running through the woods. I don't know how many people in all are running with us. I can see about a dozen, but that's just the people in view and I can hear more around us, including someone just behind me.

The bloke with the tattoos is running along in front of me. He's much taller than me, wearing a kilt or a skirt and carrying a large pink handbag.

Even though I don't have a clue what we're doing, I'm running as fast as I can to keep up with him. There's a line of security guards blocking our path and everyone except the tattooed guy is running to one side or the other to get around them, but the tattooed guy is running straight at them and I'm following him, not knowing what else to do.

As he reaches the line of security, he raises the handbag in the air and swings it around like some medieval weapon, still charging directly at them. Then he lets out a battle cry which sounds like he's channelling his inner buffalo.

The security guards dive out of his way, tripping over each other to the left and the right of him.

I run behind him.

I see a digger in front of us. It's huge; you could almost fit a small car in the bucket. Other protestors have reached it already and a number of them are sitting on it. Some are on the tracks, some are on the cab and there's a bloke in a yellow hi vis slinglet with "No New Roads" written on the back, standing up on the highest part of the digger's arm.

I run like my life depends on it and a bloke with long blonde matted hair in an orange boiler suit and a hard hat reaches out his hand and helps me up on to the tracks, which are covered in mud and therefore incredibly slippery.

I scramble from there up onto the body of the digger. I try to catch my breath. I haven't run so fast for years.

'Who's your friend, ACAB?' he asks the tattooed guy.

'This is Sketchy,' ACAB replies. 'Madcap and Prof brought him up last night.'

'Nice to meet you, Sketchy,' says the bloke in the boiler suit. 'I'm Monk.'

A Quest For Doughnuts

This was the mid 80s. I'd hardly been out in a strong wind and there I was, stepping into the unknown.

Finally, my sister has left. I've been sitting in my room, listening to the radio, waiting for her to leave. She's been in the bathroom for the last few hours. Like me, she's got impossible-to-style curly ginger hair. Unlike me, she spends her whole life in the bathroom, trying to rectify the situation. She's going through a really annoying phase at the moment, where she feels the need to correct everything I say. She's a couple of years older than me and thinks she knows it all.

This morning, the big issue was me saying 'immensely tall'. She told me that you can't say that and it doesn't make sense. I pointed out that I had said it and she'd understood it, so she's clearly talking nonsense. I think what really annoyed her was me pointing out that YTS stands for youth tea-

39

making service and that the new job she's so proud of is just a 'glorified tea-girl position'. I don't know why I said 'glorified'. It's not glorified at all. She makes tea for accountants. There's nothing glorified about that and it's not even a proper job. It only pays twenty-seven pounds fifty per week.

Our recent move from living in the countryside to living in the village of Bethersden has advantages and disadvantages. The main disadvantage is definitely neighbours. We had neighbours at our old house, but they were at least a couple of fields away. I think two fields is a good distance for neighbours. It's close enough that you can help each other in an emergency, not too far to go to fetch milk and not so close that you have to see them if you don't want to. The width of a fence panel is definitely closer than ideal for any neighbour.

I don't know our new neighbours very well yet, but from what I've seen, three fields would be a better distance between us than two. The main advantage of this village over living in the countryside is that, as we're on the A28, there's a bus route into Ashford. This gives me a level of independence I haven't previously known. No longer do I have to rely on my parents if I want to go to town.

It's Saturday, so it's market day and I'm going to catch the bus into Ashford. I love the Saturday market. It's a proper mishmash of different stalls, selling everything from jumble sale style bric-a-brac to high end antiques; from cheap food in dented tins or near its sell by date, to posh food that can't be found elsewhere in town, along with household goods and anything else you can think of.

There's something so alive about it with all the stallholders shouting over each other, trying to gain the attention of the public and draw them in to buy their goods. The way the stalls work together to create something that benefits them all is fantastic. No single stall could bring in enough trade to support itself, but together they can attract enough customers not just to make the market throb with activity, but to bring the whole town alive. The High Street shops and the pubs are all packed with people who have come to town for the market. Best of all, there's the doughnut stall selling freshly-made doughnuts, dripping in sugar and fat and all things unhealthy. The doughnut stall is definitely the highlight of the market for me.

The bus is at five minutes past ten and the news hasn't come on yet so I have enough time to make a sandwich before I go. I'm trying to decide between a cheese sandwich and a peanut butter and lime pickle sandwich.

As I ponder on this, the bus goes past the window. The news hasn't started, so it's more than five minutes early.

I grab my bag and head out of the door. The bus is now sitting at the bus stop. I run to get there before it leaves. As I get up level with the back of the bus, it indicates to pull out. I slap the back window and shout, but the driver doesn't see me, continues to pull out into the road and drives away.

I'm left standing at the bus stop, slightly out of breath. I could go back inside, have that sandwich and wait for the next bus. It'll be an hour. That's an extra hour before I get the doughnut I'm craving.

A white van is driving towards me and I decide to try hitching again. This is a little different from my last attempt, when I got a lift with the Farkases five years ago. This time, I'm going to try to get a lift with a stranger. To be precise, I'm going to try to get a lift with the stranger who's driving that white van.

I put my thumb out and look at the van, wondering if it'll stop. As it gets closer, I can see the driver. He's got long brown hair and a little red hat.

Before I know it, he's stopped just where the bus was a minute ago. This is fantastic. I've tried hitching twice now and so far I have a one hundred percent success rate.

I get into his van, put on my seatbelt and we're off. This is so much better than the bus. I still have my bus fare in my pocket, which means I can afford more doughnuts.

The driver is wearing a jacket which looks a bit

like it's made out of old faded carpet material. It's covered in little embroidered patterns and pictures of elephants and some other animal which I don't recognise. It looks like it was once brightly coloured, but it has all faded except for lines of gold stitching which shine out from its general state of disrepair. Now I can see it properly, I can see that the red hat also has embroidered patterns all over it and has little mirrors set in it. From his clothing, he looks a bit like he should be on stage.

He asks me where I'm going and says he can drop me off at the end of Godinton Road. A short walk from there and I'll be at the market.

We get talking and it turns out he's staying at a farm near Tenterden, where he's picking apples. Even though the van looks quite normal from the outside, it's not at all normal on the inside. It's set out like a camper van, with a bed in the back, a little cooker and some seats. It smells of joss-sticks or something and every bit of the van that is showing on the inside is covered in patterns; weird colourful patterns which have been painted on. It must have taken ages to paint. He tells me he lives in the van going from place to place.

I ask if he always picks fruit for a living.

'No man,' he says. 'I just do whatever feels right at the time. There's a cool vibe on the farm where I'm picking apples. There's a nice bunch of people there. We chat while we work, and we chill out together in the evening. There's no stress to the job and I get to save some money so I can go to Spain for the winter. Too many people work in jobs they don't enjoy. What's the point of life if you're not having fun?'

I ask him what he'll do in Spain, and he says he'll 'just hang out with friends, sit around campfires, chill and party'. This sounds like a lot more fun than most people's plans. Adults ask you what you want to do when you grow up, and expect you to answer by naming a job. This guy seems to have a much better answer.

My dad's always banging on about his successful career, about how he's made it through hard work. But what has he "made"? He's *made* himself into a grumpy old bastard. He's *made* people who were going to buy insurance anyway, buy insurance off him rather than someone else. He may have *made* them buy a more expensive insurance than they otherwise would. He hasn't *made* the world a better place in any notable way and he hasn't *made* himself happy.

I hope I can find a better form of success than that.

After my lift drops me off, as I'm walking to the market, I'm taking in the difference that hitching is going to make to my life. I thought that having a bus service would give me more freedom, but this is so much better. I don't need to have the bus fare, which means I can travel as far as I want. So far, this method of transport has proved to be more reliable than the bus and I get to meet interesting people.

I wonder how easy it is to hitch down to Spain. I'd have to get the boat to France. Other than that, I just have to put my thumb out and wait for lifts.

This is truly life-changing!

I've got a massive smile on my face all the way to the market and an even bigger smile as I spend my bus fare on doughnuts. I go up into town and drop two films off at the chemist to be processed and walk out towards the A28 to hitch back home.

It's quite a long walk to the A28. The bus runs from the town centre. I guess that's the downside of hitching.

I go to the big roundabout where the traffic for the A28 splits off. This looks like a good place to stand. Most of the traffic is going my way and there's a safe place for cars to stop so they can pick me up.

The first car that comes along is a red Ford Escort. If I can get a lift in this car, I keep my one hundred percent success rate at this hitching thing. As it comes towards me, I put my thumb out and look expectantly at the driver. He's got dark hair in a sort of bob-type of haircut.

I keep looking at him, but he's looking straight past me, like he hasn't seen me.

He can't have not seen me. There's nothing to see here except me. Obviously there's the road and the verge, but other than that, I'm the only object in the driver's field of vision.

For some unexplained reason, he looks straight past me and then drives straight past me.

There goes my one hundred percent success rate.

Never mind, there's another car coming; a little blue car. There's a woman driving it. She's an adult, but a young adult. If she gives me a lift, I still have a seventy-five percent success rate. That's still good and, of course, I'll be home soon.

I smile as she comes towards me, hoping that this will increase the chances of her giving me a lift. She responds to my smile with a shocked or maybe frightened look. It is hard to say for sure because she goes past quite quickly.

Now my success rate is only fifty percent. It's halved in two cars, but if the next car picks me up, it goes back up to sixty percent, which means that more cars have picked me up than not. I'd be happy with a sixty percent success rate.

There are no cars for a few minutes and I stand by the side of the road, wondering how long this is going to take. Eventually, a Ford Capri comes along. It's metallic purple, with tinted windows and a massive spoiler. It looks lower to the ground than other Capris. It might have been lowered. I can't see the driver at all because of the tinted windows, so I put out my thumb and smile at where I guess the driver's face is.

To my great relief, the car pulls up just a little way up the road from where I'm standing. It's not as close as would be ideal. The driver must have made a last-minute decision to stop, but the important thing is that they decided to stop.

I run up to the car and just as I get next to it, it drives away, wheel-spinning as it does so. I guess he thinks that's funny.

A while later, when it starts to rain, I decide to walk. I'm still hoping I'll get a lift, but if I don't, at least I'm getting closer to home. It's a shame I spent my bus fare on the extra doughnuts; there's a bus stop half a mile or so away and I could have got a bus from there.

A lorry drives towards me. If it stops, I'll still have a two percent success rate, but more importantly, I'll have a lift home. The driver beeps his horn at me, nearly deafening me as he passes.

The driver of the next car shrugs at me. Someone else did that earlier. I don't know what it means.

The next one points to the left, which I assume

means that he's going off to the left at the next junction. The next left turn is two miles away. He probably doesn't see it as that far, but it would be really nice to have a lift up to the junction. I'd be two miles closer to home at least.

The rain stops, which makes the walk more pleasant.

A white van comes along the road. As it gets closer, I can see that both front passenger seats are taken. I'm not fussy; I'll happily sit in the back, but it drives past, so I start walking again.

Two cars and a big blue van are coming my way. Is it a big van, or is it a small lorry? It's one of those vans with a big square back to them, or one of those small lorries with a van cab, depending how you look at it. The driver of the first car – a black estate of some sort – sticks two fingers up at me as he drives past. I'm not really that bothered by the insult; I could just do with a lift though.

The car behind him is a blue Peugeot. The driver smiles but doesn't stop. The ambiguous van/ lorry thing swerves into a puddle, splashing water up. I jump back to avoid getting drenched and almost fall over.

A white van, which was hidden behind the van/lorry thing, drives past without me even getting a chance to put my thumb out. My luck is in though; the white van pulls up just past where I am.

I run up to it, praying it doesn't just drive away like that Capri did.

As I open the door, I'm hit by a familiar smell of joss-sticks or something. I look up and see that sat in the driver's seat, with his little red cap and his faded jacket, is the driver who picked me up this morning.

I realise that hitching is going to be a much less reliable form of transport than I'd thought if I have to wait for this same driver each time I want a lift, especially as he's off to Spain for the winter.

Bon Jovi

I'd love to know what Bon Jovi is doing now. I have a lot of great memories of 1995 and I reckon he has too.

I've just popped into town to buy some bits and I'm hitching back.

It's a little way from here to a decent hitching spot, but I've got my thumb out while I walk and with a bit of luck, someone will pull in before I get there.

I look back at the traffic to check that it's safe to cross a side street, and who should come along but Bon Jovi. His car pulls up, completely blocking the traffic and he leans out of the window and shouts, 'Come on, Sketchy, jump in.'

Fantastic, a lift straight up to the protest camp.

Bon Jovi is one of the security guards who works up on the road protest. He's called that because he's the spitting image of Jon Bon Jovi. He's part of Unit Four. The security team is made up of

50

four units and Unit Four are my favourite. I get on well with most of the security guards, but Unit Four are more fun than the other three units, which is why they've given themselves funny names like a lot of us protestors have.

We were sat up with them last night whilst they guarded the fence. The road builders have cordoned off the whole road with some stupidly expensive fence, and now security have to guard it to prevent it getting damaged. There's no work happening on the stretch near the camp at the moment, so all there is to protect it is the fence.

Guarding it is as boring as it sounds, or at least it would be, but Unit Four don't bother guarding it at all really. They just sit down together by the fence and crack open some beers.

Karl, Prof, Madcap, Fishhead and me were sat with them until the early hours of this morning, having a beer and chatting. Obviously, Prof didn't have a beer. He hasn't taken any intoxicating substances since 1979. He doesn't even eat chocolate. He says that in 1979 he realised that he needed a clear head for fighting the system more than he needed the fun of being off his face or the enlightenment found in psychedelics.

He reckons he was already quite enlightened enough to see that he should be putting all of his energies into fighting capitalism and the establishment.

Our relationship with security seems strange to new guards and protestors. A lot of people turn up expecting a fight, especially the new security guards. Before they're allowed to come and play, they have to go through a training programme which is really more about indoctrination than teaching them anything useful. They're shown videos of protestors being violent, throwing bottles of urine and doing other unpleasant things.

I don't know where they get these videos from; my guess is that the people in them are actors. They certainly aren't protestors from this protest.

As part of the indoctrination, they're also told that we're paid to protest, but they don't tell them who pays us. This is all nonsense of course, or at least if it's not, I'm owed some back-pay.

At one point, we heard there was a rumour that we're paid to protest by Linda McCartney. We thought that that was hilarious, so we told all the guards it was true. I think some of the less intelligent security actually still believe that.

'What did Prof say to that new security guard?' asks Bon Jovi. 'The one who said he was going to tear you a new arsehole.'

'I don't know,' I respond. 'Why?'

The new guard turned up a few days ago when I was sitting on a digger, threatened, as Bon Jovi says, to tear me a new arsehole if I didn't get down, and then had to be escorted away by the other security guards.

Not only did this break our unwritten arrangement with security, but it was also quite clearly threatening behaviour as described by the Offences Against the Person Act.

I haven't seen him since. Bon Jovi says they left him on his own, guarding a bit of fence that really didn't need guarding, just so they didn't have to deal with him. Apparently he was seen sitting down chatting with Prof with his head bowed like a child who was being told off, waiting for it to all be over.

He was quite subdued for the rest of the day, so I hear, and then didn't turn up for his second day on the job. I haven't got a clue what went on there, but I'm not too upset that he hasn't stuck around.

Prof is absolutely committed to keeping the relationship between us and security friendly. He wants to convert them to our cause. On one of my first days here, he told me about the Christmas truce in World War One. He said that even though everyone looks back at it now as this beautiful heart-warming moment in history, the establishment were absolutely devastated by it at the time.

It wasn't that they were afraid it would cause them to lose the war; it was much bigger than that. It was a sign they were losing control of the populace.

The European Royal Family had always been able to sort out their disputes with each other by sending the plebs out to fight for them. A truce, even a short truce which was organised by the plebs, was an existential threat to the establishment.

If plebs from around the world communicated directly with each other, the status quo would crumble.

Prof says we can threaten the status quo here on the protest too. The security guards are not our enemies. They've mainly been pushed into these jobs by the job centre. They're only paid £3.50 an hour; they're hardly part of the ruling classes.

As he likes to say, the only thing that separates us from security is the fence. He's good with words is Prof. He can explain that sort of thing to security in a way that means they get it.

The result of all this is not just that we can sit and have a beer with them in the evening. It's also that each day is far less confrontational, and we get away with more than we would otherwise.

Sometimes they even actively help us by cutting a hole in the fence or giving us information. They'll also speak of us in much better terms when they're in the pub, or with their families and so on.

We need to elicit support from wherever we can get it and our friendly approach to security is a valuable tool in achieving this.

Our main way of slowing the road building down is jumping on diggers, or 'digger diving' as it's known. The road builders bring a digger onto site, and we jump up on it, so that for reasons of health and safety, they have to shut the engine off. Security then drag us off the digger and escort us off site. The digger can start up and if there's enough time, it can start work.

We find a way back in and jump on the digger again and so it goes on. It's not that security don't try to get us off the diggers because we're friendly with them or stop us getting on them in the first place, but it's treated more like a game of rugby with the added element of diggers than it is a fight.

It's all light hearted and we can all sit and have a beer together at the end of the day. You still get bruised. I've always got bruises all up my legs and arms, particularly under my arms. You get bad bruises under your arms where the security drag you around, but you get bruises from rugby too and this is no different really, except there's a purpose to it beyond sport.

When Fishhead turned up, he was a bit surprised by the way that security and protestors interact here. He took one of the flyers we were handing out at a free party and came down to the camp to see what it was all about. He'd been on site for all of ten minutes when we saw a digger coming towards the camp. We all went running for it and Fishhead came with us.

Turnip and Tosser had hidden, crouched down behind the tracks of the digger, to ambush anyone who tried to get on it. They jumped out and grabbed him from behind.

Fishhead elbowed Turnip square in the face, knocking him to the ground and giving him a bleeding nose. Fishhead isn't violent at all; he was just taken by surprise.

He was then even more surprised when Prof jumped on him. It's the only time I've ever seen Prof getting physical with anyone. We were all apologising to Turnip and explaining that Fishhead had just turned up and didn't know the score, when Turnip gets to his feet, announces that "tis but a scratch", wipes the blood from his face and carries on like it never happened.

By the time Prof got off him, Fishhead seemed to have seen how things worked around here and he apologised to Turnip, too. Turnip shook his hand and we all got back on with jumping on diggers.

Well, obviously, those of us who are protestors got on with jumping on diggers. The security guards got on with trying to stop us.

The story goes that Tosser and Turnip chose each other's names. Turnip decided he was going to be called Terminator. Tosser pretended to mishear him and called him Turnip. Turnip called Tosser a Tosser and both names stuck. Now they wear them with pride, as if they'd named themselves.

Some of the security have talked about leaving the job because they don't want to support the road, but we do our best to get them to stay because we'd much prefer to have security who don't want to support the road than security who do.

Even the management like the arrangement between us and security, or at least the ones here do. They all get paid. Nobody gets hurt, so less paperwork. What's not to like?

Clearly, whoever's arranging the training sees things a little differently.

As Bon Jovi and me get near the protest camp, I ask him if he wants to drop me off a little bit before the camp, so that no one sees that he's given me a lift.

'No, I'm not embarrassed,' he says. 'Anyway, they only pay me once I've clocked on. Right now I'm just a normal citizen. I can give lifts to whoever I want.'

This blasé attitude to how he's seen by his superiors soon melts away when we turn the corner and we see what's happening at the camp.

A bulldozer is sitting on the opposite side of the road and a number of protestors, including an old friend of mine Fred, are being removed from it by security.

Fred joined the protest before me. The day I arrived in Madcap's van, climbed onto my first digger and met Monk, Fred was sitting on the other side of that digger.

I didn't see her at all and didn't know she was there until I was released from the police station the next day. It's not that surprising she's involved; she definitely believes in this sort of thing and she only lives just down the road.

Right now, Fred and the other protestors are being taken off the bulldozer under the watchful eye of the sad detectives. They're known as the sad detectives because we all feel that when they chose "private detective" as a career, they must have pictured something more exciting than what they've ended up doing. We're not sure if they're employed by the company building the road, the council, or the security firm.

They mainly film the same few protestors jumping on diggers and bulldozers each day and getting dragged off by the same security guards. It's hardly the sort of detective work you see in films.

Bon Jovi has no problem with Luke or Matt seeing him dropping me off. They're his direct superiors. Guards of their rank are known as blue hats after the blue hard hats that the higher-ranking security guards wear.

They might well give me a lift themselves, but the footage that the sad detectives film goes straight to people who are not in on the cosy little arrangement between security and ourselves.

As soon as I see them, I undo my seatbelt and slide down into the footwell as far as possible. This isn't helped by the two packs of beer that are by my feet, but I'm fairly flexible and I think I'm managing to hide myself quite well.

Without saying anything, Bon Jovi drives straight past the camp and pulls up just around the corner.

'The beers are on me if you're up for it this evening,' he says, gesturing to the beer by my feet.

'Thanks,' I reply. 'I owe you a few beers.'

'Don't worry about it, but when Linda finally pays up, it's your round.'

Bike ride With Blaze

This memory isn't about hitching at all, but it's a lift that certainly helped me to get where I am today. It must have been a year or so after my second ever attempt at hitching.

Riding through this thick fog is like being engulfed in a white river. It swirls around our feet like little eddies and whirlpools, rushing past us like the froth when you're canoeing against the flow of fast-moving rapids. I feel almost weightless as the bike bounces gently over every little imperfection in the road's surface; the cool, damp air caressing my face may be the most refreshing feeling I have ever experienced.

I know these roads well, having lived in this area all my life and having cycled down them too many times to count. But somehow on the back of Blaze's motorbike, it's like I'm noticing all of this for the first time. I see a beauty in the fields and hedges as we pass them, which has never before been apparent, and as we reach the top of the hill, a view I must have looked at a thousand times has a previously unseen magnificence. I'm mesmerised by the patterns in the fog and seem to understand them as if I can see the physics behind their formation. I smell the land around us slowly warming as the sun rises and somehow I can hear the early morning calls of pigeons over the sound of the engine.

As we go around a bend, I feel the centrifugal force pulling me towards the wheels and as we straighten up again, the fog clears and I see for miles around.

I watch the patterns in the tarmac as the road flies past and then look up to see the landscape set out before me, with it's patchwork of fields created by man, and hills, streams and rivers shaped by the forces of nature. I feel simultaneously like an integral part of this whole creation and an observer, floating within the world and yet completely unconnected.

We turn another corner and we're back in the fog again, with its eddies and whirlpools. I hear, feel, smell and see everything with such new clarity, like I'm alive in a way I have never been before.

My cousin Blaze has always been more sophisticated than me. She's my older cousin, but the difference in sophistication cannot be explained away by the 18 months which separates us.

When I was struggling to put my wellies on the right feet, Blaze already had an eye for what clothing went with what and how to make a statement with what she wore. Even as a small child she seemed to have one foot in the adult world. She wasn't and still isn't trendy, far from it; she has always been alternative. I wouldn't describe her as a punk, a hippy or try to put any other label on her because none of them would fit. I guess the label 'cool' fits. She is incredibly cool.

We're riding back from a 'bonfire party' which she took me to last night. I'd never been to or heard of a bonfire party until last night. It was exactly what it sounds like, a party where people sit around a bonfire.

Other things I hadn't heard of until last night include chillums and shroom tea, both of which were being passed around the bonfire. Blaze's friends are unsurprisingly very cool and they're mainly older than Blaze. I think they might be what the news calls 'new age travellers'. They look quite rough, and I could understand how people might find them intimidating, but they were very kind and welcoming to me, even though I'm not even vaguely cool and only fifteen.

For most of the night we were just sat around chatting really. I've heard amazing stories of squats, festivals and traveller sites, battles with the police and vehicles breaking down at inopportune moments.

Gary, one of Blaze's friends, pulled back the sleeve of the army surplus jacket he was wearing and showed me the scar on his arm where he'd been bitten by a police dog. He said he felt sorry for the dog really; the police had taken an innocent dog and imposed a life of violence and fear on it. The dog handler had chosen to be in the police out of numerous possible jobs and had chosen to be a dog handler. He could leave whenever he wanted. The dog just got taken from its mother and had this life forced upon it.

Sally, who's one of Gary's mates, had been sitting quietly, poking the fire with a stick for ages. She had a dreamy smile and seemed, up to this point, completely lost in her own world.

Turning towards us quickly so her long blonde dreadlocks swung around and slapped her in the face, she stared straight through us with her bright blue eyes as if she was in some sort of trance.

'The policeman is a product of his influences, just as a dog is,' she said, and focused on our faces as if she'd only just noticed us. 'Although it looks like he made the choice to become a police officer from an almost limitless set of options, few of those options would really have fitted with his preconceived views on life. He may well have had the greatest of intentions before he joined up, but then got caught up in a culture where loyalty is to "the force" rather than to the law, and where racism, bigotry and corruption is rife. We are all a product of our influences. You can argue about how much is nature and how much is nurture, but once you look at it in those terms, none of that is actually the free will of the individual.'

Gary shut her up by saying, 'Look, Sally, he's a fucking pig and he set his dog on me. Stop making excuses for him.'

Sally laughed gently and passed him a chillum, which shut Gary up, just as effectively as Gary had shut her up.

At that point, a spark flew out of the fire and landed on this bloke who'd fallen asleep. It landed on his trouser leg and set light to it. The people next to him all tried to put it out. One did so by pouring a can of beer over it and another two tried to smother it.

One of them was using a jacket and I think the other one was trying to roll him over.

Whatever their intention was, the result was he woke up with two people seemingly attacking his now completely soaked leg. He made one hell of a noise for a few seconds, before settling down and falling back to sleep again.

Luckily, he fell asleep a little further from the fire this time.

The night was so full of stuff that made me

think, it felt like it contained a whole lifetime of experiences.

We're heading uphill now and the bike is revving higher. I can feel the vibrations going right through me from my toes to the top of my head. As the landscape flies past us, the events of the last few hours flit through my brain.

I don't know what it was about Sally, but she seemed even cooler and more sophisticated than Blaze. She was wearing a leather jacket with stuff written all over it in white and red paint. On one arm it had "fuck the system" written on it. I'd been staring at it for a while, and without really thinking said that surely it would be better to improve the system.

I immediately realised that this probably wasn't the coolest thing to say. Sally laughed, not in an unfriendly way, but almost as if I'd said it as a joke.

Then in one breath, without stopping, like she'd learnt and rehearsed the lines for a play, she said, 'The entire system is a trap, designed to manipulate you into feeding the establishment. It's one of Thatcher's ways of controlling us plebs. As soon as someone has a stake in the system, they're inhibited from rocking the boat. Even those right near the bottom of a hierarchy will protect it to get to the next rung on the ladder, or because they fear slipping down further.'

She was pacing around by the fire with deep frown lines on her forehead as she said this, looking up occasionally as if she was plucking inspiration out of the air and gesturing wildly to try to get her point across. She didn't look like she was concentrating on where she was pacing and at times, I was concerned she might take a wrong step and walk straight into the fire.

'It's like an enormous board game where a small group of winning players get to write and rewrite the rules as they go. Everyone is aware it's unjust, but either they accept their fate, or try to infiltrate that elite group of winners and start rewriting the rules themselves. On occasion, some lowly individual will attain membership of that group and partake in the rewriting of the rules, but to get there, they have to support the hierarchy at every turn.'

A woman with tatty black dreads, wearing a bright pink faux fur jacket and a cowboy hat, walked up to Sally, grinned at her and said, 'Come on, Sally, It's a party. Have a drink.' She then opened a can of beer right in Sally's face, spraying her in the mouth.

When this failed to get a reaction, she walked away, swigging from the can.

Other than having her words briefly muffled, Sally carried on as if nothing had happened.

'Other people regard these "successful" players as evidence that they too can win. Some work on the assumption that if they can get into the winners group, they can rewrite the rules to be more equitable, but that's not feasible. You can't spend your whole life supporting the hierarchy and investing yourself in it and then change those habits and discard everything you've built up. Human nature just doesn't allow a complete about-face like that. Some of those who are serious about changing the system get nowhere because they try to change it from the start and they are penalised for doing so.'

I think Sally would have continued for a while; she seemed to just be getting into her stride and I'd have loved to have heard what she had to say, but Gary butted in with, 'Yeah, mate, and we're going to burn that fucking board game to the ground,' which sort-of ended that conversation.

Overall, Gary seems a lot blunter than Sally.

Even though I haven't slept, I don't feel at all tired, just too full of new information to be able to process it all. They were talking about anarchy and how people view it as a violent, disorderly state of affairs. They explained to me that it's actually about relying on your own morals rather than legal restrictions.

I've never thought about anarchy before and what it actually means. It's not like they teach this stuff at school.

They also talked about whether society was ready for anarchy and if not, how we can move closer to being ready. A friend of Gary and Sally's whose name I don't remember reckons that we were moving further away from being ready, because capitalism relies on the breakdown of society into individuals who can trade with and compete with each other.

Moving from tribal societies, to extended families, to nuclear families is a move away from feeling a responsibility towards others and therefore away from being able to play a productive role in an anarchic society. He said that some hunter-gatherer tribes have no rulers and are in effect anarchic societies. I don't know if any of that is true.

At some point in the early hours, two police officers walked across the field towards us. I'd had a whole night of stories about various confrontations with the police. Some of which had been quite violent and all of which involved unfair behaviour on the police's part. As such, their presence worried me.

I warned Gary they were there.

He turned around to look at them and said, 'Don't worry, mate. It wouldn't be a party if the pigs didn't turn up.'

I don't really understand what they were doing.

They didn't do anything. They turned up, made their presence known and then I didn't see them again. I can't see that anyone would've complained. There's a woodland between us and the nearest house. They can't have heard the party from there. My parents anniversary party was louder than last night's bonfire party. The police didn't turn up to that and they were playing Elvis. Surely, if there's a music crime, it's Elvis played loudly.

The fog is clearing again, and everything has a newfound clarity. It's like I've just put glasses on that bring everything into focus. I don't want this to end, but we're turning on to the A28, so I know we'll be home soon.

One part of the night keeps replaying in my mind.

A few hours ago the fire died down and Sally and Gary's mate, who's name I can't remember, got up to get more wood. The hedge at the edge of the field had been laid at some point over winter. A lot of the sticks which had been cut out were just left in piles by the hedge. It was these sticks we were burning on the fire. We were pulling them out from the grass which had grown over them, trying to avoid the thorns, which wasn't easy in the dark, and he said it was a great example of people's desire to contribute.

I didn't know what he meant at first, so he

asked me why I was helping him to get wood.

'I don't want the fire to go out and to get cold,' I said.

He pointed out that he was getting wood anyway. It would have been more work for him if I hadn't helped, but I'd have been warmer, because he would have got the wood and I wouldn't have left the warmth of the fire. The only reward I got from helping was being seen as helpful, therefore gaining elevated status within the group and seeing myself as being helpful, therefore gaining self-respect.

He said that both of these were a much more powerful motivation than they're given credit for and that even when people have paid jobs, a lot of the motivation comes from these two factors. It certainly works to get me to collect wood for a fire.

I don't know how much this applies to life in general.

It's been a long night and when I think about these things, my head feels as foggy as the journey home has been. We're on the final straight heading towards my house and now we pull up on our driveway.

Blaze comes in and I go to the kitchen to make her a coffee before she rides home.

By the time I take it to her, she's fast asleep on our sofa, snoring loudly.

Hyp Or Hypnot

Thoughts flow through us like water flows through a landscape. (Summer '95).

I'm hitching into town to get some bits.

Ironically, the reason the traffic is terrible today is because of the new road. It's supposed to save everyone time on their journeys, but in order to build it, they need to redirect the traffic at one of the junctions. This means they've had to put temporary measures in place, including two sets of non-functioning traffic lights. One set is jammed on red and the other is jammed on green.

People are only prepared to wait so long for the red light to change. Eventually, they drive out gingerly into the road, stopping the traffic coming through the green light. The drivers coming through the green light are understandably displeased at being cut up when it's their right of way.

I'm trying to hitch a lift from drivers coming

off this junction. On the plus side, I have a decent amount of traffic going past me; it's crawling along, practically at walking pace and there's a fairly reasonable lay-by for folks to pull into to pick me up.

On the downside, pretty much every driver is in a bad mood by the time they get to me. I smile, keep my thumb out and wait for a lovely person who wants to give me a lift.

Eventually, there'll be one in this long line of cars driven almost entirely by irate people. In the meantime, I'll try not to let their anger get to me.

A massive articulated lorry has gone through the red light and properly snarled up the traffic. It's crawling along towards me and where they've narrowed the road down with bollards, it's having problems getting past the oncoming traffic.

I have my thumb out, but there's no way I'm getting a lift from the lorry. The driver looks like he's sat on a wasps nest, his face is that red. I smile at him, and he scowls back at me. He almost pushes me into the hedge as he passes.

Once he's past, I can see who that lovely person who's going to give me a lift is.

It's Prof. He's driving towards me in Madcap's van.

I don't think Prof even realised the lights were on red when he entered the junction, but he's got through it OK. He's waving at me to show he's seen me and that's caused him to lose concentration and momentarily mount the kerb.

Then he oversteers and goes over into the other lane in front of the oncoming traffic. A car coming the other way swerves away from the van and then back towards the middle of the road. The Volvo behind Prof has skidded to a halt so as not to hit it. There's a little red car behind that, which seems to have run into the back of the Volvo.

By the time Prof pulls up to give me a lift, there's a trail of chaos behind him.

The bloke in the Volvo steps out into the road and starts screaming at the driver of the little red car. He's accusing him in rather strong terms of having a visual impairment and asking in the least polite way possible for his insurance details.

Prof pulls in and as I jump in the passenger seat, he jumps out of the van and ventures back into the chaos he's caused.

I have to admit, I'm strongly in favour of us just driving away and leaving them to sort it out between themselves.

Prof clearly has other plans. He runs back down the road, waving his arms in the air and shouting something. He's got his back to me and I can't hear the words.

Should I get out and help? I don't really know

what I'd be helping with.

Prof and the Volvo driver seem to be exchanging words. The Volvo driver is shouting at Prof. I think he's going to hit him. He's stepping towards him, but now he looks like he's crying on Prof's shoulder. Then he takes a step back and goes to give a hug to the driver of the little red car, who looks confused and recoils. He's backing up as far as he can before his car prevents him going further.

Prof points towards Madcap's van, like he's giving the Volvo driver directions, then walks up to the van himself. He climbs up into the driver's seat, with his big grin and his eyes the size of saucers, turns to me and says, 'It was just a bit of a misunderstanding really'.

As we drive off, the Volvo driver pulls into the lay-by where the van had been parked and the other traffic starts to move again.

'So what you did back there, Prof, was that hypnosis?' I ask.

Many times I've watched Prof elicit strange and unexpected reactions from people, just by talking to them. Mainly those people are security guards or police. I've listened to his words and it doesn't sound like the hypnosis you see on the TV, but the effect is definitely extraordinary.

'It depends on your definition of hypnosis,' comes the reply. 'What you're doing now can be classed as hypnosis. Whether consciously or unconsciously, you're communicating with me in a way that alters my mental state. That would be a broad definition of hypnosis. A narrower definition would be that it's only hypnosis if it's a conscious and deliberate method of communication to alter someone's mental state, or put them in a trance, if you like. You could narrow it down further still, by saying that it also has to be for a chosen purpose. That definition still allows for a lot of everyday hypnosis.'

This sounds a bit like he's avoiding the question.

'When you break bad news to someone, you might talk in softer tones to lower their anxiety. You might change their environment to make it more conducive to getting the response you desire by, say, getting them to sit down first. You might lead into the bad news with some sort of preamble to get them in a more resilient state, like saying "I'm really sorry to be the one to say this, I know you may find this news difficult to take, but…". There's no purpose to these words other than to induce an advantageous mindset in the context of the news that you intend to impart. Is that hypnosis? I don't know. It's just semantics.'

I'm sure there must be a more straightforward answer than this. Prof's a great communicator;

75

couldn't he just tell me straight?

'The example I gave there is, of course, benevolent, but there's plenty of malevolent everyday hypnosis. Advertising is the obvious example. The world's best paid psychologists work in advertising and are assigned the task of writing hypnotic scripts, so they're actually the world's highest earning hypnotists. They have meetings where they discuss each hypnotic script and how to make it more effective. They use visual as well as oral hooks and prompts, select the demographic to induce into their chosen trance, carefully choose the best context in which to present this to their audience and pay millions to deliver it to them. It's little surprise they're so effective at hypnosis. Right now, all across the world, people are choosing products in shops, thinking that they're making a choice out of free will, but actually they've been conditioned by hypnosis to purchase that product.'

Prof is always banging on about advertising. Not in a bad way. He's always got something interesting to say on the subject, but it is one of his favourite topics and I've heard some of his rants on the subject a number of times. He's never described it as hypnotism before or ever talked about hypnotism, which seems strange as it turns out he's clearly very interested in that too.

'So if advertisers are using hypnotism on us,

why isn't this common knowledge? Do they have a secret society of hypnotists, who they recruit from?'

'Not at all, Sketchy. They probably don't define it as hypnotism themselves. Just like employers. Employers are often fairly proficient hypnotists, even though they may not realise that's what they're doing. Especially long-standing, large, institutional employers. They determine how to be effective in eliciting the desired response over generations. As a result, they discover hypnotic methodology accidentally if not deliberately. The army is the most extreme of these. The police are up there as well, but the army are more extreme. There's a lot of crossover with conditioning and hypnosis, but like I say, I'm not really big on semantics. The military completely breaks a recruit's way of thinking and replaces it with an extreme form of obedience. They require them to act on commands, not their own decision-making process. You can often identify people who are military, or ex-military just by their stance. Having been so heavily conditioned they've even changed the way they hold themselves. Even after years of civilian life, they still slip straight back into their conditioning when the correct stimulus is presented to them. If you walk up to them, hold yourself in the correct way and confidently bark an order at them, quite often they'll have acted on your command before they realise what's going on.'

I've seen Prof do this. A couple of weeks ago, we were trying to get on a digger, which security had completely surrounded. Security had easily four times the amount of people we did. It looked like a completely impossible task.

We were having a fun exchanging banter with them, but there was no opportunity to stop them working on the road. Then Prof walked up to two of the security guards, stood bolt upright and shouted, "Step aside" at them.

Without even thinking, they stepped aside and let him past. They only stepped aside for a second, but it was long enough for him to slip past them and get onto the digger. All the other security were taking the piss out of them something chronic. It was fantastic!

We went from watching a digger working and exchanging banter with security, to watching security exchange banter with each other whilst Prof sat on the now stationary digger.

'When I first discovered the effects of hypnosis, I wasn't trying to investigate hypnosis at all,' Prof continues. 'I wanted to know what had happened to my mate Craig. We used to spend all our time together, having fun and getting into trouble. We were only kids, but we got up to some real adventures. Then one summer, he went off to America. He had family over there. When he returned, he was completely transformed. He'd got in with the wrong crowd in my opinion, not that he wanted to hear that. He'd gone over there and joined one of those evangelical churches. I'd never heard of them back then, but they were quite big in the states.

'When Craig returned, he didn't want to party any more. He didn't want to have fun at all from what I could tell. All he wanted was to be a good Christian and he was only interested in hanging out with me if he could convert me to his new-found nonsense. There was a branch of this church he'd affiliated himself with in Dover. He went there multiple times a week and invited me to go along in the hope I would see the light. I definitely didn't want to join any religion and I was a bit scared of his church, having seen what it did to him, but I also had a burning desire to find out what had happened. I speculated that if I could find out what had influenced him to be religious, I might be able to cure him. I didn't cure him. I offended him. In doing so, I drove him away.

'The loss of Craig's friendship just left me more determined to find out what they had done to him. I started attending churches and synagogues and any religious places I could find. I listened to what they said and, more to the point, how they said it, and I saw they were all using the same tricks. I don't know how many of them understood the tricks and how many had just copied the style of successful preachers. I read books on mind control from a military perspective. There was an extremely interesting book on the experiences of combatants who were in POW camps in Korea. It explained how they had been brainwashed into believing in communism and that America should get out of South East Asia. Obviously, they didn't go into how they had, prior to that, been brainwashed into believing in capitalism and how America should be involved in South East Asia, but the book had some interesting information. It was hard to find much on how mind control works, because it's not in the interests of those who practice it to explain it.

'Then one day, a girl I knew asked me if I wanted to go to see a stage hypnotist who was performing in town. I wasn't really interested in stage hypnotism, which I just saw as cheap tricks and below my intellectual level. I have to admit I was a proper snob in that way. I was, however, interested in the girl. This was before I met Madcap.

'I went along and the hypnotist was using the same rhythmic way of talking as I'd heard preachers use in churches, synagogues and temples. Then he started using other tricks I'd seen them using. Seeing that opened my eyes to how the whole hypnotism thing worked and was used by organisations like churches. As a result, I think I was probably a bit too excited about the hypnotist and didn't pay enough attention to the girl. Certainly, it didn't go anywhere. I can't even remember her name.

'Subsequently, I studied hypnotism from any available source. I think everyone should study it really. Not that everyone should practice hypnotism, or at least, not more than we all do anyway. It would be advantageous if people could at least recognise what it is and understand a little about how it works. It's easy to believe your thoughts are your own and to be uncritical of them as a result. Once you start looking at your thoughts less as part of you and more as something you picked up somewhere, and then questioning how they arose and whether they are useful, your way of thinking changes dramatically.'

Old Ladies

Less effort than cycling, more reliable than the bus, hitching had become my main form of transport. This was the late '80s, probably '88.

I popped in to see a friend for a cup of tea on my way back from college, got caught up chatting and a number of hours have passed. I'm now walking to the roundabout, where the traffic for the A28 splits off, to hitch a lift back home. I could have got a bus pass to get me to and from college, but it's quicker to hitch. I've been hitching this route most days for a number of months, so a lot of people who regularly drive this way recognise me and pick me up whenever they see me.

I stop just off the roundabout where the traffic hasn't picked up speed yet and there's a good safe space for a car to pull in. I watch the cars as they come towards me and hope I'll get a quick lift home soon.

A police car pulls onto the roundabout and

comes off it in my direction. I keep my thumb out as if I'm trying to get a lift off them and sure enough they pull over.

It would be lovely to think they're going to offer me a lift home, but something tells me that is not their intention.

I walk up to the car, playing it as if I'm hitching and they're giving me a lift.

Two police officers get out of the car. One is very tall and thin, the other looks too short to be a police officer. I guess he must have worn platforms for the interview.

'Where are you going?' says the taller of the two.

'Bethersden,' I say. 'Are you going that way?'

They both just look at me like they don't know how this hitching lark works.

'Why are you going there?' says the short police officer.

'Are you going that way?' I ask again, ignoring his question.

'What are you doing in Bethersden?' he asks, as if his first question wasn't clear enough.

'If you give me a lift, we can chat about it on the way,' I suggest, and then repeat, 'Are you going that way?'

The short one is clearly not in the mood for stupid questions, or at least he's not in the mood to answer stupid questions, but he's more than happy to ask them.

'What are you doing out here?'

'I'd have thought that was remarkably obvious,' I say. 'I'm hitching to Bethersden.' Then I add, 'Are you going that way?' just in case he didn't understand the question up till now.

Who knows, maybe they'll decide to give me a lift. It's as obvious that they're not busy as it is that I'm hitching to Bethersden.

'Don't get fucking funny with me, sunshine.'

'If you're not going to Bethersden, I don't think you can help me. It's been nice chatting, but I really should get hitching and you've probably got crimes to solve.'

I turn around and start to walk back to my hitching spot.

'Stop right there,' he says.

I stop as if the music had stopped in a game of musical statues, with one foot off the ground.

'Stop playing stupid games,' he says.

'Can I move again then?' I don't wait for an answer as I haven't chosen the best position to stop in and I'm either going to fall over or get cramp really soon if I don't move.

'What have you got in your bag?'

'My possessions.'

'OK, enough of your lip. Show me what's in

the bag.' He's got his best serious face on now. I can tell he's practised this face in the mirror, along with the serious voice that he's using.

'What's your reasonable suspicion?' I ask.

'Just look at the way you're dressed.'

What I'm wearing is mainly army surplus, with the addition of a colourful waistcoat. I try to explain to him that the army wear these same clothes and that if he thinks these look suspicious, there's a barracks just up the road with loads of people wearing clothes just like this and his time might be better spent up there.

'It's the way you wear them,' he says.

'Thanks,' I say.

'Show me what's in your bag.'

I quote the section out of Baker and Wilkie's Police Promotion Handbook about how the clothes that someone wears cannot amount to reasonable suspicion. I got my copy of Baker and Wilkie's in a charity shop. I've memorised a few lines from it for just this sort of occasion.

The radio in their car gives a short burst of scratchy sound and the tall one who is closer to the car indicates to the short one they should leave.

I'm in full agreement they should leave.

They jump in the car and go.

A few minutes later I'm sitting in a car heading to Bethersden.

Back at home, I reassemble a moped I bought last week for twenty-five pounds. I've cleaned up the carb because a friend who knows about these things said that's what was wrong with it. He actually pointed out there was a lot wrong with it, but apparently a dirty carb was probably why it wasn't running properly.

The moped isn't a serious form of transport and is unlikely to stop me having to hitch any time soon. I certainly wouldn't ride it into town. Not only is it not road legal, but it's so far from road legal you can tell from a distance it's not. Even if Ashford Police didn't seem to have some vendetta against me, I wouldn't ride it into town.

On the back roads, however, there are rarely any police, so going to see friends in the sticks should be fine.

Having put the carb back on, I kick start it and to my surprise, it fires into life. I'd half expected that me cleaning the carb would be its death knell.

I head out onto the road to test it out and it's working much better. I kick it up through the gears and the engine is screaming away. At the corner where the Whiston is, I turn around and head back. It seems that not only is the bike still working after my interfering with it, but it's actually working better than it was.

Being the fun and exciting guy that I am, I

spend the rest of the evening writing an essay for my law A level about the role of magistrates in the criminal justice system. Of the subjects I'm doing, it's the only one that really interests me. You'd want to know the rules before you play a board game, yet we all go through life, subject to rules that we neither know nor understand.

Hitching back to Ashford to go to college in the morning is less eventful. Toby, who apparently works for a building firm but seems to spend all his time driving up and down the A28, picks me up as I'm walking to my hitching spot. He gives me a lift at least once a week and, assuming that I'd be hitching into town, pulled over when he saw me walking down the road.

I tell him about the latest bout of harassment from the police and we laugh together at their expense.

After another day at college, I'm heading back to my hitching spot again.

Again, I've popped in to see my mate and again, I was there for longer than intended. I walk down and stop just off the roundabout where the traffic hasn't picked up speed yet and there's a good safe space for a car to pull in.

I watch the cars as they come towards me and hope I'll get a quick lift and get home soon.

A police car pulls onto the roundabout and

comes off it in my direction. I keep my thumb out as if I'm trying to get a lift off them and sure enough they pull over. It would be lovely to think they're going to offer me a lift home, but something tells me that is not their intention.

If this feels familiar, there's a reason. This is the fourteenth time in as many days the police have stopped me in this spot, each time with the same pointless questions: What are you doing? Where are you going? What are you going there for? What's in your bag?

This time, when they ask what's in my bag, I take out two books. One is Smith and Hogan's Criminal Law. The other is Baker and Wilkie's Police Promotion Handbook. Smith and Hogan is by far the larger book and is only in my hand for theatrical reasons. I have Baker and Wilkie's bookmarked on the appropriate page and offer to show it to the two police officers who are insisting they have the right to search me.

They're not happy I'm not showing them what else I have on me; they're not happy they can't legally search me, and they're certainly not happy that I'm taking the piss out of them.

As unhappy as they are, they walk over to their car and get in. They then just sit there, in their car.

At this point, the police car is sat right where a car would pull up to give me a lift, which is going to make hitching quite difficult.

I breathe a sigh of relief as they start the engine. I assume this is the last I'll see of them, at least until tomorrow. They then put their car into reverse past me towards the roundabout. It looks like they're going to reverse right back onto it. I know the police are quite happy to break the highway code, but reversing onto the roundabout seems unnecessarily reckless and I'm intrigued as to what their game is.

Just before they get to the point where cars exit the roundabout in my direction, they stop. A big black Mercedes driven by an elderly chap with a shirt and tie exits the roundabout in my direction. It has to move over to the middle of the road to get past the police car.

By the time it sees me, it's already too late to safely pull in to pick me up and it's in the middle of a dangerous manoeuvre, so picking up hitchers is the last thing on the driver's mind.

The police have made it almost impossible for anyone to pick me up here. They grin at me from their car.

I smile back, put my thumb out and pretend this is not really a problem.

The Mercedes drives straight past.

Even though I'm obviously not going to get a lift with the police there, I figure that if I act cool enough, they'll get bored, or get called to a real crime.

The next car is a tatty Ford Escort, which looks like it's held together by rust and luck. By the way it swerves around the police car, there's either something wrong with the steering, the driver or both.

The driver, who is probably in his twenties, looks extremely nervous and stares in his rear-view mirror as he passes the police. He's either too concerned they will pull him or too relieved that they haven't to even think about giving me a lift. He's made a sensible decision not to stop for me; if he had stopped, they would have easily found something wrong with his car they could have caused him grief over.

The road goes quiet and I'm left looking at the police, still trying to pretend that they're not inconveniencing me in any way. I'm putting on as good a show as I can, but it's not working and they're sat there laughing at me.

I'm praying someone robs a bank or does something else to cause them to get called away.

A little white Metro pulls onto the roundabout and sure enough it's coming off in my direction.

As it gets closer, I can see two old ladies in the front. They've both got their hair set into big hairstyles that were probably the height of fashion when they were young and their hair was not so white. It's unlikely they'd pick me up in the best of circumstances, and these are not the best of circumstances.

I smile sweetly at them, but my smile is really for the benefit of the police.

To my surprise, the Metro pulls up. I run up to it and the woman in the passenger seat speaks to me in a somewhat plummy accent and invites me to get in to the car.

As I open the back door, I can see one of the police officers running up the road towards us. He looks pissed off and a bit out of breath.

I get in the back and hope the driver will go before he gets to it.

She winds down her window as he approaches. When he gets to the car, he's unable to get his words out, allowing the driver time to speak first.

'You really shouldn't park there, young man,' she says, gesturing back at the police car. 'You could cause an accident.'

'Do you know him?' he says, pointing to me.

'Are you detaining me?' she responds.

'No.' From his intonation, this is definitely supposed to be the beginning of a sentence, but she's driving away already.

I turn around to watch the baffled expression on his face disappear into the distance. My expression is just as baffled, but a happy sort of baffled.

'Was that policeman harassing you?' asks the sweet-looking old lady in the passenger seat.

'They really are the most terrible bullies,' says the driver. 'We used to fight them before the war, you know.'

'You used to fight the police?' I say, in the tone of someone who has been transported into another dimension and is trying to find their bearings.

'Well, they just got in the way, didn't they, dear?' says the driver, more to the passenger than to me. 'Indeed, we were supposed to be fighting the fascists.'

'There was little difference,' says the passenger. 'Many of them were paid up members of the British Union of Fascists back then. They had no qualms about hitting a woman and their hands always went where they weren't wanted.'

There's something quite dis-concerting about hearing someone saying these things in such a posh, old fashioned accent. These two old ladies look and sound much more likely to be having tea with the vicar than fighting with the police.

'They were not all like that,' the driver interjects. 'The better behaved police stayed back out of the action. They just stood around looking embarrassed, but not one of them would stop the supposed "bad apples". It was not limited to them, of course. Everyone saw those of us who were against the fascists as idiots or agitators in those days. The press absolutely hated us. They wrote some truly awful things. The BBC would happily give airtime to fascists, but we were seen as not respectable enough to be given a voice.'

She slows down to about thirty miles per hour from the steady forty-five she's been doing until now, along this very straight and wide road.

I look ahead and see that a car has pulled onto the road a good two hundred metres ahead of us. As it speeds off into the distance, she steadily accelerates back up to forty-five. She's possibly the most cautious driver I've ever had a lift from.

'Of course, in times of hardship,' she continues, 'and believe you me, the 30s were a time of hardship, people turn to either fascism or socialism to look for a way out of the situation. The authorities, or to be more precise the powers-that-be, see socialism as a threat to their very existence, whereas fascism is no threat to them at all. When socialists are fighting fascists, they will always take the side of the fascists.'

All the way home they tell me of their exploits in the 30s. It's hard to believe that these seemingly respectable old ladies were once hardened anti-fascists.

When they drop me off, they tell me to take care, just in the way your granny might when you part after a visit.

No sooner am I out of the car than I'm face to face with the police again. It's a slightly different situation to the one I faced in Ashford though.

Our village policeman stops to talk to me. He's a towering figure at something over six foot six and three times as broad as me at least, although I have to admit, most people are broader than me. Unlike the police I've been dealing with in Ashford, he's not a bully and doesn't push his weight around. He's firm and I definitely wouldn't want to cross him, but he's not out to make trouble.

'So then, Jason,' he says. 'I think you need to realise that if I see someone riding a motorbike in my village without a helmet, I'm going to have to ask them questions about their tax, insurance and MOT.'

On that note he walked away without giving me a chance to respond.

He's one of the good ones, I'm thinking. He'd have stayed back out of the action, well out of the action, in a village somewhere, not getting involved in that sort of stuff at all.

New Boy

I have no enemies, only misguided friends. Some are very misguided. (Late summer '95)

I'm in real trouble if this vehicle doesn't stop.

I'm kneeling on the ground, with my head bowed. It's been hot recently and the first shower in weeks passed over a few minutes ago. It was only a short shower, but it's released that fragrance you get after rain hits hot dry soil.

With my head so close to the ground it fills my nostrils. My right leg is crossed over the left, meaning not only that I can't stand up quickly, but also that anyone looking at me can see I can't.

My eyes are gently closed and my facial expression is entirely relaxed. I hear the engine of the approaching digger as it revs higher. Hearing that, I know it's not one of the regular digger drivers. It must be someone new. I'm on good terms with most of the digger drivers and I've spent a lot of time chatting with them whilst they wait for security to remove me from their vehicles.

There are digger drivers who are not so friendly, but none of them would bother to rev their engine like that because they would know I'm not moving.

A few have tried playing chicken with me. They've all lost. They know they would relive the moment of my death again and again. They know they would always regret it. I know that so long as the vehicle is moving at a sufficient speed and I position myself so that it strikes the top of my head, I will relive nothing. I won't suffer. I won't feel anything.

Everything will just end at the point of impact.

I know there is nothing I can do which would be more effective at highlighting the environmental damage of the road than losing this game of chicken.

The digger is still roaring towards me. The security guards and the protestors who are out today are screaming at me to move.

When we went for the fence, I was the only one who managed to get over. Security caught the others and there isn't time for either the protestors or security to get over the fence and intervene now.

Whatever is about to happen is going to happen and there's nothing they can do.

From what I can hear, this may be my final

game.

The digger is probably too late to stop now if it wanted to. In the position I'm in, it's too late for me to get out of the way. I could try, but that would be more likely to prolong my suffering and I would rather a quick death than a slow one.

I concentrate on my breathing. I breathe slowly and deliberately. I want to die with a calm look on my face. I don't want anyone to see my fear.

I've always been able to do this. I can switch off the emotion in my face in a desperate situation and look calm. It's not the greatest superpower, but I may as well use it now.

I hear the crunching of machinery and the ground under the digger as the driver has a last-minute change of mind and decides to stop. I hear however-many-tons of digger skidding towards me and I hope it either hits me hard enough to kill me outright, or stops in time.

I feel the air and dust engulf me as it approaches. Then it stops.

I open my eyes. The bottom of the bulldozer blade is just below my face.

As I lift my head, I knock it on the unforgiving metal.

Luke, the blue hat is first on the scene. The rumour is that him and Matt are ex-special forces. Certainly, they're handy in the way you would expect of special forces and they have short military-style haircuts.

All the protestors and all the other security are still on the other side of the fence.

Luke's job now as a security guard is quite clear. I'm still in the track blocking the digger's way. He should be dragging me out of the way so that the digger can pass.

Luke is a very physical bloke; often too physical. Road protest is a full contact sport in his eyes. It's not rare for him to overstep the mark.

He's only done it once to me. He threw me up against the fence one time, right into one of the metal fenceposts. I hadn't really done anything other than try to run past him when he was in the wrong mood. One minute I was dodging his arm as he tried to grab me, next thing I knew I was flying up against the fence.

It was completely uncalled for and he apologised afterwards. He's rough though, just as a general thing. When he grabs you, he grabs you as hard as he can. If he tackles you, he doesn't care if you hurt yourself landing badly. He sees it as all part of the game.

I've never seen him lose it like this before though.

Luke is screaming at the digger driver, asking him if he really wants a "dead fucking protestor" on his conscience and telling him that if he wants to keep his job, there are rules like "not fucking killing anyone".

When he's finished tearing strips off the driver, he calms down and walks towards me.

'Come on, Sketchy,' he says, as if we're friends and we're going to the pub. 'Let's go.'

I stand up and we walk towards the nearest gate so that he can escort me to the other side of the fence. In the same way that his role is to drag me away from the digger, mine is to resist. It's all gone a bit wrong today and although I could buy myself an extra thirty seconds, maybe even a couple of minutes of delaying the digger, I stand up and walk with him without argument.

As I go through the gate, I'm greeted by the security and protestors who are waiting there. It's a security guard, whose name I don't know, who speaks first. He's an alright bloke. Even though I don't know his name, we've played plenty of games together and he's got a fair attitude.

'You OK, Sketchy?' he asks in a concerned tone.

'Yeah, I'm fine,' I say. 'It didn't hit me, did it?'

I'm lying of course; physically I'm fine, but mentally I feel a bit distant, like the world isn't real and I'm just watching all this on TV. It's like I'm one step removed from reality. I'm not shaking, and I don't feel upset or scared. I'm not angry with the digger driver or anything, I'm just a bit numb.

The digger has gone and there's nothing to be done here, so we leave security and walk away to decide our next move. Madcap has to go into town soon, so she's calling it quits for the day. Karl asks her for a lift into town, so he's not sticking around. Fred and Yuppy decide to go and work on the defences back in the woods, so it's just Fishhead and me left.

That's not such a bad thing; Fishhead's a good person to have around when things go wrong. He's very level-headed and sensitive towards what's going on in people's heads. Right now, I could do with that.

We follow the route of the planned road, but at a distance to avoid being seen. We're looking for a digger to dive on and a route to get to it that's not too out in the open.

After a while, we see the digger that nearly killed me. There are two security guards nearby and two of the sad detectives, who are sat on the bonnet of their van looking bored. One is leant right back looking up at the sky and the other is sat on the very front of the bonnet with his chin rested on one hand and his other hand on a newspaper, which looks very crumpled, like they've both read it cover to cover already.

They probably have no more of a clue than we

do what the digger is actually doing. They spend hours each day watching diggers dig holes and fill them in, scrape earth back or build it up. Sometimes they'll spend a whole day watching diggers without seeing a protestor at all. The one supporting his chin with his hand is at least trying to keep an eye out, in case there is something worth looking at. The other bloke seems to have given up entirely.

Fishhead isn't too keen. He asks me if I'm really sure I want to risk it, being as the driver has already proved himself to be a complete nutter. I know his concern is purely for me. However much I insist I'm fine, he knows me well; we've been in a lot of situations together and he can see that I'm not fine at all.

If it was just him, he'd be heading towards the digger already. I insist as convincingly as I can that I'm alright and what I need is to stop that digger from working, so we try our luck.

The route to the digger is quite easy. There used to be a ditch crossing the site. They've filled parts of it with concrete pipes. They run under the fence and right up to where the digger is working, at which point there is an open section of ditch before the concrete pipes start again.

We can get into the pipes through the end, which is on our side of the fence. They didn't just leave this all open for us. We removed the metal bars which blocked the entrance to the concrete pipe a couple of nights ago. We thought it might be a useful way in.

The pipe is just big enough to crawl along on our hands and knees. It's hard on the knees, but it means we'll be right up next to the digger before anyone sees us. Luckily, other than that brief shower earlier, it hasn't rained, so it's fairly dry in our little tunnel. This is a vast improvement on last time I was in here. We checked it out before they fitted the bars. That was just after heavy rain had washed tonnes of mud into it. The result was that my feet were so caked in mud I could hardly walk on level ground, let alone climb on a digger.

The open section of the tunnel is almost the length of the digger's tracks and the tracks themselves are right on the edge of the bank. From here, we just have to choose our moment, jump up onto the track and from there onto the body of the digger.

We're both a little cautious because the side of the ditch is beginning to crumble under the weight of the track.

We look at each other, knowing the timing isn't going to get any more promising than this. We're just about to step out of the tunnel and jump on the digger when the engine cuts out. We stop completely still.

Up until this moment, any noise that we made has been drowned out. Now with the engine off and us being in an echoey tunnel, the slightest sound is going to be heard by everyone in the vicinity.

We hear the click of the door to the cab opening, then the sound of it slamming shut.

We've got a very limited view here. I can see one digger track and a bit of sky, that's about it. Fishhead is just behind me in the tunnel. He'll be able to see even less than me.

I see a flask being placed on the digger track and then an arse appears next to the flask as the driver sits down for his tea break.

The driver has his back towards us, which is advantageous. He opens the flask and pours himself a drink.

Fishhead slowly and carefully leans past me to see what's going on, then moves back again.

If this tunnel was just a little bit larger, we'd be a whole lot more comfortable. As it is, we're crouched over with our heads bowed in a position which would have been fine for a few seconds, but is now starting to make my neck ache. We could lie down, which would make my neck ache less, or move to another position, but we can't risk being heard.

Eventually, the driver finishes his drink and heads back to the cab. We hear the door slam, and we jump out of the tunnel.

The bucket is on the ground just in front of the track. I jump on it and move up the arm, so that I'm halfway between the bucket and the joint.

I get a position I can stay in for a while without slipping, with my feet jammed between the hydraulic hoses and the arm. Fishhead is up on the roof of the cab.

There are two security guards running towards us. I don't recognise them, so they must be new. They'll need more than two of them to remove us, so we'll be here until backup arrives. One is talking into his radio as he runs, so we probably only have a few minutes, but a few minutes delay a few times a day all adds up.

I hear the engine start up. This can only mean one thing.

Unfortunately, I'm not in the greatest position, halfway up the arm like this. Having my feet jammed between the arm and the hose is fine if the digger isn't moving, but as soon as it does, I could be in real danger.

I lower myself down so that I'm standing on the bucket, just in time. The boom rises, the arm stretches out and the bucket with me on it is lifted into the air.

Then we start to move clockwise, round and round, faster and faster. I'm in a pretty secure position now. He can turn this into a fairground ride and my guess is I'll be fine.

The amber light on top of the digger is on a little pole and Fishhead is hanging on to that for dear life.

I get a quick glance at the guards as I swing past them; one of them is shouting at the digger driver; the other is on the radio.

A little way behind them, the sad detectives are stood filming this impromptu rodeo, no doubt pleased to have some action to liven up an otherwise uneventful day.

The arm suddenly jolts to a stop and starts swinging the other way.

Well, that was unexpected and it almost made me lose balance, but I'm still here.

Now he's realised that hitting the bucket on the ground as it goes around is a good way to knock me off. It certainly makes the ride uncomfortable.

The driver tries moving the bucket in a scooping movement so that my feet can't grip it properly. He really is trying to kill me here.

I don't know if he's thought this through, but I can only see two outcomes. One is that Fishhead and myself walk away without injury, leaving him looking like a bit of a pratt, and the other is that he gets a criminal conviction for killing or injuring us.

I don't really see how either of those work to his advantage.

Now he's lifting the bucket high in the air and shaking it like he's trying to shift some mud which has got stuck to it. I'm just hanging on to the hydraulic pipes with my feet raised off the bucket.

He lowers it again and goes back to swinging me around.

Suddenly, the whole digger moves underneath me. The bucket with me on it goes crashing towards the ground.

I jump off just before it makes contact and to my great relief, I manage to land uninjured. The bucket crashes down beside me, kicking up a cloud of dust and grit.

The side of the ditch has collapsed, and the front of the track has slipped down the bank and into the tunnel. This created enough space for the back of the digger's track to slip down the ditch too.

The cab has come down hard on the other bank of the ditch and smashed all the glass on that side of the cab.

Fishhead is hanging off the roof, just a couple of feet above the ground. He lets go of the little pole which has been his saviour until now and falls to the floor next to me.

The digger now has both ends of its track just inside the two sections of concrete pipe. The driver tries to move the arm, but the cab is leaning hard on the bank of the ditch. The arm just flails around pointlessly with it's very limited movement.

I can't really see how you can get the digger out without removing some of the sections of tunnel. Luckily, that's not my problem.

The sad detectives film Fishhead and me walking away for a bit, then turn the camera back towards the digger.

I don't think we'll see that driver again. I don't know if they'll do anything about the clear breaches of health and safety that just occurred. My guess is they'll sack him.

Even if they don't, everyone on site is going to want to see that video and, if he sticks around, the piss-taking will be unbearable.

It's a shame really. There was no gain in any of it for him. He could have just been in a bad mood today and decided to take it out on protestors, but it would have to be an extremely bad mood to justify his actions.

Maybe he sees us as a threat, but I can't see how we're a threat to him. All he had to do is stop when a protestor makes it unsafe to do otherwise and accept it as a paid break.

One of the drivers brings in a book of crosswords for just that purpose. Quite a few of them bring in more tea than their arranged breaks would allow for and maybe a paper to read.

He's sat there in the mud, with his digger on

its side, unable to right itself, shouting abuse and kicking the dashboard out of anger.

He started a new job today and he'll end it today as well.

It's a shame we wont get a chance to chat with him and explain our side of things. I don't think trying to talk to him now would be very productive.

A Quest For Orange Juice

I can't remember exactly when this was, but I was still just a child and it was the first time either Toby or I heard Bobby McFerrin's Don't Worry, Be Happy. We were singing along by the end of the track.

I'm going to pop into town in a bit to see if the library has a book on fungi.

I heard on the radio that until the mid-nineteenth century, the Anglican church classed the study of fungi as witchcraft. They used to actually burn people at the stake for knowing too much about mushrooms. Apparently that's why, as British people, we know so much less about fungi than people in the rest of Europe.

I'd never really thought about it, but I know very little about fungi, compared to what I know about plants and animals. They also said that when early forms of life divided into kingdoms, animals split off from plants and then fungi split off from animals. Therefore, fungi are more closely related to us than they are to plants. I think it would be

109

interesting to know more about our fungal cousins.

First things first though, I've just had breakfast and I'm going to grab some orange juice at the shop to wash it down with, then I'll hitch into town.

I was sure I put my wallet down in my room, but I can't find it anywhere. My room is a proper state though. I look under a pile of clothes and find a mug of cold tea. Miraculously, it's managed to stay upright even though it's entirely buried. That could have been messy!

As much as I look, there's no wallet. I head downstairs and there it is on the kitchen table. I chuck my boots on without doing them up and head out to the shop, which is next door but one.

No sooner do my feet touch the pavement than a van pulls up. It's Toby. He must think I'm hitching. I may as well forgo the orange juice and catch a lift into town with him.

'Mornin', Jason,' he says as I open the door. With a big grin on his face, he adds, 'Your taxi awaits.'

It's the third time he's picked me up this week.

'Cheers, mate,' I reply, as I get in and put my seatbelt on. 'Picking up materials in Ashford again?'

'Not today. The boss has only decided to send me to Exeter to get some posh bathroom suite for this job we're doin'. It's got to be fitted tomorrow and they can't deliver until next week, so I get to spend the day drivin' to Exeter and back. It's goin' to be a long journey, but it's better than diggin' up the old drainage. That's the other job he offered me.'

A while before we get to Ashford, Toby floats the idea that I spend the day with him and keep him company on his drive. I mention that my mate Gavin lives in Exeter and suggest that we drop in to see him for a cuppa whilst we're there.

It seems like learning about fungi will have to wait for another day.

Me and Toby start to talk in a way we never have before. We've never really talked about anything serious. It's only seven miles into town from my place and he drives fairly fast, so we only have a few minutes.

Normally, we joke and take the piss a bit, but that's all. There's not really time to do more than that.

As we head up the motorway, we swap stories about our childhoods. I tell him about our old place in the sticks, how much I hated school and always wanted to get back home to spend more time in the woods. I tell him about the time at primary school when I realised a lot of what I was being told to do didn't seem to have any point to it. I'd been told I was there to learn and I was happy to learn, but rather than blindly go along with pointless instructions, I decided to ask 'why'. This infuriated my teacher, Mr

Craddock.

He stood over me one day, all red in the face in his ill-fitting Victorian-style three piece suit, and bellowed at me that the only reason I needed was because he 'bloody told me to'. When I pointed out he shouldn't use that word, he told me to put out my hand for him to hit with a ruler. This seemed unfair to me. He had sworn and I was getting the punishment.

I, of course, asked why.

He grabbed my hand and held it whilst he hit me with the ruler and then the school threatened to expel me if I continued to question the teachers.

It turns out that Toby spent a lot of his childhood in Germany on an army base. He says his family are a military family and he was expected to join the military himself.

'There was never any question about it. It's what my dad did and his dad before him. My brother served in the Falklands. My uncle died in Northern Ireland. They'd always just assumed I'd follow suit. I don't mean that I'd die, but I'd join up and serve. I didn't see any way out of it really. If I didn't sign up, they'd disown me, so I applied. I thought if I didn't put the effort in, I could fail the entry exams. That way, I'd have tried my best and failed. I thought that would be a fair get-out. I would have been seen as the idiot of the family, but I can live with that.'

This all seems very familiar. Not the military thing. I don't think anyone in my family has had a career in the military. The expectation though; the expectation is very familiar. My dad has always just assumed that I'd work for him. I'm expected to get whatever education I can and then join his firm, so I can continue his life's work of selling people insurance which they may or may not need. If I work really hard and follow his lead, maybe one day I can be as miserable as he is. Delaying that is certainly a good reason to stay in education. College is far better than school was, but I'm sure there's something better out there.

'It didn't work out though,' Toby continues. 'The exams were easier than I thought. I failed to fail, if you get what I mean. I've always been pretty fit, so the physical wasn't an issue. I didn't put the effort in that most of them did, but I got through. I was bloody depressed to be honest. I couldn't see any way out. Then they called me in for a psychological assessment. Genuinely, psychologically I was not in a good place.'

He looks at me with a serious expression on his face and shakes his head.

'My nerves just came out as a terrible sense of humour. When they asked me "Are you a homosexual?" I said "No, but I'm up for learnin' if there's a special force". Well that didn't go down well at all. Next thing I know, the bloke who's interviewin' me says, "You're not really fitted to being in the army, are you?" I couldn't disagree and they turned me down.'

'That must have been a relief,' I say. Personally, I couldn't imagine anything worse than being in the army. I couldn't stand being told to do pointless things at school. The army seems like an exaggerated version of that nonsense, with added killing. At least nobody will die if I joined my dad's firm. I might think I'd die of boredom, but I won't actually die.

I'm hoping to find a way to avoid it by the time I leave education. It would be much easier if I knew what I wanted to do. When I was five, I wanted to be a fireman. I don't know why really. I guess they're heroes, which is a good thing to be. Since then, I haven't really seen any career path that looks attractive. I'd like to do something useful and preferably something fun. I don't know what though.

'Well, yeah, and I thought that I'd got away with it,' Toby says, rolling a cigarette with one hand and steering with the other. 'My dad was pissed off I didn't get in. But he had to agree, I'd tried my best. I thought he'd get over it in time. Trouble is, he's got connections, so he asked around and found out what happened. He went apeshit at me. Absolutely lost it. Kicked me out onto the street. Hasn't spoken to me since.'

'Shit. Were you OK? I mean, did you have anywhere to stay?'

'Just friend's sofas and that. Luckily, I got this job soon after. I was labourin' at first, before I got my drivin' licence. It wasn't the best, but it put a roof over my head. My boss is pretty good to me. He's always done well by me and now I get to drive around pickin' up materials most of the time. I can't complain at all.'

By the time we get to Exeter, we know each other's back story pretty well and we've chatted about all sorts of stuff. We both thought it was great that Reagan was visiting Russia. Hopefully, tensions will subside in the Cold War. It's a miracle that neither side has set off a nuclear weapon.

Who knows, maybe sanity'll prevail and we'll stop pointing them at each other.

Whilst Toby's picking up the bathroom suite, I find a phone box nearby and phone Gavin. His mum answers and says he'll be back in a bit.

Toby says he can't stick around as he has a long drive ahead of him. I make a spur of the moment decision, phone again and ask Gavin's mum if it's OK for me to stay over tonight. I figure I can hitch back in the morning. I haven't seen Gavin for ages and I'm in Exeter now; it seems a shame to miss the opportunity.

Toby drops me off at Gavin's place and heads back to Ashford.

As soon as he drives away, I have a sinking feeling as I realise how long the hitch back home is. I've only ever hitched up and down the A28. I've daydreamed about hitching long distance and seeing the world for free, but my longest hitch to date is Tenterden to Ashford, which is just over twelve miles and I'm never more than seven miles away from home on that route. I only have a few coins in my wallet and I'm a lot further than seven miles from home, so I'm committed to hitching now, whether I like it or not.

It's great seeing Gavin, and his mum cooks a fantastic curry.

Next morning, his dad drops me off at a hitching spot so I don't have to walk, which is really cool of him. He says he's seen plenty of people hitching here and they're not here now, so they must have got lifts.

I put my thumb out and wait. The traffic here is quite fast. But there's a good place to pull in when someone decides to give me a lift.

After about three hours, no one has stopped. An extra wide lorry goes through the junction, slowing everyone down to a snail's pace. This is ideal. Now I have time to look the drivers in the eye properly and they have time to think about giving me a lift.

A tatty old Allegro goes past, driven by an old bloke with a flat cap. He's staring intently at the car in front and doesn't seem to notice me at all.

A woman in the daftest looking hat I've ever seen is driving the car just behind him. Her hat is small and black and appears to be stuck to the side of her head, unless it's slipped down whilst she's driving. It's got black and white feathers on it, which seem to be blocking her view a bit.

They clearly haven't blocked her view entirely; she certainly sees me. I can tell, because she's looking at me in absolute disgust.

I guess I'm not getting a lift from her today.

Behind her is a lorry. The driver smiles down at me from his cab, but makes no move to stop.

A few more cars drive by slowly before the traffic speeds up again. Now I'm watching cars drive by at speed again. There's an earth bank a little way away from the road. I keep looking over at it, wondering if the skeletons of the hitchers who were here before me are behind it. I don't want to seem pessimistic, but this is a terrible hitching spot.

A car coming towards me pulls up in a lay-by a few yards before it reaches me. At first, I think it's stopping for me, albeit in a slightly strange place. A bloke gets out who's dressed in patchwork clothing from head to foot. He only needs a hat with bells on it and he'd be your classic court jester.

Once the car drives away, he comes bounding over towards me. He's carrying a bag and a hitching sign. They're dropping him off rather than picking me up. Now I have to share this lousy hitching spot with another hitcher. That's not going to speed things up at all.

'How's it going, man?' he says in the happiest voice I've ever heard. He has the enthusiasm in his voice that you'd expect of a children's TV presenter. But then he hasn't been standing here as long as I have.

'Well,' I say, 'that's the problem. I don't seem to be going anywhere.'

'Where are you trying to get to, man?' he asks, giving me an incredibly intense stare.

'I've got to get back to Ashford, Kent,' I say, trying not to sound too annoyed about the whole situation.

'See if this helps,' he says, pulls a piece of cardboard out of his bag, writes 'M25' on it in big letters with a marker pen and hands it to me. 'Enjoy the adventure.'

He gives me no time to respond, or even take in what just happened. Clearly a man on a mission, he turns to face the traffic, puts his sign out and starts walking backwards away from me, whilst holding it up to the oncoming cars. He's got an unbelievably friendly smile, one that oozes confidence. A smile which says, 'You really would be missing out if you didn't take this opportunity to spend some time with me.'

I've pretty much given up hope of getting a lift and I watch in disbelief as a silver Audi pulls up almost immediately to give him a lift. He jumps in and he's off. From his arrival to his departure must have taken all of thirty seconds. I would be left doubting that he was even here, were it not for the hitching sign that I'm holding, which proves his existence.

As I hold out my new sign, I'm curious as to whether the magic will work for me as it did for him.

The first car is a big blue Peugeot estate. I smile at the driver in the friendliest way I can, but it drives past, followed by a green van with a florist sign on the side, a white van and a little yellow Metro. The car behind that though, a battered old Astra pulls in to give me a lift.

I wish I had some way of thanking that bloke in the patchwork clothing.

The driver of the Astra is immensely tall and just as notably thin. He has mousy brown hair, but his hairline has receded almost all the way to the back of his head, leaving just a crescent shape haloing his scalp. His smile is warm and welcoming, and he invites me to get into his car with the softest of voices.

I thank him sincerely for picking me up, because I really was concerned I was going to spend the rest of my life there, waiting for a lift.

'I always pick up hitchers if they're going my way,' he says. 'I feel I owe it to the world. I did a lot of hitching myself. I even tried to get funding for research into hitching.'

'What research was that?' I ask. I can't imagine there's much call for research into hitching.

'I wanted to study why people give lifts to hitchers and as importantly, why people don't.' he says. 'It's an interesting area in my opinion and if I'd managed to get funding for it, I could have been paid to hitch around having adventures, but I couldn't find the funding, so I had to get a real job.

'On the face of it, people give hitchers lifts out of pure altruism, but there's much more to it than that. Some people give lifts for the company, some because they want to get stuff off their chests. Hitchers are great people to confide in. They have no preconceived ideas about your life and you'll never see them again. I used to have lots of people unload their issues on me. Sometimes, quite deep and personal stuff. I give people lifts because I've been given lots of lifts myself and I feel I should repay society. That's interesting in itself. If we could persuade more people that society was a supportive thing and they were in debt to it, they would be more inclined to do people favours, which would leave those people more likely to believe that society was a supportive thing, like some sort of virtuous cycle.'

This all makes sense to me, but how would you start this virtuous cycle?

'The other side of this coin is, of course, the people who don't give lifts. Contrastingly, this is often down to their negative view of society and a fear of strangers. The fear of hitchers is quite markedly exaggerated. People think that every other hitcher is a serial killer. If I was advising serial killers on how to be effective, or successful or however you want to put it, I'd say don't bother hitching as a way to find your victims. To get a lift, you have to stand where the drivers can see you, generally for quite a long time. This leaves hundreds of witnesses. If you cover up your face, you'll never get a lift, so you can forget that. Serial killers are usually seeking a certain demographic as I understand it. Hitching is an extremely inefficient way to meet up with your chosen demographic, so unless you're a very unfussy serial killer, you're going to have to get lots of lifts before you find your victim. This leaves lots more witnesses, so raises your chance of getting caught. There are much better methodologies for serial killers to adopt, methodologies which also don't involve standing around in the weather so much.'

My lift takes me all the way to Potters Bar

services on the M25. He tells me story after story of his hitching days, travelling around Britain and Europe, including stories of hitching in Italy, a country which he seems to be completely in love with.

I've seen the value in these hitching signs and figure I need one for the next leg of my journey, which says 'M20', so I ditch the 'M25' sign and go into the shops to look for a marker pen and something to eat. I'm now faced with the ridiculous prices that a service station charges.

They have no marker pens. For all of my money, I can get a pack of three felt tips, or I can get a sandwich. Whilst I'm trying to make this decision, I see the pen at the checkout. The one on a chain for signing cheques. There is, of course, one at every checkout and there's an unused checkout, so I figure I could use that pen without anyone minding.

I buy the sandwich, which turns out to be the poorest quality sandwich I've ever encountered, and go off to find some cardboard. There's a crate of broken-down display boxes. One of the shop assistants gives me a funny look when I'm going through it, but no one objects to me taking a piece of cardboard.

I go over to the empty checkout and start making a sign. A marker would make this task much easier.

I've drawn an outline. It's not the greatest, but it'll do. I then start to fill it in, which takes ages. I'm about halfway through the 'M' when a store manager comes over to tell me that the pens are 'not for customer use'. They clearly are. I understand they're specifically for customers to sign cheques with, but he's wrong to say that they're not for customer use.

Soon, I'm in the carpark with a half-written sign, which isn't going to help at all. Now I've seen the difference they make, I really don't fancy hitching from here with no sign.

I wonder about asking someone for a pen. I also wonder about asking in the garage if they'll let me use one.

Then in a moment of genius — OK, maybe not genius, but with some semblance of a good idea — I realise that if I fold the M25 sign over, it would say M2. I'd prefer the M20, but a quick lift to the M2 is better than living at this service station for the rest of my life.

If I can get to Canterbury, I can hitch down the A28 to Ashford and on to Bethersden using just my thumb. I go to the bin where I threw the sign away to see if it's still useable. An empty coffee cup has been thrown in on top of it. There's coffee on the back of the sign, but the important side is fine. I shake it to remove the excess coffee and wipe it on the grass. I wouldn't want to eat off it, but it'll be fine to wave at passing cars.

I head over to the exit and hold up my sign. Three cars drive past before an old Mini Countryman pulls up. The back is full of furniture and the legs of a chair are sticking out into the front, either side of the top of the passenger seat.

I squeeze in with my head between the legs. This is fine, but I have very limited vision to the sides, which means I can't see the face of the driver without straining my neck.

In theory this shouldn't be a problem; he should have his eyes on the road, but it's a bit socially weird. If I look down, I have a reasonable view of where his brown and black chequered trousers meet his matching waistcoat.

The driver is an antiques dealer. He's just picked up the furniture in a barn in Oxfordshire and he's taking it back to Kent. The 'barn' part of that explains the musty smell in the car.

I wouldn't say it was particularly offensive as smells go, but certainly distinctive.

He's going to Upper Harbledown which is fantastic. If it comes to it, I can walk from there to the A28.

I tell him all about my journey to and from Exeter, how I clumsily found myself there without considering my journey back and how I was saved by the chap who was dressed like a court jester.

He chuckles away through the whole story. He tells me about his life as an antiques dealer, travelling around looking for bargains in barns and boot fairs. It sounds like a lot of wild goose chases with only the occasional worthwhile find.

When we get to Upper Harbledown, he keeps driving. At first I think he must live just on the other side, which is handy for me, because it takes me closer to the A28.

Then I realise we've gone past Upper Harbledown completely, and not long after that he drops me off at the junction of the A28.

He's been great company as well as a useful lift and he's ended the journey going a couple of miles out of his way to drop me off where I want to be. It's not every day that a complete stranger is that generous to you.

When we stop, I thank him profusely, but he says not to worry, sticks his hand in his pocket and passes me a marker pen.

'It sounds like you might find this useful,' he says, before turning around to drive back home.

I now have a marker, but I don't have anything to write a sign on. I still have the M2/M25 sign, but the back is too covered in coffee to use. I'm sure I could go for a wander and find something, but I decide instead to go for the traditional approach and stick my thumb out.

The first car, a brown Ford Fiesta, drives straight past, followed by the next car and every other car that turns up for at least half an hour.

A few cars later, when I'm just wondering if it would be a good idea to go find some card, a blue Ford Transit van pulls up. The two front seats are occupied, but the passenger gets out and unlocks the back.

'Ashford town centre any good?' he asks.

That sounds great. I jump in the back of the van.

He slams the door shut hard and I hear a key in the lock as the van is locked with me in it. It's pitch black in here. There's nothing to sit on other than the floor.

I suddenly feel very unsafe. I'm not sure that getting into this van was such a great idea. I feel the van pull out onto the road and we drive for what seems like a long time.

The van is turning and slowing down.

It stops, then speeds up again. There are a number of left and right turns. I don't have a clue where we are.

The van stops again. It's reversing and I feel it hit something, not hard, but it definitely hit something.

A door opens and someone walks around to the back. I don't have a clue what's going on, let alone how to get out of whatever situation I've got myself into.

I hear keys in the lock of the back door. Whoever is opening the lock seems to be struggling a bit and having to jiggle the key around to get it to work.

I hear the lock click open and the door latch being opened.

The doors swing wide open and standing in front of me is the bloke who locked me in.

'Sorry about locking you in, chap,' he says with a smile. 'The catch doesn't work on the back doors on this one.' Behind the van is a brick wall and a bollard lying on the floor. We must have hit the bollard, I guess.

I look around and I'm in Ashford Market. He probably thinks I'm a bit weird from the nervous way I thank him for the lift, before I hurriedly walk away.

It's only as I'm walking away that I take in how badly I'd misjudged that situation. I really thought that something terrible was going to occur.

I head into the market cafe building and grab a bit of cardboard for a sign. I don't need a hitching sign to get to Bethersden, but it can't hurt, and I have the marker that the antiques dealer gave me.

A short walk later, I'm standing by the roundabout with a sign saying 'Bethersden'. The 'B' is quite big and the letters get incrementally smaller from there on, as I realised I was running out of space on the piece of cardboard, but it's readable.

I hold it out as a white van drives up and I realise it's Toby.

'Check you out with your posh sign,' he says, laughing as I get into his van.

Fens And Fields

I've always liked writing poetry. Road protest gave me no end of inspiration. (Autumn '95)

It's not really my thing this.

I quite like writing poems, but I find reading them out a bit awkward. I'm only really here because Fishhead insisted I send the poem in.

I guess it's an opportunity to highlight the protest, but I'd prefer to spend the day jumping on diggers, to be honest.

I didn't really expect the poem to get picked. Sure everyone at camp says it's great, but they're a lovely bunch of freaks and they can truly relate to it. I'm now going to perform it in front of a whole roomful of strangers.

Strangers who've deliberately come here to judge poetry.

I know it's only the judges who are supposed to be here to judge poetry as such. The audience would all say they are here to enjoy the poetry, but afterwards they'll also say, "I liked so-and-so's poetry: I thought that was very moving, but I thought that other chap, well, I thought his poetry was a bit flat." And so on.

They'll all be judging me when I read out my poem and to be frank, I'm not that convinced it's any good.

They brought our group of poets into the wings at the side of the stage a little while ago. We've been slowly shuffling forwards towards the stage itself since then.

Are we poets? Am I a poet?

I've written a few poems, but I've never sold one.

Is being a poet like being a murderer? You only have to murder one person to be a murderer, or is it like being a builder? You can't call yourself a builder just because you've built a wall in your garden. You have to build professionally to call yourself a builder.

There's only one person between me and the stage. He's an elderly gentleman. "Elderly" might be a bit harsh, but he's more than a generation older than me. He's a short, rotund man, almost as wide as he is tall, with a large handlebar moustache and a huge, flattened red nose which entirely dominates his face. He's wearing a tweed jacket and matching trousers, which make it look like he might be going out shooting pheasants or something after this.

He's very well spoken and has a big booming voice. He offered me a glass of water earlier. I mean, the water was free, but he offered to pour me a glass, whilst he was pouring one for himself, which was nice of him.

He doesn't look like much of an environmental activist really, or at least he doesn't look like the poets I expected when I thought about a poetry contest for poems about environmentalism.

I expected the other contestants to be cooler and more streetwise than me. Which isn't difficult.

The audience applaud; the poet who's just been on walks off the stage and the bloke in tweed walks up to the microphone.

He introduces himself as Charles Reynolds and says he's a farmer from Cambridgeshire. This explains the rural attire. He speaks for a bit about how honoured he is to be here and how pleased he is that someone has read and enjoyed his poem.

Then he starts to recite it. It isn't helping my nerves at all that he speaks like a thespian. He has that way of delivering his words as if he'd spent his whole life on stage.

He starts his poem really slowly and speeds up a bit as he gets into the pace of it.

'As a child I loved our farm as if it were a
living creature.
It's body adorned with a display of life,
flowers, mammals, insects, birds.
It showed magnificence in every feature.

But then, when I became a man,
I was taught to see it in a different way.
Agricultural college made me throw this
childish view away.

This creature surrounding and supporting
us,
Was to be harnessed as a resource.
Techniques for achieving this were the
content of the course

My task was to tame this beast or to
harness it at least,
to turn the post war famine into feast.'

He expresses the thought behind each word
perfectly. I know my delivery will not be anywhere
near as proficient as his.

'With guidance from The Ministry
and all the techniques they showed me,
I broke that land like you'd break a wild

and feisty pony.

Through that rough, wet, tussocky moor,
My tractor, plough and harrow tore.
Until just a plain flat field remained,
where abundant life was there before.

I drained the life right from the body
when I drained the land,
and the peaty dark brown blood did run
from cuts that I made by my hand.
That blood it ran into the ditches, newly
dug or newly cleared.
I was a hero of the nation,
fighting the shortages we feared.

I poisoned the land with chemicals
and drugged it up with NPK.
Planted the latest modern grass
designed to grow in an efficient way.

Admired by my fellow farmers,
praised by the ministry,
I had tamed this wild fen
And much honour was bestowed on me.

I look out now upon the corpse of what
once was there,

the lifeless ground which I have left.
No birds, no butterflies, no vitality,
and I mourn the beauty of which it is now
bereft.

I stand witness to my own crime;
The murder of this once beauteous fen.
Killed by chemicals and machines
To serve The Ministry and men.'

The audience applauds, as do I. You could hear it was truly heartfelt and far better than my poem.

The poet-farmer bows a low theatrical bow, thanks the audience and leaves the stage.

So here goes!

I walk up to the mike, say 'Hello' and introduce myself.

The audience's positive reaction to me talking about road protest helps my confidence a bit. They're clearly on my side, but this is still horribly uncomfortable.

As I start to recite my poem, it's like I'm in a trance. I've recited it so many times now, that I don't really hear the words properly, or at least, I can hear them but they sound distant, like they're not coming out of my mouth. Like I'm just hearing someone else saying them.

It only seems like seconds before it's over. The audience is applauding. I consider taking a bow but think better of it.

I look at the audience, wondering if I should at least nod my head like a little tiny bow. My face probably looks painfully uncomfortable right now. If it doesn't, I don't know why not.

I mumble 'Thank you' into the microphone and walk off stage, trying not to trip over.

There's a "meet the poets" thing happening in the bar now that we've all finished reciting our poetry.

For the other poets, I think this is a chance to see if someone here can help their poetry career. Personally, I'm hoping I can find myself a lift back. There's a lot of people here who have all travelled to be here and will travel back afterwards.

They're generally going to be like-minded when it comes to the environment at least.

I must have a certain amount of kudos. My poem did just win a prize. This looks like quite a fair opportunity to get a lift without having to stand in the rain.

I chat with a journalist from the Guardian, who has said he is going back to London after this. He seems like a nice guy and I eventually ask if he can give me a lift, but he came here by train.

I talk to a woman wearing a long flowing

Indian-style dress and a white cape, sort of like a druid might wear. She tells me how much she enjoyed my poem and asks if I'd be interested in performing at a festival she's involved with.

Then she starts telling me how "sacred" this festival is and that it's held in a sacred space on a date chosen for its fortuitous astrology or something.

Now, I'm just being lectured by her on her hippy-religious views. I'm being polite and smile and nod in the right places, but I decide not to ask her for a lift.

That farmer chap is holding court. He has a little group of people surrounding him, who all seem to hang on his every word. He gestures wildly as he regales some tale or other. Maybe he's reciting another poem. He's certainly entertaining them.

I decide to go out and catch people leaving the event as they drive out of the car park. Surely someone will give me a lift. I have a sign saying 'M4'. I show it to all the drivers as they leave, but to no avail.

There are only three cars left now. There's a blue Ford Mondeo, an old Rover and an even older Ford Escort. The Escort doesn't look like it's moved in a long time, there are leaves and sap stains all over it from the tree which overhangs it.

I may as well walk out to a proper hitching spot. It was raining when I first came out here, but it's brightened up now, which will make the walk more pleasant.

Just as I lift my rucksack on to my back, that farmer chap, Charles Reynolds, comes out.

'Are you hitching?' he asks.

I explain that I'm trying to, but with no success, and he offers me a lift.

'Us prize-winning poets have got to stick together,' he explains.

The interior of his car is immaculate. There are covers over the seats to stop them getting dirty and even these are immaculate. I look down at my boots and hope they don't leave too much dirt on the immaculate foot well.

We soon get chatting and it turns out this is his first poetry competition, too. I'm surprised; he seemed to be such a practised performer.

He asks me about road-protesting. He says that although he "doesn't really approve" of trespassing and breaking the law, he thinks it's commendable that I'm standing up for the "preservation of the countryside". He says he has always stood up for it and has been a member of the CPRE for over thirty years.

I've not heard of the CPRE, but he explains that it's an environmental charity which looks after the countryside. He says he knows his local CPRE rep very well, because they're both officers of the

Conservative Club and they go shooting together.

I can see that we're at very different places politically, so I try to steer the conversation away from politics and try to find common ground by asking about his farm. I've heard about some really cool agricultural projects where wildlife is flourishing alongside agriculture, and I'm keen to hear about his farm.

He tells me he owns two hundred acres of Cambridgeshire.

'Not the most productive land, but a good solid working farm which pays its way.'

I ask him if he's been able to restore the habitats on the land that were destroyed.

'It's not really economically viable to do so,' he says. 'There really isn't enough profit in farming to be able to spend your time worrying about every bird and every wildflower. It's a game of efficiency. We're competing on a global stage, you know. We have to compete with farmers from all over the world. It's all very well to reminisce about the wildlife that was there, but we have to live in the real world. Food doesn't magically appear and nor do farm profits. If the farm isn't profitable, it cannot continue. I don't have time to be tinkering around making homes for birds and bats and so on. I have a farm to run. And anyway, what's the point? When I die, the farm will get sold. Even if I restored it back to the nature-filled place it was when I took it over, the next farmer would have to destroy it all again to make it profitable.'

'Are you not concerned about the habitats?' This all seems a long way from the sentiment he expressed so eloquently on stage earlier.

'Well, environmentally I've left the world with an extremely good poem which hopefully will encourage future generations to look after the planet and all that sort of thing. I think that along with all my other achievements, the positions I've held and the good works I've done, that's not a bad legacy if you want to look at it on those terms. My poem was judged to be the best, after all, even better than yours.'

I'll give him his due; this is the first time he's mentioned that his poem beat mine in the competition and I did rather push him into a corner there.

Up To The Smoke

This was in the morning on the 31st of March (I think 1990). I can still picture the poster with the date on.

If I hadn't slept in this morning, I'd be sitting on a coach, going up to London with Mick and my other friends from Maidstone.

As it is, I'm standing by the side of the road, hoping for a lift.

My sign says London on it.

I did think about making a sign saying Poll Tax Demo. From what they've said, it's going to be big. Someone's bound to drive past here on their way. It would be nice to get a lift with someone who's also going on the march.

A little red car pulls up. I run up to it, but it drives away just as I get there.

It's a shame I've got no way of contacting the driver. He or she really deserves some sort of comedy award for that.

Cars go by, followed by more cars, which also go by. A minibus comes towards me with a banner in the window which says 'Fuck the Poll Tax'. It drives by. The woman in the passenger seat shrugs at me in a friendly looking way.

In all fairness, it is absolutely crammed full of people; it really doesn't look like there's room for me.

A bloke drives past with his window wound down and shouts something at me. I can tell by what I can hear of the tone that it's supposed to be aggressive or insulting, but I can't make out any of the words.

What a complete waste of energy on his part. Hopefully it made him happy.

A big white, brand-new Volvo comes towards me. It looks very posh. I do get lifts in posh cars, but I get more in cars that aren't posh.

I smile and hold up my sign. It comes to a halt just in front of me. The woman in the passenger seat winds down her window and leans out.

'Excuse me, would you like a lift to London?' Her home counties accent says as much about her social status as the car does.

The question seems a tad unnecessary in the circumstances, but they're offering me a lift and soon I'm sitting in the back of the Volvo with their two children.

'Are you attending the demonstration to protest against the Community Charge?' asks the driver, a man who's just as well-spoken as the woman whom I assume is his wife.

'Yes,' I say cautiously. You never know what politics people have and it would be a shame to cut this journey short.

'Jolly good, so are we,' he says, much to my surprise, 'This will be Hugo and Isabella's first demonstration. We feel it to be terribly important, not just that we stand up for what we believe in, but also that they grow up with an understanding of the importance of participating in a pluralist democracy.'

This is a lovely thought, but Isabella only looks about three. I'm not really sure how much she's going to learn about pluralist democracy today.

We all play I-Spy to entertain the kids. Isabella does surprisingly well at it, so long as you make the sound of the first letter. Hugo, who is probably about five and has a very neat haircut with a side parting, tells me all about his horse. He goes into great detail about the white markings on this otherwise brown horse as if he's making sure I'll recognise it if I see it.

Their mother explains that it's not actually his horse, it's the one he rides when he goes for lessons. He tells me he wants his own horse when he grows up, then he says that he'd need two, so that they're not lonely if he's not there. Then he realises if he has two and rides one, the other one might be lonely, so he thinks he should probably have three.

He thinks about this for a while and I'm waiting for his justification for four horses, but after much deliberation, he sticks with three.

After a while, Hugo says he's hungry and his mother gets out some snacks she's prepared for the journey. She offers me some as well, which is lovely of her, but it does leave me eating a sausage roll, quite self-consciously whilst trying not to spill crumbs all over the interior of their very posh car. The kids don't seem to find this a problem and from what I can see have not dropped a single flake of pastry.

We have a tray of buffet style party food, which as well as the sausage rolls, includes pineapple and cheese on sticks and vol-au-vents, which are filled with some sort of creamy sauce with delicious, but unidentifiable, lumps of something. I spill sauce down my front along with more pastry crumbs, but I clear it up quickly and I don't think anyone has seen.

Isabella announces that she's going to sing a song for me. She sings Twinkle Twinkle Little Star five times, missing out and repeating the occasional line. Her mother tells her she's sung it enough times now and Isabella says that this is 'the long one', but her mother insists we've heard enough.

She's gentle with the way she says this, but I get the impression she's heard the song more times than would be ideal. We return to playing I-Spy.

As we get closer to London, we see more and more people on their way to the demo. There are coaches with banners on display in the windows and cars crammed full of people who also have banners. There must also be a lot more people who are going, but aren't making it obvious by carrying or displaying banners.

A coach passes us, which is full of punks. They all have brightly-coloured hair. I wonder if they've all done their hair especially for the demo.

Isabella points at one and says, 'Mummy, that man's got red hair'.

Her mother tells her not to point at people because it's rude. I think that as well as wanting her daughter to grow up with good manners, she's a bit intimidated by a whole coachload of punks.

I see a coach with someone on it who looks like Mick. I only get a quick glance, but it does look like him sitting there gesturing madly as he talks to someone.

If so, that's the coach I'm supposed to be on. It probably wouldn't be such a comfortable ride as my present lift, but it would be more fun to be going up with a group of friends.

With the number of people on the road who are clearly going to the march, I realise my chances of meeting up with that lot when I get to London are pretty much non-existent. They'll have no way of knowing where I am and vice versa.

A convoy of police vans overtake us. Hugo starts to count them but loses concentration. The traffic builds up and slows down.

By the time we're in Central London, we're crawling along at a snail's pace when we're moving at all. I keep hoping we'll get past whatever is slowing us down, but it becomes more and more apparent that what's slowing us down is the sheer volume of 'us'.

People are walking past us on the pavement on their way to the demo. A police officer tries to divert us towards somewhere where we can park, but the father of this family that I'm getting a lift with says he's going to park at his office.

We're within walking distance of the protest. It's plainly obvious there's no point me staying in the car, so I suggest I could get out here. I'm happy to jump out just where we are, but the father insists on pulling over. There's a slightly curt tone to his voice.

It's the first time he's been anything other than super-calm and well measured in his communication. I'm a bit late in realising that he sees me getting out in traffic as a bad example to set for the kids.

We wait for the traffic to move and then he pulls over the short distance between us and the curb, and I get out in a safe and respectable manner. I thank them for the lift and say goodbye to Hugo and Isabella.

They wave goodbye vigorously as if they're trying to dislocate their wrists.

As I walk towards Kennington Park, there's a celebratory atmosphere. That might seem like a strange way to put it, but it feels like we're celebrating our resistance to the injustice of this tax and celebrating the fact that so many others share our opposition to the injustice.

People are chanting in an unorganised, almost anarchic way. We're here to make our voices heard and we're proud of it.

I'm not even at the demo yet and already it feels very moving to be part of such a large crowd who have gathered for one purpose and to feel the sense of camaraderie that that brings.

Fred's Camp

Sometimes, beauty and fragility go hand in hand. (Spring '96)

'Well, you've caused a right commotion with folk around here, there's no question about it.'

My lift, a woman who may be in her 30s with a soft voice and what I think is the remnants of a Scottish accent says. She's got long ginger hair. Not bright red like my hair and not in irregular shaped and sized dreadlocks like mine. Her hair is almost strawberry blonde and it's perfectly brushed.

She's driving me to the village where Fred and some friends have set up a protest camp.

'Folk in the village are completely against the road, that's for sure, but they're fairly split over the idea of a protest camp.' She grins as she says this. It seems like she might be quite enjoying this particular commotion.

'They're a funny lot here,' the woman

continues. 'And they don't like change at all. The road is change, so they don't like that and then you lot come along and set up a protest camp and they don't like that either. If they built the road and then decided to demolish it and return it to nature a few years later, I reckon a whole load of them would likely object to that too.

'Now, that Maureen Powercourt, she's one to be on the lookout for. She led the campaign against the road. Indeed, she said she would do anything to stop it. In one meeting, she even said she would lie down in front of the diggers herself, if that's what it took to stop it being built. Well, that was fine until folk came along who were actually prepared to lie down in front of the diggers, then she did the most hilarious about-face and since then, she seems to be devoting a heap of her time to objecting to the protest.'

She looks over at me and smirks. Her green eyes stand out in a stunning contrast against her hair.

'She's always got something to object to, has Maureen. Mainly folk with untidy gardens which let the village down, and at one point she ran a campaign to limit the colours that folk in the village could paint their houses. Somebody painted their house bright pink, you see. To be honest, it does look hideous, but instead of just accepting it like everyone else, Maureen decided the village needed a by-law to prevent it happening. She brought it up in parish council meetings and wrote to the local MP. She tried to get a petition going, but only a handful of folk were up for signing it. It was a real storm in a teacup and it came to nothing. When we get to the village, you'll see the pink house. It really is truly hideous.'

We're on a winding lane from the main road to the village. We're just going over the second hump back bridge. They're both stone bridges with carvings of wild animals on them. There are foxes, wild boar and various smaller animals which are harder to identify as they're more worn. The bridges are only wide enough for one vehicle to cross at a time and the road is widened either end of them to create a passing place.

'Now, the petition that she got together to oppose the road, that's a different story. Like I said, everyone in the village is against the road. It doesn't even serve the village. You'll have to drive three miles in one direction or four in the other to get onto it. We'll all see it and we'll definitely hear it, but it won't be useful to local traffic at all. When she started the petition, it was just in the village, but the population of the village is only three hundred. She was never going to get many signatures here, so she went to town set up a little table in the High Street and started persuading folk in town to support it. They say it had thirty thousand signatures in the end, a lot of them tourists apparently. Likely most just signed it to get Maureen of their backs, so they could get on with enjoying their holidays. The council's planning committee made a big point of how much weight they gave the petition when making their decision, but they still backed the road, so at the end of the day, it was all a complete waste of time.'

I've heard a lot of these tales of bureaucratic battles failing, leaving setting up a protest camp as the only option for opposing construction. I guess they must be successful sometimes, but then there's no need for the protest, so we never get to hear about them.

'When I heard you lot had arrived, I had images of Maureen carrying out her promise to lie down in front of the diggers, but it turns out that if there's one thing Maureen can't stand more than the road, it's hippies. Dirty hippies with dreadlocks in the village is her worst nightmare. No offence meant.'

I laugh. I'm not even vaguely offended and I appreciate knowing how the land lies.

'Annie Sharland,' she says in a noticeably softer voice. 'She's a completely different kettle of fish. She acted as Maureen's deputy in getting the petition together, staffed the stall with her in town and everything. When she heard about you lot, she was over the moon. She'd given up on the whole idea of opposing the road. Once the council had made their decision, there didn't seem to be anything else that could be done. Practically everybody in the village had already written to our MP. Folk had talked about challenging the decision in court, but nobody believed that would go anywhere. Now there's a protest camp, she's up there every day, doing what she can to support the protestors.'

As we drive into the village, I can see why its occupants might be so opposed to change. It truly is a beautiful place and the very epitome of an English village. There is indeed one pink house, and it is indeed hideous. It appears to be the only blemish in sight.

The village is centred around an ancient church and a thatched building, which houses a pub and a shop. The buildings look out over a triangular village green, where the three roads that come into the village meet. All the gardens are neat and tidy. There are cast iron benches dotted around the green and everything is immaculate and well maintained.

'That's where they're building the road,' my lift declares, pointing up towards a woodland which sits on high land above the village. 'I may as well drop you off there and save you the walk.'

We take a left and head uphill towards the tall oak trees which dominate the view. The entrance to the woods is through an old gateway, marked by two rotten gateposts, next to which lies the remains of an old wooden gate. From there, the track opens up to form an enormous cathedral-like space, with dappled light between the high oaks.

This must be the gateway Fred described as a "defendable position" and to an extent it is. The narrow entrance certainly gives an advantage in that respect.

Up in the canopy above is a walkway made of blue polyprop rope connecting two treehouses.

Underneath the oaks, the shrub layer of the woodland is dominated by huge overstood hazel coppice stools. Like so much hazel coppice, this looks like it was worked up until World War Two and then neglected. Men left their roles as woodsmen and went off to war. When they returned, the shortage of labour and the efficiencies of mechanisation made coppicing impractical to continue.

From the size of the stools, they must be well over a thousand years old. Hundreds of woodsmen will have cut them over that time and their shape has been moulded by their hands and their decisions. The height and angle that they cut the coppice and the regularity that they returned to the stools will have all had an effect on what we see before us now.

A woodsman cutting a bit high because their bad back makes it difficult to bend down low means that the next cut will also be higher than it would otherwise and so on for generations. Cutting at the wrong angle or not leaving a clean cut would have allowed rain to collect and cause rot, distorting the shape and reducing the size of the stool.

Young men would have learned their trade in these woods from wizened old woodsmen, mastered it and then, as wizened old woodsmen themselves, passed it on to future generations. They would have seen the cycle starting with newly-cut coppice where light hits the woodland floor, creating a space full of wildflowers and butterflies and a rich foraging area for birds and mammals alike.

Then comes the stage where it seems impossibly swamped by bramble creating safe nesting sites for birds and food for all manner of species. Finally, the hazel breaks through and shades the bramble out and provides hazel nuts for dormice, nuthatches and jays, before time comes to coppice it and start all over again.

As generation after generation repeated this cycle, the ecosystem that is here today evolved alongside their work.

Nothing looks so natural to the human eye as an ancient woodland, but like almost all ancient woodlands, this is a manufactured landscape, created by man working in harmony with nature. None of this work was carried out for the sake of wildlife; it was all for practical reasons, to provide fuel and fencing, tools, tool handles and other items of use.

It was the unchanged continuity of this work which allowed rich ecosystems to form. Lichens and mycelium which take hundreds of years to colonise a woodland had hundreds of years to do so. Plants which slowly spread by sucker or seeds falling close to the parent plant have had a chance to find every suitable niche in the woods through hundreds of years of slow encroachment. Birds have returned from their migration year after year to always find a suitable habitat in which to live and forage. As a result, their young have multiplied to build up healthy populations which are resilient to the vagaries of the weather, predators and other natural threats.

The petition didn't save this woodland and nor did writing to the local MP. Realistically, we have to accept that the protest won't either. If we can get journalists interested, they'll film the mighty oaks being felled and crashing to the ground and they'll film the protestors crying when it happens. People will agree it's a sad sight to watch, even if they agree with building the road.

Few people will note the destruction of the coppice, which looks to many like unruly scrub. Those stools which have been cut and maintained and cared for and worked for over a thousand years will have one last cut, not by billhook, axe or bowsaw this time, not even by chainsaw, but by digger bucket and bulldozer blade.

Their limbs will be crushed and splintered. Their roots will be torn from the ground, exposing the centuries-old network of mycelium to the air where it will be desiccated by the sun and the wind and destroyed completely. As is the way with mycelium, no one will notice it. It goes unnoticed as it passes nutrients and information from tree to tree, and it will go unnoticed in its destruction. Invertebrates will be crushed into the compacted earth along with rodents, rabbits and any other small mammals who dwell beneath the forest floor.

Just like the road protest site in Kent and the woods I played in as a child, this woodland and all the life in it will be replaced by concrete and tarmac. Birds will return from their migration to find there is no home or forage waiting for them and the birds that do not migrate will watch the landscape which supports them being destroyed. The generalist birds, the robin, the blackbird and the wren, birds who can adapt to many habitats will mainly move on to new places. The specialist birds, the wood warblers, the willow tits, the lesser spotted woodpeckers and other birds which require a specific habitat, will mainly die.

I thank my lift and she drives away, leaving me to walk up the track towards the camp.

I meet Fred on the way. She greets me with a hug and starts to tell me all about the camp and the woods and the people who are involved as we walk further up the track.

Soon we're at an outdoor kitchen in a glade where a dozen or so people are milling around. Even though I've never been here before, walking into the camp evokes a feeling, like coming home. The people here are my people. We have a common cause and I find comfort in the feeling of camaraderie that creates.

A blackened kettle is boiling away on the campfire and people are carrying out the various tasks that are required to create and maintain a protest camp.

Fred introduces me to the other people there. Yuppy I know from the Kent protest and a grey-haired lady, who's sitting by the fire having a cuppa, turns out to be Annie, who my lift told me about. The others are mainly Fred's friends, some local teenagers and a few friends of friends who have come down to help out.

Annie, who is surprisingly fit for her age, offers to show me around the woods. She's lived in the village her whole life and played here as a child. She knows every nook and cranny and shows me an old hollow tree where bats and owls live, a little waterfall which comes straight out of a rock face at the height of my head and an amazing display of orchids and other wildflowers in a clearing created where a large oak has fallen and allowed light to the ground, just as cutting the coppice would have done many years ago. She tells me that she and her late husband used to come up here when they were "courting" and that, later, they used to camp overnight here as a family when the children were young.

'It truly is a magical place, isn't it?' she says.

'Yes,' I say. 'It's such a shame we're going to see it being destroyed.'

Back To The Sticks

This was in the afternoon on the 31st of March (1990?). Newspaper headlines the next day, confirmed that his cynicism was well placed.

I'm hitching back to Ashford on the A20.

Unfortunately, I'm not on the best part of the A20 for that purpose; I'm still very much in Central London. I don't have any money or food. That was in my bag, which I lost earlier.

I do have a hitching sign which says Ashford on it. Luckily, my marker pen happened to be in my pocket, not my bag. I lost the bag somewhere not far from Trafalgar Square. I don't know if it caught on something or if the police grabbed it.

I didn't look back. I just let go of it and kept running.

I ran until I realised there were no police around any more. I don't know how far it is to a decent hitching spot, but I guess, if I keep heading along the A20, I'll find somewhere eventually. At least I'm safe now.

It was all fine until we got to Trafalgar Square. Sure, there were a few people throwing empty beer cans, but that's the only violence I saw.

Then we got into the square and it all changed. I don't know what I expected, some sort of stage with people giving speeches, I think, or something like that. Then we'd get to a point where we felt we'd done our bit, and all go home, I guess.

I've never been to a big demonstration or been in a big crowd like that. I didn't really consider the possibility of it getting violent. Even if I had, I would have thought I could just walk away, but it wasn't like that.

You couldn't just walk away.

Once we were in the square, police with loud hailers gave us orders to disperse. I didn't want any trouble; we'd shown our opposition to the injustice that the Poll Tax represents.

I was more than happy to disperse, but I couldn't see where to go. I couldn't go back, because the crush of the crowd was pushing me forward. I could see what I thought was a potential way out, but the police were blocking it.

I stood on a bollard, with this bloke helping me to balance. He wanted to know the way out too.

All the exits I could see were blocked by the police. Then the crowd surged towards us. I don't know what happened to the bloke. He just disappeared.

I fell off the bollard and only just managed to stay upright as I was carried along with the crowd. I had no control at all over where I was going; I was crushed between people who were moving one way and another.

There was a banner pushing into my side at one point, digging into my ribs. I couldn't see who was holding it.

When momentarily there was enough space that it wasn't being pressed into me, it just fell to the ground, because whoever it belonged to was no longer there. Then I was being crushed from all directions again.

All around me, people were panicking. You could hear people shouting out that they were being crushed and the noise of shouting and screams would build up on one side or another, just before the force of the crush would come from that side, like the way a flash of lightning pre-empts the sound of thunder.

There was an overwhelming smell, which included a mix of sweat and vomit and smoke as well as all the normal smells of the city. I don't know what was burning, but I definitely smelt smoke.

All I could see were the people crushed up against me, their terrified faces, the backs of their heads and their coats.

There was a black and grey coat; it was a thick coat like you'd wear in winter, with big shoulders, like it had rigid shoulder pads. It was just in front of me when something pushed against the back of my head.

My face was pressed right into this coat; it was rough against my skin. It felt like I was there for ages crushed up against this rough, possibly woollen coat. It had a strong smell of cigar smoke.

When whatever was pushing against the back of my head moved, I could see a bit more. I could move my head to see the sky and there was enough space to see between the people around me.

I started looking for a way out again. The police were charging the crowd behind me, so I couldn't go that way. There was a line of police ahead, holding the crowd back, so I couldn't go that way either.

I tried to go off to my right and get out that way. The line of police in front of me were wearing normal uniforms. They were being pushed by the crowd who were trying to escape from the police behind us.

Suddenly, this line of uniformed police disappeared. Directly behind them was a line of police in full riot gear. Each of them stepped forwards past the uniformed police officer in front of them and swung their batons at a protestor's head.

Right in front of me, there was a bloke who seemed to be pleading with a uniformed officer. I don't have a clue what he was saying, but the officer was communicating with him in what seemed like a fairly calm manner, considering the situation.

Without warning, that police officer was replaced with another in riot gear. Before the bloke who was pleading even knew what had happened, there was a baton flying through the air and making contact with the side of his skull.

His head was knocked to the side and bounced off his shoulder. He stood upright, with this confused look on his face for what seemed like ages, but must have been less than a second. Then he fell back onto a bloke who was just behind him, and blood started pouring from the side of his head.

He just collapsed on the floor, completely unconscious.

I found myself standing there, frozen to the spot, trying to process what I'd seen. It was like someone had turned down the volume switch on the world around me, but not just the sound; I was numb to all my senses.

Then the whole situation suddenly came back into stark focus. There were cracked heads all over the place. Everyone was a target, no matter what they were doing. I saw a woman holding her kid in her arms. The kid was not much more than a baby.

There was blood gushing out of the woman's head and down onto her kid. She clearly wasn't rioting. No one riots holding a small child like that.

The police weren't trying to police the demonstration, they were attacking it, like an army attacks it's enemy. I was just trying to avoid getting my head cracked. I was terrified.

Most of the injuries I saw were cracked heads. The main police tactic seemed to be to swing batons at protestor's heads.

There were other injuries too. I saw people being carried by other people. They must have had injuries to their legs I guess, but those injuries aren't visible in the way that cracked heads are.

The mounted police were above us, looking down on us, which increased their ability to dehumanise us. They were swinging their batons indiscriminately, lashing out at anyone in reach. Like the other police, they were aiming for the head wherever possible.

In amongst that ultra-violent situation, there are horses; innocent, beautiful, magnificent creatures.

You can't help but be concerned about them and their welfare.

If a person attacks you, your natural reaction is to defend yourself, but if they do so on horseback, even with all the adrenaline and fear, you have concern; concern for this poor animal, who will also be suffering from the same fear as you.

The police, sat high on the horses' backs, showed no such concern. They ignored the welfare of their horses as they rode them into the crowd, to swing their extra-long batons at the heads of anyone they could reach.

I don't know what order the rest of it happened in. I was pushed one way and another by the crowd as we all ran. The police seemed to be attacking us from every direction.

At one point, I remember this girl's face in front of mine. She was a really cute looking girl, with long black hair. She might have been about fifteen or sixteen.

I don't know if she was with people or just on her own. She was just suddenly there in front of me.

Then behind her was a police officer in full riot gear. He lifted his baton to swing it at the back of her head. She hadn't seen him at all, because he was behind her. Her face didn't register what was going on because she was completely oblivious to what was just about to happen.

I pushed her out of the way. I'm no hero. There was nothing heroic about what I did. I was terrified. I didn't do it thinking my action posed any risk to myself; I didn't think at all.

With the crush of the crowd, I was then forced into the space I'd created by pushing the girl out of the way. The police officer's baton was now swinging towards me. I looked him straight in the face. I couldn't do anything else; I was immobilised by the crushing force of the crowd.

He stopped his baton inches from my face. Somehow, this man who could baton a girl around the back of the head, couldn't hit me when I looked him in the eye.

'Would you like a lift?'

I hear the voice, but I don't really process what's going on.

'Are you OK? Would you like a lift?'

I look up and there's a bloke standing next to the open driver's door of his car. I'd almost forgotten I was hitching.

'Would you like a lift?' he says again.

I try to talk, but no words come out. I nod and then manage to say, 'Please.'

We drive along in silence for a couple of minutes.

'Are you ok?' he says, breaking the silence.

I don't know how to answer this. I'm surprisingly ok considering what's gone on, but at the same time I'm not ok at all.

'Your arm,' he says. 'Is it ok?'

I look down at my arm and it's absolutely covered in blood; I've got blood all over the door of his car and all over the seat.

'Oh shit!' I say. 'I'm sorry about your car.' I undo the seatbelt and remove my jacket by turning it inside out, trying not to spread the blood any further.

'Don't worry about the car,' he says. 'Is your arm OK?'

'It's fine,' I say. 'I think it's fine'. I check my arm and it seems fine. I run my other hand across my neck and my head to see if the blood is coming from there, but I don't seem to have any injuries. I don't know who's blood this is, but it's not mine.

I try to explain everything that happened. It all comes out as an uncontrolled stream of words and I don't know if any of it makes any sense.

I tell him about my whole day, about the lift up in the Volvo, the march and how great it felt to be part of that mass of people who were all there to oppose an injustice.

I tell him about the police attacking the march, about them blocking us in and telling us to disperse.

I tell him about the bloke I saw being dragged by the neck by a mounted policeman.

I tell him about everything I saw and thought and felt. He sits there quietly, listening to it all. I really am babbling, and I really don't know how much of what I'm saying makes any sense.

I tell him that tomorrows papers will have shocking reports of the police violence because it was so horrific to anyone who was there.

'No they won't,' he says. 'What purpose would that serve?'

'It would serve the purpose of telling the truth,' I reply.

'There is that, I suppose,' he says with a dismissive snort.

Hanging Around

This was late summer or early autumn 1996. It was an early start and there was a nip in the air when we woke up in the woods that morning.

I'm standing by the road with a sign.

The road is in the very centre of London and the sign says 'Capitalism Kills, Kill Capitalism'. This is the same as the wording on Monk's banner.

Monk is about half way up the lamppost that he's climbing. We've been planning this protest for weeks. The bank which we're outside is funding both sides of the conflict in the Zaire. The bank's directors know that however many people get killed and whoever wins, the bank will get a generous return on its investment.

I'm chatting with a smartly-dressed woman who came up to find out what we're doing and seems genuinely shocked by what we're telling her. Karl has given her a flyer, which she's put in her pocket to read later.

Generally, we're getting a warm reception. A few people have shouted abuse as they drive past.

Whenever someone shouts 'Get a job!', Fishhead replies 'Get an education!'. I don't think this helps, but it amuses us. Mainly people seem to either agree with us or not care one way or the other.

Monk is sitting on the top of the lamppost now, getting the brace out of his pocket and fitting it diagonally between the upright post and the arm which the lamp is on. It fits around the arm and has an eyelet which is right over near the lamp. He clips a karabiner into the eyelet, puts the noose around his neck. You can't make an omelet without breaking any eggs and what we're trying to achieve is far more important than making an omelet. What people are about to witness is going to shock them. Hopefully, it'll shock them into thinking about the message Monk is trying to get across with this dramatic and extreme form of protest.

Emotions are, understandably, running high.

I'm rushing with adrenaline and a lump forms in my throat as I watch.

He checks the noose one last time.

Looking straight ahead, with a blank expression on his face, he stares into the distance and jumps.

Although the free-fall is only a couple of metres. It seems like minutes have gone by before the rope tightens and his body suddenly jerks to a stop. He bounces from the force of the fall and then just hangs there, suspended from the lamppost, limp and seemingly lifeless.

I hear the crunch of two vehicles colliding as the banner hanging from his feet unrolls to say, 'Capitalism Kills, Kill Cap'.

Monk hangs there, his head flopped to one side, completely motionless. The look on Madcap's face drops and she starts playing nervously with her dreads. She spent ages getting everything together for this and now the banner hasn't unrolled properly.

Then Monk flails around in what looks like some sort of death throes and the banner unrolls to reveal the full message.

Madcap smiles; her part in this has worked.

I'd believe that he was dead myself if I hadn't watched Monk practising this again and again over the last couple of weeks, hanging himself from various trees in the woods. The noose is attached by Velcro, so it won't harm him if it snags on anything and he's hanging in what he reports is a very comfortable harness. He slept in the harness last Tuesday night, hanging from a big oak tree over the clearing where we have our campfire. He said it was fine once the fire died down and the smoke stopped blowing in his face.

The police arrive in force almost immediately. Two vans pull up across the road, two more arrive and park on the pavement either side of us. Having surrounded us, they shout at us over a loud hailer. A number of the protestors are playing musical instruments and singing, which makes it difficult to hear what the police are saying.

For some reason, one police officer strides forwards on his own, coming right up to where Karl, Fishhead and a few other protestors are standing handing out flyers, and he properly loses it. He starts shouting at the protestors, raises his baton and takes a swing at Karl, who quite sensibly steps back. The baton swings through the air, failing to make contact with anything and the police officer loses balance momentarily. This gives everyone a chance to jump back.

Whilst everyone else is getting out of the way, Prof turns around swiftly to face the police officer and I see an angry look on Prof's face; so angry that it seems unreal. Not angry like he gets when he's ranting about politics, but an out-of-control anger, which comes from the most primeval part of the brain.

Just like the copper, he's red in the face and his eyes, which are normally so full of inquisitiveness and love, are protruding from their sockets as if he is trying to kill this angry policeman using only his stare. His hands are raised like the copper's, but he doesn't have anything in them. The copper's baton is going to give him a distinct advantage over Prof's empty hands if this becomes a fight.

'I can see why you're so fucking angry,' he shouts at the copper at the top of his voice. 'Like me, you can't stand this shit,' he continues, still shouting right into the copper's face and gesturing to the side. His tone has dropped very slightly, but he is still clearly out of control.

As I glance to the side where he gestured, there's nothing there of significance, just passers-by carrying on with their normal business. The copper looks as if he doesn't know how to react to this.

'When will these people show some respect?' Prof cries out. He looks slightly saner now. His eyes seem to have gone back into their sockets and he's less red in the face, but he's making no sense.

What does he mean by "these people"? Does he mean us, his fellow protestors?

'Like me, you've clearly worked hard to get where you are. Surely, we're due some respect for that?' he says. His voice is raised, but he doesn't seem angry now, just disappointed and he's talking more slowly than he was before.

The copper looks less angry now too. He also looks confused.

'How are we supposed to take this weight on our shoulders?' Prof asks in a firm but calming voice. 'You feel that weight, don't you.' This is said as a statement not a question, and whilst he says it, he nods and lowers his arms.

The copper then lowers his baton as if he was mimicking Prof.

I don't hear what Prof says next as I'm somewhat distracted by the arm around my neck and the police radio digging into my back as I get grabbed from behind.

I'm pulled backwards. My windpipe is being crushed and I can't breathe. I try to turn my head to the side and a voice in my ear shouts, 'Don't fucking try it!'

My neck is being squeezed so hard that it feels like my head is swelling up. Everything in my vision is getting darker and has a dark blue tinge. I can hear my friends shouting, but I can't make out the words.

I try to raise my hand to pull the arm from my neck, but my arm seems too heavy to lift. My vision has got even darker and the voices are muffled, as if I have my hands over my ears.

I'm lying face down on a hard surface, trying to catch my breath. The back and top of my head hurt as if I've been hit with something.

As I open my eyes, I can see a hard black rubberised surface underneath me and white metal like the inside of the body of a vehicle to my side. It takes me a moment to realise that I've been thrown into the back of a police van.

My right arm is twisted up my back and my left arm is spread out across the floor. I look around without moving. I'm alone in the van. I don't think I'm in the level of pain which indicates broken bones or other serious injury, so I start to straighten myself up.

Something slams against the side of my face and the back of my head hits the panelling of the van. I look up to see that Karl has been thrown into the van on top of me.

A police officer drags me to my feet by my jacket and throws me into a seat. He then turns to Karl and starts to do the same. Karl is much more together than me and manages to slow himself down so that he lands in the seat in a more controlled manner than I did.

I look out of the window and there's absolute chaos. The police are charging in from all sides, grabbing anyone they can.

Meanwhile, Prof is sitting on the grass still talking to the angry policeman, who doesn't seem angry at all anymore. They're sitting together chatting, like none of this madness is going on around them.

Yuppy is next into the van. His hands are cuffed behind his back and he's being carried by two police officers. They throw him in so that his head hits one of the seats. This causes his legs to swing around and hit another officer who's sitting in the van.

'Don't kick me, you little shit,' says the officer and kicks him hard in the leg.

Another copper is dragging Fishhead towards the van by his neck. He's got both hands on the copper's arm and is trying to pry it from his neck, but to no effect.

The copper turns him around to face the van and tries to push him in through the door. Fishhead manages to put one foot on either side of the doorway and pushes back, causing the copper to fall backwards. They roll around on the floor for a bit before another copper jumps in and soon Fishhead is in the van, too.

Outside the van it's mayhem. The police are swinging batons all over the place.

The next person thrown into the van is some poor girl who none of us know. I don't know how old she is. She might be an adult, but I doubt it. She's screaming and shouting at the police as they drag her over and chuck her in.

I think she was just in the wrong place at the wrong time and the police grabbed her thinking she was with us. As she's pushed down into a seat, I see a small trickle of blood coming from her ear. I don't think it's serious.

I look out of the window and Prof is in handcuffs. The officer he was talking to is still sitting on the ground. Two other police are standing over the now very confused and upset-looking policeman and seem to be shouting at him. They drag him to his feet and escort him to another van as if they're arresting him too.

Prof is brought around to the open door of the van and steps in as if he's just getting a lift somewhere. He looks unbelievably serene.

The door slams shut and we're off to the station. I knew there was a possibility I'd get arrested today, but I assumed that if I did, it would be because I did something stupid. I didn't expect to get arrested for standing around in a public place with a placard.

As we drive past, I see Monk, still hanging completely motionless from the lamppost, with his matted blonde hair moving gently in the wind. Passers-by must think he's dead. It's been a long day already and personally, I'm wondering if he's sleeping.

The girl who I don't know is crying and Yuppy is still on the floor and is screaming at the top of his voice. A number of the other protestors are screaming at the police as well, telling them to let Yuppy take a seat. He's bouncing around as the van swerves at high speed through the city. His head crashes into the bottom of the seat every time the van stops a bit quickly.

To put it mildly, this is a clear breach of the

officers' duty of care, but the issue here is that they don't care.

I'm quite quiet myself. My neck hurts and I have a terrible headache. I'm dazed and confused, and I feel a little sick.

When we arrive at the station, they take Yuppy out. Four officers come out of the station and pick him up, one on each arm and one on each leg. They carry him face down into the building.

Then they come back for the girl. She has blood right the way down her face now and is clearly in shock. Four more police come out of the station and take Karl and Fishhead, just leaving me, Prof and one copper in the van.

Prof and the one remaining copper are at the front of the van, one on each side, and I'm at the back. Everything has gone quiet. No one is screaming, shouting or crying. In fact no one is making any noise at all.

The copper, who has said nothing and done nothing up to this point other than sit in the van looking slightly embarrassed, breaks the silence.

He turns to Prof and says, 'Don't worry, fella. You shouldn't be here for long. You didn't do anything really. They only arrested you to get you out of the way.'

'How do you feel about that?' asks Prof calmly. 'How do you feel about your part in all this?'

'I'm only doing my job,' says the copper. 'Some of that was a bit heavy handed, I have to admit, but we can't have anarchy on the streets.'

'What "anarchy on the streets"? Like people acting outside the law?' Prof chuckles to himself. 'You know none of those arrests were lawful, don't you?'

'You have to look at the greater good,' says the copper, shifting in his seat as if he's sat on something uncomfortable. 'As I said, you shouldn't be here long.'

'But how do you feel about your part in this?' asks Prof again, shifting in his seat and then turning to face the copper. 'How do you justify it? You can justify it, can't you?'

'I don't think it's as bad as you're making out. You'll be released in a few hours at most.'

'Oh, OK, fella,' says Prof gently. 'What if they were going to keep me in overnight? Would you have assisted in my arrest if you knew that would happen? You know it wasn't a lawful arrest.'

'OK, I would probably still go along with it,' admits the copper. 'A night in the cells isn't that bad.'

'That's a fair point,' agrees Prof and leans in, slightly closer to the copper. 'What about a couple of days?'

'We have to keep order,' the copper says. 'What are we supposed to do?'

Prof nods as if he's in agreement. 'I understand keeping order is important to you and is fundamental to your job, so would you have still gone along with it, if I was going to get a week in the cells?'

There's nothing confrontational about either man's tone. They're talking like friends in the pub might if they were discussing some made up dilemma.

'Yes,' the copper says. 'I probably would have.'

'What about two weeks?' asks Prof. 'I guess two weeks isn't that long either?'

'Why would you spend two weeks in custody?'

'Well, I mean theoretically,' says Prof. 'Theoretically, if it was going to be two weeks?'

'Theoretically, it would still be better than theoretical anarchy.'

'And a month?' Prof nods again as if he's deep in thought.

'Yes, a month.'

I can't believe he's just said that. I can't believe that this copper who seems to be talking this through in a reasonable and rational way is prepared to be part of locking someone up for a month who by his own admission "didn't do anything really".

'What about three months?' says Prof. 'Is three months any different to one?'

'I guess not.'

'Would six make the difference?'

'You're just being ridiculous.'

'No, but theoretically, if it came to that, would you do it to protect order?' Prof says in a tone so gentle I can only just hear it.

'Yes, I probably would. We have to have some semblance of order.' The copper's tone is less certain now. I think he may be questioning his own words.

'You're a good man and you're here because you want to make the world a better place. I can see that. I'm interested in what you say for that reason. What about if it turned out to be a year in custody?'

'If the circumstances required, I'd still do it,' says the copper. He seems to have gained confidence now and is more certain about what he's saying.

'Two years?'

'Yes.'

'Three?'

'I guess so.' The doubt is coming back into his voice. A frown is forming on his face and he shifts as if he's uncomfortable again. He slouches forward and raises his hand to his face so that it partially covers his mouth. He has an extremely despondent look on his face.

Leaning forward so that he's in the same slouched position as the police officer, Prof looks him straight in the eye and whilst scratching his nose says, with a warm tone to his voice, 'You're proud to wear the uniform, aren't you.' This is stated with absolute certainty. I can hear now that Prof is reassuring him so he can push him further.

He then moves his hand away from his face and back down onto the seat. The police officer moves his hand away from his face, too. Prof shifts around in his seat, stretches a bit and leans back to sit with a more upright posture.

As he does that, his concerned expression transforms into a gentle and friendly smile.

The police officer also leans back into a more upright posture. The despondent look has gone from his face now.

'Overall, if I was going to spend five years inside, it would still be worthwhile overall, wouldn't it?'

'Yes,' says the copper thoughtfully and with absolute certainty. "It would."

'Ten years?' This is asked as a question, but all three of us know there is only one possible outcome.

'Yes.'

'Twenty five years?' says Prof, nodding gently to the rhythm of his words, 'To uphold law and order and prevent anarchy on the street, that would be worth it, wouldn't it?'

'I'm afraid it would,' says the copper.

Then, with an abrupt change of tone, Prof asks, 'Would you pull the lever in the gas chamber?'

The spell is broken.

'No, no I absolutely wouldn't!' The copper sits bolt upright. 'Of course not. How can you say that? I could never do that. What are you saying?'

I can see that he's absolutely horrified.

'Do you think,' says Prof slowly and gently, 'that it would be a good idea for you to refuse? Would you really refuse to pull that lever in a situation where people who have committed no crime are being sent to prison for 25 years? You have to think of your family now as well as yourself. What would happen to them and to you if you did refuse? What would you really do?'

The van door slides open to reveal two more police. One of them points at Prof and says, 'You next.'

Prof calmly stands up, steps out and follows the police inside without looking back.

Now it's just me and the cop in the van. I'm at the back, facing him He's at the front, looking towards the door that Prof just left through.

He doesn't move at first. He just sits there.

I'm beginning to think he's forgotten about me.

Eventually, he turns around and wipes a tear from his face.

Squat Party

It was quite a party! My memory is a bit hazy, but I think this was the summer of 1990.

I'm standing at my spot, hitching into town when a bus pulls up.

As it is actually a bus stop, logically this should happen much more often than it does. It says something about the infrequency of the bus service, or the speed at which I get a lift, that this is the first time I've seen a bus here in ages.

I wave the bus driver on, but he doesn't seem to understand. He looks in his mirror, first a look of confusion, then impatience, then anger. He doesn't understand any of the hand signals I'm using to tell him I don't want a to get on the bus, so I decide to walk up to him to tell him.

As soon as I take a step towards him, he pulls out and drives away, grinning in his mirror at me, like he's got one over on me.

Oh well! With my hitching spot free of buses, I'm now able to hitch into town.

The first car that comes along is a BMW. As I put my thumb out, it slows down, ready to stop.

No, my mistake; it was slowing down to turn left into the village. I would have expected an indicator to have come on. I guess it must not be working.

After that, there's a long gap in the traffic before a bicycle comes my way. I put out my thumb and grin at the driver, who, without slowing down, shouts 'Go on then!' and indicates for me to jump up on his handlebars.

It's not a lift, but it made us both smile.

Our next-door neighbour pulls out of his drive and turns towards me.

Here's a dilemma. He can see I'm hitching. If I don't put my thumb out when he drives past, he could take offence. It would be quite a statement to say, 'I want a lift, but not with you'.

The fact is though, I do want a lift and I'd prefer not to get one with him. If I do put my thumb out, he might feel it would be too rude not to give me a lift. Then, I have the journey into town in his car, which is going to be less pleasant than standing here all day long, even if it rains.

It's an impossible situation really. I put my thumb out and risk the socially uncomfortable ride.

He pretends he hasn't seen me and drives straight past. What a relief!

One of them Robin Reliants is coming my way. Fantastic! I've never been in one. Hopefully the driver is in the mood for picking up hitchers.

Thumb out, big grin on my face, I watch as it comes towards me. With a bit of luck, I could soon be sitting in that quirky little vehicle heading to town.

I try to soften my grin into a warm and friendly smile and to my great pleasure, the driver smiles back and pulls up. I run up to the car and jump in the passenger seat.

My lift is a few years older than me. He has a massive head of jet black hair which looks like it's never been brushed and an old army surplus jacket. He looks familiar, but I can't place him, at all. He probably just looks a bit like someone I know. He's a big guy and he fills his half of this very small car.

As we pull away, the car moves in a slightly strange way. I don't know if this is how Robin Reliants are, or if this one's out of balance for some reason.

'What are you going to Ashford for, mate?' he asks.

I tell him I'm looking for work. Since I dropped out of college, I've had a few short-term jobs, but the last one, cleaning graffiti, came to an end a few weeks ago.

I'd been to a temp agency in town and that's what was going. The hourly rate wasn't fantastic, but it was something, so I'd said yes. The work turned out to be in London and they picked us up in a van at eight in the morning to take us there.

Of course, they didn't pick me up in Bethersden, so I had to hitch to Ashford.

The first day went alright. I got there just in time, got the lift and spent the day scrubbing graffiti off the walls of a shopping centre. It was hardly my dream job, but it was work and it was all that was on offer.

The next day, we got stuck in traffic on the way to London. They don't pay you for your travel time, so I lost out on two hours pay. That seemed a bit tight to me. I appreciate I wasn't working, but I was giving up my time for the job.

Day three was when it all went properly wrong. It took me a while to get a lift and I only just made it to the meeting point in time. When I got there, there was another bloke waiting for the van. He said he'd been there for half an hour, which was a relief, because I knew that I hadn't missed the lift.

Then this girl turned up a little bit later. She was more relieved than me, because she was about five minutes late and she really thought that she'd missed it. She told us her mother was looking after her baby so she could work and she really needed the cash.

We waited there for about half an hour before the bloke who was there before me gave up and decided the van wasn't coming.

I stuck around for about ten or fifteen minutes after he left. The girl was still there when I gave up. She was going to stick around as long as it took.

I hitched back home and phoned the agency to ask what had happened to the van and they said there wasn't any work that day, so they'd phoned my house at quarter to eight to let me know. Of course, by quarter to eight, I was on my way to Ashford. If they had half a brain, they'd have realised that was too late.

I pretty much told them that on the phone. I don't think they'll be offering me any more work. My dad is still insisting I should go and work for him, but he's become even more grumpy because I don't want to, which makes the prospect of working for him even less attractive than it already was.

'What would you want a job for mate?' my lift asks with a theatrical level of disgust.

'I need the money.' I think this is fairly obvious.

'That's understandable,' he says, 'Watch out though,. You think you're just going to do a little bit of work to get some money together, one thing leads to another, you get into bad habits and next thing you know, you could find yourself in a career.'

Then his whole tone changes, like he's had a sudden moment of realisation. 'Mate, I know you! We've sat round a fire together, haven't we? You're Blaze's cousin.'

I realise why he seemed familiar. This is Gary, Blaze's friend. We have indeed sat around a fire together.

We chat a bit about the night around the bonfire last summer. He's forgotten my name, which is fair enough; I was just some kid he met at a party. I ask him what he's doing in Ashford and he tells me he's just moved into a squat there and he's sorting out the electrics.

'Are you an electrician?' I ask.

He laughs and says he isn't, but he's had the electricity cut off in enough squats that he knows what to do to put it back on. He points to a big, industrial-looking fuse in the glove box in front of me and tells me he's just been to pick it up.

I ask him where the squat is and he says it's Appleby Court, just off Bank Street. I don't recognise the name, but when he describes where it is, I do know it.

There used to be a washing machine repair shop there.

It turns out the shop was owned by Gary's uncle and aunt. He says they'd run it for 30 years, but now they've been evicted along with the tenants in the flats and houses.

I can see he's pissed off about the evictions. I think that might have been his motivation in choosing to squat this particular place.

'I'll tell you what, mate, we're the number one topic of conversation in The Burlingford Club where all the snobs hang out,' Gary says. 'We get to hear all about what they say, because we have a friend who works there, Gail. You might have met her, she was at that bonfire party.'

I have no memory of anyone called Gail at that party, but my memories of the night are somewhat lacking order and clarity.

Gary looks at my blank expression and carries on. 'Mate, while she's pouring them drinks, they're pouring out their hearts about how we're lowering the tone of the neighbourhood. She was doing a shift the other week and Mr Savory who owns our squat comes in, all dressed up in a three piece suit, which was bursting at the seams around his fat fucking gut. He goes up to the bar, orders his drink and announces that they're having a meeting and he'll need a tab, as all the drinks are on him. He looks at her, with this pompous look, like she's supposed to be impressed. All she can think to say is 'Are you some old, fat version of the fucking Milkybar Kid?' so she shuts up. Then some quite high-ranking pigs come in, followed by various councillors and other local business owners. She knows all these people because they're all regulars. She can't hear all of their conversation, but voices get raised when the pigs have to explain to some of the other people there that they can't just kick us out of the squat because we're legally allowed to be there, and they can't arrest us unless we actually commit a crime. Mr Savory starts ripping into them about it being their job to keep order, then starts having a go at the councillors, who turned down his proposal to knock down Appleby Court and build an office block. The councillors who are there remind him that they voted for it, but say they don't control how the other councillors vote and that the office block he proposed was an absolute eyesore. He says it's better than a boarded up derelict courtyard. That's what Appleby Court has become since he boarded it up and left it to become derelict. Then one of the councillors says they're sure that if he puts in another application, the other councillors will see the light and support it.'

I think it's quite funny that the people in the Burlingford club speak so freely in front of Gail, never suspecting that she's feeding information back to the squatters. I guess it's the advantage of their arrogant worldview, where, as bar-staff, she's seen as so low status that she's almost totally dehumanised.

I ask Gary if it really looks derelict just by having the windows boarded up.

Surely, unless it's actually derelict, it would just look like a building with the windows boarded up.

'He didn't just board over the windows, mate, he boarded over the carvings along the tops of the walls and the engraving of the date it was built. By covering up everything that makes it look attractive with tatty boards, it really did look derelict. We removed the boards, which is technically criminal damage, but the only people who saw us are the neighbours. They understand his fucking game and don't want to live next to a derelict building. I really don't think they'll say anything at all, mate.'

We drive into town and up to Appleby Court. When I get out, I look up at the carvings at the top of the wall, just underneath the Kent-peg roof.

The building consists of a courtyard, surrounded by terrace houses, with one entrance and the old washing machine repair shop opposite. It has fancy little details carved and built into it all over the place.

It really is quite ornate and beautifully built. You can see that, although it's a bit run down and uncared for, it would have been quite grand when it was first built. I'd never noticed it before but then I've never had much reason to come here.

I guess I'd never really paid attention to the building itself and certainly hadn't bothered looking up at the roof. The people who built it put a lot of work into that décor, just for other people to walk around without ever noticing it.

Gary invites me in for tea, but although I'd love to chat more with him and look around the squat, I really need to get on with looking for a job, so I decline the offer.

He says there's a party tonight to celebrate their new squat and I'd be welcome to come along.

I'm definitely going to the party. If it's anywhere near as fun as the bonfire, it'll be fantastic.

I walk out into Bank Street and then up to the High Street and around town, looking at all the fancy features on the buildings which I'd never noticed before.

I'd never realised how many of the buildings have beautiful Kent peg roofs.

There are loads of ornate features that you'd expect to find on famous historical buildings.

I wonder how much more hand-crafted ornamentation has been lost behind the UPVC shop fronts and plastic signs. I also wonder if anyone knows the names of any of the craftspeople who carved and moulded and formed these features with great skill and calloused hands.

The people who paid them to do the work will

be remembered in historical records and may even have plaques up with their names on them in

The Burlingford Club, but the people who did the work, the people who actually built this town are probably entirely forgotten and we all walk past their works of art every day without even looking up to see them.

Fishtruck

I must have listened to a thousand hours of lorry driver's tales, but this guy really had been around the block. This was about a week after Monkey pretended to hang himself.

'I wanted to see the world mate. I didn't have any cash so this seemed like the best option. I could've joined the army I s'pose, but it didn't really appeal. I don't like the idea of having to kill someone and I've got no appetite at all for being killed, so I decided to become a lorry driver.'

My lift, a bloke who must be closer to sixty than fifty and has a belly which is trying to escape through the gap between his trousers and his t-shirt is staring straight ahead at the empty motorway. He has a certain stoicism to him, as if it was always going to turn out this way, so he has had to accept it for what it is.

'My plan to see the world had a slow start. I had to stick with the company who paid for my training for five years, or else pay back the costs. They kept hinting they'd send me off long distance, but I was pretty much always in the home counties. There was the occasional drive to such exotic places as Swindon or even Leeds, but mainly just Surrey. As soon as the five years were up, I joined a company which did more overseas work. The first job they gave me took me to France. I was hoping for Spain or somewhere else warm, but at least it wasn't bloody Guildford. I delivered a load to a little industrial estate in Normandy.'

There's a woodland on my side of the road. The sun is large, reddish orange and low in the sky behind it. This creates an orange strobe effect. The flickering light feels warm on my face.

'I was off the ferry for all of an hour before I arrived there and then had to stop overnight before heading back. I got to see a few French roads and the countryside next to those roads. I got to the place I was dropping my load and it was in the middle of nowhere. There was nothing within walking distance, just a closed warehouse at the end of an empty road. I didn't get to have a meal or even a drink in a French cafe or anything like that. I ate a pasty and some beans in my cab and listened to the radio. I picked up a load nearby in the morning and headed back. I grabbed breakfast on the ferry. I had a fry-up, but I had a croissant with it. I wanted to have some taste of French grub during the trip. It was a disappointing start to the job, but after that, they sent me all over Europe.'

We're past the woodland, heading down a slight incline towards a fairly flat section of land. The road cuts through the landscape, dividing the habitats on one side from the other. Everything in my view other than the road is formed of soft rounded shapes of vegetation. The road looks alien to its surroundings, like it's a foreign object plonked on the land without thought or care.

'I took hops to Germany and brought wine back. I took a whole lorry load of locks over to Luxembourg. I came back with an empty load because something went wrong with the paperwork. I had the highest winds I've ever known on the way back. People think a heavy load is a problem, but trust me, a light load and high winds is much more of an issue. I had to pull into a service station and wait for the storm to pass. You can imagine how chuffed my boss was. Not only was I returning empty, but I was delayed as well. He gave me no end of grief. Then I was heading down to Spain with some doors, I think it was doors, but I might have mixed that up. Anyway, I was heading down to Spain and I stopped at a service station and got chatting to another British lorry driver who was taking a load down to Morocco.'

There's a dead deer on the hard shoulder. I

can't see how it got over the tall fence either side of the road. I guess its ancestors must have crossed freely, back and forth across the arbitrary line that is now a road.

'Now, to me, Morocco was more like it. I'd been all over Europe at this point and I wanted to see more of the world. That's what it was all about for me, like I said. The firm the other driver was working for specialised in Africa and the Middle East. He gave me his boss's number and I gave him a call. My first job for them, and my last as it turned out, was delivering Belgian chocolates to Jordan. Well, I got as far as the Syrian border and this chap in a uniform with a rifle in his hands tells me to pull over and turn off the engine. So I do what he says and I sit in the cab, waiting for his next instruction. Then he comes over, all angry and starts shouting at me. I don't understand what he's saying at first, which only makes things worse. Then I realise he's shouting at me to turn the engine off, but the engine is off already. I try to tell him, but he's having none of it. He's jumping up and down and shouting and frankly, this is getting us nowhere, so I take the keys out of the ignition and show them to him to show the engine is switched off.

'He's getting more and more irate and showing him the keys hasn't helped at all. So he tells me to get out of the cab. I climb down and he's absolutely bloody apoplectic! I have no clue what he's being so pissy about, so there's little I can do to calm the situation down. Once I'm down, he starts pointing at the fridge unit, which is whirring away like mad in all that heat and he shouts at me again to turn the engine off. I try to explain to him that this is a fridge unit not an engine, but he's having none of it. He raises the gun and sticks it straight in my face.'

He throws his head backwards into the headrest of his seat as he recalls this. I've seen this exact movement and expression before, when a previous lift of mine, Felix, recalled having a gun pointed at him in Afghanistan.

'Now, like I said, I have no appetite at all for being killed, so at this stage, I'm up for doing anything he bloody says. If he'd have told me to set fire to the lorry, if it was that or him shoot me in the face, I'd have done it straight away. So I turn the fridge unit off and then try to explain to him that it's not an engine and the chocolate will melt if it stays off. You've got to realise it was bloody hot that day. I don't know how hot it normally is down that way, on account of I've never been back, but it was properly scorching. I know I'm going to be red as a lobster in five minutes if I don't find shade. He isn't taking any notice of anything I say. The more I try to explain, the angrier he gets.

'He tells me to go into the customs building

and raises his gun in my face again. For obvious reasons, I go along with what he wants, hoping this is going to be real quick. I didn't know how long it would take for the chocolate to melt, but in that heat, it wasn't going to be long.'

Where the motorway crosses a river, the banks are faced in concrete, from the rivers edge right up to the road. You can see the meandering river, twisting and turning off into the distance in either direction to accommodate the varied geology of the land. The route it's taking will have changed constantly over time as it wears through the soil and stone beneath and around it. Then where it approaches the road, it's straightened and boxed in by the uncompromising walls of concrete which contain it.

'The customs building was lovely and cool, once I got inside. It was one of them traditionally built square buildings like they have out there. I have to admit that briefly I was so relieved to be somewhere cool I forgot how bad this situation was. I went up to the counter and a man in all them Arabic robes and that took a form out of a drawer under the counter and gave it to me to fill in, but the form was in Arabic. I asked him if he spoke English and he just replied in Arabic and pointed at the form. Of course, I didn't have a clue what he was saying, so I try again, this time pointing to the form and saying slowly in English that I can't understand it. So, he takes the form off me and examines it. He says a few words in Arabic as if he's reading them off the form and gives it back to me. I can tell he's telling me just to fill the form in, but of course I can't because I don't have a bloody clue what's written on it.

'Another bloke who works there steps in and says something to me, again in Arabic, and I try to explain to him what the problem is, but he just does the same as the first guy. Luckily, a chap in the queue just behind me steps in to help. He talks down to the customs officers in a way I wouldn't have the balls to do, even if they were unarmed British customs. He takes the form off me and throws it at them. Then he shouts to them something which must have translated roughly as "Just give him the English version", because that's what they do. They take another version of the form in English out of the drawer and give it to me. I thank the chap behind me in the queue and fill in the form.'

'They only wanted a few details, name, address, age that sort of thing. I give the form back to them and the customs bloke says something in Arabic and points to a seat, so I go and sit down. After a bit, I go back to the counter to see if I can speed things up. I knew the shelf life of those chocolates was getting shorter by the minute. I stand in the queue for a bit, then when I get to the front and try to explain, the bloke behind the counter just tuts at me and points to the seat where I'd been sitting. Well, there's only so much you can do, so I sit back down and wait.

'I waited for ages. I was fairly sure by that point my load was ruined, so there was nothing left to lose.'

He shakes his head and lets out a deep sigh.

'Eventually, one of the customs officers calls me over to the counter and says "passport". I give him my passport. He looks at it, then he looks at me, then he holds it up so he can compare my face to my passport photo side by side. Then he passes it to another customs officer, who does the same, looks at me, looks at my passport photo, holds it up to compare and passes it to another customs officer. My passport travelled around the whole bloody office like this, with each of them comparing my face to my photo. The looks on their faces were full of concern and suspicion. You'd have thought I was some wanted criminal.

'All this time, I'm trying to keep my composure, but I'm terrified I'm never going to be let out. When absolutely everyone in the office has had a look, probably even the bloody tea boy, it's returned to the bloke who took it off me. He looks down at it and then up at my face as if he's having one last check. Then he picks up the rubber stamp on the desk, stamps my passport and hands it back, whilst saying "Welcome to Syria" in a perfect English accent.'

'So was the chocolate melted?' I ask. 'How long does the back of a lorry stay refrigerated in that heat?'

'Buggered, mate. Completely buggered!' he says. 'I didn't find out straight away though. I didn't want to open up the back because that would only make matters worse if it wasn't ruined yet, so I turned the fridge unit back on and carried on my way. I think I thought the boxes might provide some extra insulation and, I don't know, maybe it wasn't as bad as I thought. I didn't really know what to do then. Who knows, it could have been fine, so I took it all the way to Jordan.'

There's a junction and a road which crosses the motorway. Another strip of destroyed ecosystem, dividing habitats, disappearing out of sight into the distance in either direction.

'When I got there, they started unloading and everything was fine and dandy till they opened one of the boxes up. You've got to understand here that these weren't just any chocolates. They were the poshest chocolates I've ever seen in my life. They were in these beautiful hand-painted velvet-lined boxes, with ribbons around them and a little wax seal thing like old kings would use and that. As soon as they opened that box, all the smiles disappeared. The bottom of the box was filled with a mix of chocolate and fillings which had all melted to liquid and set again into one messy lump along with their wrappers. It looked like a right mess. So all the chocolates were loaded back on the lorry and they refused delivery. I had to phone the boss. You can imagine he wasn't best pleased. He's only been my boss for five minutes and I'm phoning him up with this absolute shitshow of a situation.

'So when he'd finished screaming down the phone at me, I turned around and headed back. Eventually, I got to the Syrian border. After my last experience, I thought at least it doesn't matter if they get me to turn the fridge unit off. Those chocolates are not going to get any worse, whatever I do to them now. So I pull up and I get told where to park and I go into the customs building and they look at my passport. No problems there. They seem a little less confrontational at this border, which obviously I'm happy about. Then they're looking at the paperwork for the truck and they ask me what the load is. I explain the situation and they tell me the load is no longer classed as food, it's now contaminated food waste.

'My paperwork would have been fine to bring the load back as food, but I don't have the paperwork for contaminated food waste, so I'm back on the blower to my new boss, who's already made it as clear as day he isn't going to be employing me after this disastrous state of affairs and he's just as happy as you probably imagine he would be.

'So he's shouting abuse down the phone at me and I'm standing there in the customs office, holding the phone away from my ear so he doesn't deafen me, much to the amusement of everyone working there. Anyway, cut a long story short, I'm stuck there for four days while they sort the paperwork and shortly after that, I was back in Blighty looking for another job.'

There's police tape where a vehicle has come off the road and crashed into an area of scrub. The vehicle has been removed, just leaving the smashed up remains of the saplings it crunched its way through and some broken glass from its lights.

'There's always work for drivers luckily, so I was back to delivering all over Europe for another firm. My first job was taking some olive oil down to Greece which seemed strange as I'm pretty sure they make it there. But I just get paid to drive, so there you go. I was working for this lot for about three months when they asked if I'd like to go to Russia. Well, it wouldn't be top of my holiday list, but I'm up for an adventure, so why not?

'I met another driver on the way out there who scared the crap out of me. He had all these tales of bandits and all this. He said it was the "Wild East" and you had to be careful, 'cos there were desperate people in Russia. He said you should keep a fifty

Deutsch Mark note on show in the cab, because if bandits see that, it's enough money that they'll just grab it and run. I was never convinced about that, but I did clip a 50DM note to my clipboard in the cab just in case. I was nervous as hell all the way.'

A kestrel is hovering above the embankment on the other side of the road, taking full advantage of a small section of hunting ground which has been spared from concrete and tarmac.

'Now, Russia is a big country, and I was going all the way up to Siberia, so I got to see a lot of it. As always, I only got to see the roads and what you can see from them, but it did feel like an adventure. I saw a lot of countryside and an awful lot of snow. It was bloody cold. Cold like I've never known. Where Syria was approaching forty degrees centigrade, Siberia was around minus forty. Luckily, I'm in a brand-new, top of the range Scania and the heating in the cab was top notch, so that wasn't a problem, but if you stepped outside, your nose would start to freeze up.

'Where I was going was an oil refinery or something and when I got there, I met this Russian lorry driver who knew about ten words of English, which is about eight words more than I knew in Russian. He lived right by where I was parked up. We got drinking in this little bar. We continued until the early hours. It was quite a sesh. Last I remember of the night was him trying to explain something about plum vodka.'

A family overtake us, with two children in the back of the car. They wave and smile at us and my lift waves and beeps his horn at them.

'Then I woke up on the floor of the bar the next morning, with my head spinning and feeling as sick as a dog. My new Russian friend woke me up before leaving the bar himself. I guess he must have slept there too.

'I get up and go out to the truck and it won't start. It was so cold the diesel had frozen. Well, I've never had to deal with that before. Diesel doesn't freeze in England, so I don't know what to do. Well the Russian chap is sitting in his cab on the other side of the car park and I can see from the exhaust fumes and the steam as it heats up that he's got his truck started. He jumps out of his cab and comes over. In his hands, he's got this metal thing that's like a camping saucepan. You know those rectangular ones that the army use? It's like one of those.

'He says "OK, I help". Then, before I can think about what he's doing, he lights whatever is in this little camping saucepan type thing, which from the way it goes up clearly contains some diesel in the mix and shoves it under the engine block. This apparently is normal procedure in Siberia for starting a truck in minus forty.'

More roadkill. A fox this time, lying on the verge by the hard shoulder. It almost looks like it's sleeping.

'Well, there's a difference between a Russian truck and a brand new top of the range Scania. There's actually quite a few differences and most of them mean that the Scania is the better truck, but the key difference here is that the Russian truck has metal pipes and metal everything else and the Scania pipes, including the diesel pipes, are plastic or rubber or something, as are a lot of the other components of the engine. Within about thirty seconds of that saucepan thing going under the engine, the whole bloody truck was up in flames. I'm stood there a few metres from it, watching it burn.

'Luckily it was too cold to get out without grabbing a jacket, because all I had now was the clothes I stood up in. All the rest of my clothes were burnt, my passport and the other bits of paperwork were burnt, my money was burnt, my address book, even that 50 DM note and the clipboard it was clipped to. The whole lot, up in flames in front of my eyes.

'That wasn't a good day, I can tell you! So they flew me back. They didn't sack me, luckily, but I got all the crappy jobs from then on. So I started looking another job and I found this one. It's steady and reliable. I know where I'm going, and I don't get into trouble. You can hardly claim it's "seeing the world", but it's seeing the bits of the world between Aberdeen and Spain. That's where I go now, from Aberdeen down to Spain and then back up to Aberdeen. I pick up fish in Aberdeen and take it down to Spain and then I pick up fish in Spain and take it up to Aberdeen.'

'Could they not all eat their local fish?' I ask.'It seems like a waste of fuel.'

'It's worse than you think,' he says. 'It's almost always cod. I pick up cod in Aberdeen, take it down to Spain, then I pick up cod in Spain and take it back. It makes no sense at all, but it pays the bills.'

Meteorologist

*Ten minutes or so with this guy was not enough. I could
have chatted with him for hours. ('91)*

I think I'm going deaf in my left ear.

I've been standing here for four hours now. If
it was a few degrees colder, this rain would be sleet,
if not snow. The wind has been consistently blowing
cold rain into my ear, which caused it to go numb a
while back.

Then the feeling came back in the form of
terrible earache. I can't turn around, because I'd then
have my back to the traffic. But having stood here for
four hours, I'm painfully aware I could have stood
with my back to the wind ignoring the traffic for all
that time and it wouldn't have made any difference.

I could indeed have just gone and sat
somewhere out of the wind, and I wouldn't have
missed out on a lift.

For all my efforts, I haven't got a lift, just

earache. That is the benefit, or rather disbenefit of hindsight in this situation.

The next car to come along might give me a lift and therefore might be worth the pain of continuing to face my left ear into this somewhat unpleasant wind. I won't know of course until it comes and if it just drives past like every other car has so far, I'm just pointlessly causing myself pain. Oh the joys of hitching!

Well, here's the next car. It's an old Hillman Imp. They're really cool cars, but they're not massive. I'm wearing a big rucksack and carrying a fairly bulky bag. Unless the car is completely empty, apart from the driver, I'm guessing there probably isn't space for me and my luggage.

I'd give up on this whole thing and go home, but the only way to get there would be to hitch. It would mean hitching the other way, so my left ear could take a rest from the elements whilst my right ear went numb and then developed an earache.

It's hard to know which is worse, terrible earache in both ears or absolutely excruciating earache in one.

I put on a big smile for the driver. Hopefully this doesn't look like the manic grin of a serial killer.

On reflection, it probably does.

I can just see myself being found here having frozen to death, my left ear becoming frozen first, then slowly spreading until the whole of my body was frozen solid. It's probably not a helpful thought, but it's what's in my mind.

To my great surprise, the car stops. I run up to it and the driver beckons me to get in and starts moving box files which are stacked up on the back seat. My rucksack and bag are dripping with rain and the driver is telling me to put them in the back with the box files.

I put my jacket over them first to stop the rain from soaking the contents. Rain drips from my rucksack onto the floor of the car.

When I sit down in the front, rain drips from me onto the seat and pours from my trousers into the footwell. I'm cold and wet, but at least I'm in a warm car and I'm moving.

This is going to be a quick journey. The driver, an almost entirely bald man in a bright red jumper which is severely frayed at the cuffs, tells me he's only going 10 minutes down the road, but he's going past a service station, which will be better for hitching than this cold and windy spot.

Here has proved to be poor for hitching, so I hope he's right. I apologise for getting the car wet and say that I hope I haven't got the contents of the boxes in the back wet.

'Oh, don't worry,' he says. 'It's only a bit of rain, which is what's in the boxes as well, or at least a study on rainfall. It's quite apt that it gets a bit of rain on it.' He smiles almost to the point that it's a chuckle.

'A study on rainfall?' I ask.

'Rainfall patterns are my thing,' he says. 'I've made quite a career out of studying them.'

'You're a meteorologist?'

'That's right. I started off doing a physics degree and then... I don't actually know how I ended up studying rainfall patterns, but they turned out to be very interesting. Then somehow, I've ended up in meteorology. It's actually the patterns rather than the rainfall that interests me.'

'So as a meteorologist, do you think that global warming will kill us off?'

'Well, it really isn't my subject, although I probably have more of a clue than most people about it. You really need to ask a climate scientist.'

I feel like a bit of an idiot now. He's already told me he studies rainfall patterns and I'm asking him about something completely different. It seemed like a fair punt when starting a conversation with a meteorologist, but now it seems a bit daft.

'If I had to have a stab at it from what I know as a meteorologist,' he continues, 'I don't really think global warming should be an existential issue. It is going to cause us serious problems, there's no question about that, but if we take the right actions and deal with the situation, we really should be able to get our emissions down to a level where they're not problematic. Sure, it requires compromises on our lifestyle. We have to account for the environmental cost of everything, just as we do the monetary cost on a personal, organisational and governmental level. When you view it on the basis of a cost benefit analysis, the cost of acting on the information that we have is miniscule in relation to the benefit of continuing to have a habitable planet. It's just common sense to act. I know all sorts of people bandy around the phrase 'common sense' to mean agreeing with them, but purely on a rational and logical basis, we are compelled to act.'

'So you think it'll be fine?' I say. 'You reckon people will just see sense and make the necessary adjustments and it'll all be fine?'

I guess he's right. It's in everyone's interest to ensure that the planet remains habitable. It makes sense that we'll all look after it.

A motorbike comes up behind us. My lift pulls over, almost into the gutter at the side of the road to give it space to pass.

It passes us, the rider lifts the fingers of one hand as a signal to say thanks and accelerates off into the distance.

The meteorologist continues, 'Well,' he says, 'logic does suggest that people will see the data and act to mitigate the worst effects of global warming and everything will be fine in the long run. Unfortunately, my wife, who's a psychologist, sees it very differently. She'll tell you that it's far more complicated than that. Firstly, she blames me. Well, all scientists really. We're not great communicators and we tend not to make absolute statements. Where sceptics will tell you absolutely without doubt that the whole thing is a lie based on no information at all, us scientists tend to talk in terms of there being a strong evidence base or the data being clear. People are stuck between two arguments, one of them being expressed in clear terms with absolute conviction and the other presented in a slightly woolly way as if the person making it doesn't want to commit themselves. In that situation, it's easy to believe the former, even if the person making it happens to be an uninformed idiot.'

This guy's tone is one of deep concern and concentration. He sounds like he's trying to find the solution to some complex puzzle. Every now and again he runs his hand back across head, as if he's trying to flick back the hair that used to be there.

'My wife talks about this as a propaganda war, between those of us who can see a clear and present danger and wish to avoid it and those who have a vested interest in dismissing the issue. Take the motor industry, for instance. They've spent decades persuading people through advertising that cars and motorbikes are sexy and exciting and getting people to see them as an extension of themselves. You have lots of men with frail egos who rely on their vehicles to substitute their belief in their own virility and masculinity. They've spent their whole lives watching car adverts and motor industry sponsored motor sports. This has conditioned them to trigger a dopamine response when they cause an engine to roar. We've all seen the sad little men who've reached late middle age and bought themselves a sports car or a motorbike. They do so because they're not content with what they've achieved in life and possibly because their penile function is somewhat below par, but also because they've been conditioned to.'

My lift taps the dashboard as he says this as if to underline his point and the frown on his face grows. 'Psychologists have apparently shown that rats can be conditioned to create a dopamine response to almost anything. You can make them push buttons, pull levers, solve mazes or anything you choose by rewarding them with a shot of dopamine. The behaviour that you reward, inevitably becomes a compulsive behaviour and then they provide their own dopamine, or something like that. Look at this here.'

He points to the car in front of us. It's a very

sporty-looking, metalic blue boy-racer car with a comically oversized exhaust and spoiler. I can't see what make it is. It's got go faster stripes and a word written down the side of it in joined up writing, like a signature. It looks like it says 'distortion', or 'destruction', or 'distraction' or something. I can't make it out properly.

As I'm looking at the car, the driver looks at me in his mirror. I can see the bumfluff on his chin. He can't be much older than seventeen.

'This young man has probably spent money he can't afford to buy and insure a car like that. The spoiler makes little difference to performance in reality and go faster stripes obviously make no difference at all except psychologically, yet he feels compelled to buy it. Some women have also been conditioned to see the flash car as a sign of power and wealth. This is true, even though the man driving it has actually lowered their wealth by buying it and may well have no significant wealth other than the car. All of this is, of course, generalisation but it has a powerful societal effect and that effect has been brought about by multinational corporations spending billions on advertising.'

He lets out a big sigh and looks at me to check I'm following him. I am, but I'm also caught up with the bit about rats. When they're pressing levers in lab experiments and giving themselves a dose of dopamine, do they really feel anything akin to the exhilaration of driving a fast car? How would you know if they were? Are corporations really treating us like rats in a laboratory?

He clearly thinks I'm following him well enough, because he continues.

'Then, on the side of maintaining an inhabitable planet, you have scientists making cautious, rational statements. We don't present the message with all the bells and whistles that advertisers use. There are no dramatic scenes, scantily clad women or even background music, so no dopamine or serotonin is triggered. People are only connected to the information rationally, rather than emotionally. Therefore, we really have no effective way to counter the propaganda from the motor industry. That's only one sector. There's also the aviation industry, the energy industry and the food industry.'

The volume and tempo of his voice increase as he gets more agitated by what he's describing.

'Each of these industries spend more per year on propaganda in the form of advertising than the scientific community spends on getting the message across about global warming. All this advertising has the same message, that message being, 'Buy this product and you will be happier'. They hire the world's greatest communicators to implant this message in your head. The USSR has never been able compete with capitalism for the amount of propaganda consumed by its citizens. Westerners will happily sit and watch advert after advert, all telling them that consuming more will make them happier. Trying to persuade them to consume less for the sake of the planet goes against all of their conditioning.'

The thing where he brushes his imaginary hair back has become more and more frequent, like an uncontrollable tic. The concern in his voice has turned to utter despair as if listening to his own words has brought home the severity of the situation. He barely takes a breath before he dives back in again.

'Then you have the economic and political aspect. I'm not an economist, I don't study politics and I don't have the advantage of living with an expert in either field, so I'm just talking as a man on the street here. As I see it, we can give everyone in the world a decent standard of living and do so sustainably. We can allow some people to have lavish lifestyles where they own multiple, high-value houses, fly around the world on private jets and own massive yachts. What we can't do is both. Logically, we need to curb the consumption of the super-rich. Unfortunately, they control the world and the media. As such, they control the politicians. Their interests come before your interests, my interests and the concept of an inhabitable planet. It's not that there's some sort of mysterious cabal that are conspiring against us. It's just about vested interests. If all the most powerful people in the world have the same vested interest, they'll all act to ensure that things go their way.'

He looks over at me again, but this time it's not to check that I'm following him; it's to confirm we both see this in the same way. He wants company in his despair, someone to share this unfortunate worldview with.

'It's entirely possible to mitigate the worst effects of global warming. I can tell you that as a meteorologist, but both my wife's view from a psychologist's standpoint, and my own understanding have persuaded me that it is highly unlikely we ever will. So, if you ask me generally what I think, I think we're probably all doomed'.

My lift taps the steering wheel with his fingers in a nervous way and laughs a slightly uncomfortable laugh.

Second Lift With Morag

It would seem healthier to forget this day, but it's part of me. (Autumn '96)

It seems fitting that Morag is giving me a lift away from here, as she was the one to bring me here in the first place.

Soon I'll be on my way back to Kent and I'll probably never see this hill again.

This has been my fifth eviction and the first one where I haven't been arrested. Those oaks coming down and the coppice and scrub being removed was the extreme destruction I always knew it would be.

Annie has been sat away from the action huddled up in her raincoat, not wanting to leave the site, but unable to act. She insists she's fine, but she's been crying since the first tree came down and has hardly said a word to anyone, accept to say that she's fine. She hasn't even accepted a cup of tea.

I've never known Annie refuse a cup of tea

until today.

The last two trees to come down were the two at the entrance, connected by the walkway of blue polyprop. It took eight hours to remove Fred and the others from the treehouses. They had defences all the way up the tree to make them difficult to climb, but eventually the bailiffs used diggers and levelled the ground around the trees enough to get a cherry-picker up there.

Fred tried to keep out of reach of the cherry-picker for as long as she could by running up and down the walkway, but that only bought an extra few minutes. She's sitting in the back of the meat-wagon now waiting to be taken to the police station.

There's a great big pile of debris at the side of the site. They've pushed up all the smaller wood, along with soil and anything else that was in the way into this pile. There's too much earth for it to burn properly. I don't know what they'll do with it, but I guess the object of today was just to remove us and any other living thing from the area, and they've achieved that.

Maybe they'll just bury it under the new road. We've watched rabbits run from the diggers as their burrows have been destroyed. I've also seen the squashed remains of rabbits which didn't manage to escape in time pushed up into the pile along with everything else which made up their homes and their habitat; indeed, everything else that made up their world.

The structures which made up our outdoor kitchen along with utensils, a sleeping bag and various other items are compacted into the mess. One of the coppice stools came up almost complete and you can see the details of its carefully-crafted shape and the remains of the root system that supported it up high on top of the pile. It's lying on its side, smashed like it's been in a car crash with the roots torn apart and exposed to the sun.

Maureen Powercourt was up here earlier, talking to the reporters. Although she's always been against the protest, which she said when she was interviewed for the TV, she also said she thought we were courageous and that we were fighting for a just cause. She's chair of the parish council now, so she came up here to represent the parish. She looked tearful and I thought she was going to cry.

She didn't, or at least I didn't see her crying. Almost everyone else has.

I was chatting with a security guard earlier who said to me that I'd look back at this as the worst destruction I had seen in my life, but I'd know that I'd done all I could to prevent it. He said he'd always look back, knowing that he was part of the destruction. When he got a tear in his eye, I didn't know what to do. I felt completely ill-equipped for the situation.

He's just some bloke who's in a situation which he didn't create, playing a part which he just kind of fell into.

None of this is his fault. I wish I had some way of putting that across to him, but I didn't, and I was just silent.

Morag drops me off in the same spot as she picked me up all those months ago. I thank her. She offered me a place to stay for the night, but I said that I'd rather be on my way.

When cars drive past, I can't smile at them. I'm normally great at faking a smile for a lift, but I seem to have lost the ability. I know I need to get back to Kent, but I don't care if it happens or not. I don't care if I get a lift and I don't care how long I'm standing here.

The sun lowers in the sky and creates the most magnificent sunset, but it does nothing for me. It's like something inside me has died.

As well as being the first eviction that hasn't ended in arrest for me, this is the first one where I haven't cried. I've had people crying on my shoulder today and I've tried to comfort them, but I've felt nothing.

I watched them push up all the life in those woods into a pile of death and destruction and I felt nothing.

The hideous pink house in the village normally

never fails to bring a smile to my face, but today I saw it for the last time and felt nothing. Even looking up from the village and seeing the skyline which used to be dominated by those massive oaks and is now dominated by a large brown scar on the hillside left me completely unmoved.

I feel like giving up.

I don't mean giving up protest, I mean giving up entirely. I have no motivation to get a lift. I don't care if it rains and I get soaked.

I don't care about hunger or thirst or living to see another day.

I'm not angry or sad.

I'm not anything.

I don't even want to curl up into a ball and disappear.

I don't feel anything.

I just stand here, holding my sign whilst cars drive past.

Marek

The start of my European adventures in '91. I really hoped that travelling around Europe would give me some direction, some clue of what I wanted to do with my life. It certainly changed me.

This service station is showing all the signs of closing for the night.

The cafe closed a good hour ago and soon after that the shop closed as well. As I watched the lights go out with my travelling companion Fred. Both she and I knew the chances of getting a lift tonight were rapidly reducing.

We're now watching the petrol attendant putting away the various items which are outside the kiosk, so we're pretty sure the garage will close soon too.

The attendant goes into the kiosk and comes out again with a broom and starts sweeping up. We're very much hoping we'll get a lift in the next few minutes because there's nothing left to attract someone off the motorway once that garage is closed.

A car pulls up to get petrol, but the attendant waves him away. The lights are still on for the moment, but the place is now, it seems, closed.

This car is probably our last chance of a lift. It's a little sports car; we could probably just about squeeze in with our rucksacks, but it's not going to be the most comfortable of rides.

Its lights flash as it comes towards us. We hope this is a signal that it's going to stop, but it keeps going and drives straight past us and back out onto the road.

The garage lights go out, leaving the service station lit by a smattering of street lights.

The petrol attendant gets in his car and heads towards us. There's always a chance he could give us a lift. We only need to get to a 24-hour service station or a busy junction and we can carry on hitching.

He winds down his window and shouts something at us in a friendly and enthusiastic way whilst waving vigorously.

We don't understand, because we don't speak French.

Now there only appear to be four people in the whole of the service station; Fred, myself and two other hitchers twenty metres or so further along the slip road. They're two blokes who, like us, are in their early twenties. They're dressed in clothing designed more for practicality than style and have old fashioned leather rucksacks with them. They both have jet black hair. One has his long hair, tied back in a ponytail, the other's hair is short, which looks a bit like his mother might have cut his fringe to get it out of his eyes.

We've been communicating with them through smiles and shrugs ever since we arrived here. Mainly we've been communicating about the lack of lifts in this silent mime-like manner. We look at them, they look at us; we shrug at them and they shrug back. We all know we'll be camping here tonight.

The other two hitchers walk towards us and say hello. The one with the longer hair is called Marek, his mate is Vaclav and they're from Czechoslovakia. They've been here all day, which is only a few hours longer than we have.

Even during the day when this is a fully functioning service station, it's not a great hitching spot. Hopefully we'll be luckier tomorrow.

We've been thinking for a while we might end up sleeping here tonight and we've spotted a promising patch of grass on the edge of the service station where we'd be tucked away out of sight, so the four of us go over to check it out.

It's very flat, but the ground is parched and hard, so we decide to get some cardboard to go under the tent for padding. We ask Marek and Vaclav if they'd like some cardboard too. They don't seem to understand, but come with us as we go to the back of the shop and cafe area to look for some.

There are stacks and stacks of flattened cardboard boxes and some cardboard sheets from the bottom of pallets. We grab four of the cardboard sheets, two for each tent and have a look to see what's in the skips.

The first one has stinking food waste in it. The second is empty except for three sacks of baguettes. Fred grabs two baguettes as I struggle to carry the sheets of card.

'These are free?' asks Vaclav, gesturing at the baguettes.

'Welcome to the efficiencies of capitalism,' Fred announces.

Marek and Vaclav both look a bit surprised. We've brought some food with us and so have our new friends, so along with the baguettes, we make a passable meal for the four of us.

I'm gutted it was only bread we got from the skips. Fred's line about capitalism would have been so much better if it was accompanied by cream cakes or at least some nice pastries.

My first experience of 'skip-diving' or 'skipping' was much more fruitful than this.

I'd just moved into Appleby Court and on my first night, one of the other squatters, a bloke called Paul, asked if I wanted to go skipping. I didn't know what he meant at first. Paul walks with quite a limp; it seemed unlikely he was going to be skipping using a skipping rope, or prancing down the pavement, hopping from one foot to another.

When he explained that he meant taking discarded food out of supermarket skips, I was understandably wary of the idea. I thought there must be something wrong with the food if they're throwing it out and it didn't seem very hygienic to get food from a bin.

As I saw it, shops are in the business of making a profit and throwing saleable food away didn't seem like any part of a sensible business plan. I was both curious and hungry though, so I went along.

We went through a little gap in the fence that led to the area at the back of Safeway's carpark where their skips were. You had to be careful getting through, because there was a bramble bush on one side and the gap wasn't very wide, but I've always been quite slim so it wasn't a problem. I ate a blackberry as I came through, so I already knew the trip wasn't completely wasted. We went into a little undercover area where there were three blue skips, each about five feet tall and almost as wide.

Paul lifted the lid of the first skip and we both leant in to see what it contained. There were cardboard boxes sitting on the top.

He ripped one open. It was full of smoked

salmon with a use by date which ran out the next day. It had clearly just come out of the fridge as it was still very cold to the touch. It was sealed in plastic packaging in an unopened box, so no chance of contamination.

We took the box.

The rest of that skip was full of office waste, so we moved on.

The next one was literally fruitful. As well as two trays of avocados, there was crate after crate of blackberries all in little 100g trays, each priced at 80p and then reduced to 40p. It must have come as a shock to the manager of Safeway's that people weren't prepared to pay £8 per kilo for blackberries in blackberry season. They weren't even great blackberries. The one I ate coming through the gap was a lot more flavoursome. I don't know if it was the type of blackberry or whether they'd lost some flavour in the journey from Germany to Ashford, but they were not the best.

The avocados were unripe. The only reason we could see for discarding them was the best before stamp. It looked like whoever had stamped it on had walked away half way through, leaving an unreadable smear instead of a clearly stamped date.

You really don't need a best before date to tell you that rock solid avocados are not ready to be thrown out yet. Apparently, the manager of Safeway doesn't know that.

Underneath the blackberries were some loaves of bread and some rolls. We took the bread rolls, but the loaves were pappy white sliced bread and it was a bit squashed so we left that.

I lifted the lid on the third skip with anticipation, but it was completely empty. We grabbed a trolley, loaded the food into it and headed back across the town centre to the squat, me pushing the trolley and Paul limping along behind.

Since that first time, I've often eaten food from skips. There's generally a fair amount of baked goods because they have such a short shelf life. It's not just that it's impossible to accurately judge the amount people will buy, but supermarkets want the look of abundance, which comes at the cost of waste.

To that extent, waste is part of their business plans. The person cooking off the last batch of baked goods in a supermarket knows some will be wasted. If there was a chance they'd all be sold, they'd bake more.

A downside of relying on skipping for food is the lack of balance. There are lots of cakes and pastries and just like growing vegetables you have your gluts. Unlike the gluts from the veg patch, the skipping gluts are rarely healthy. I once found a whole skip of chocolate truffles. The first box was great, but a few days later when they were the only food that we had in the squat, I felt sick at the sight of them.

Although by no means a great haul, the baguettes that we've just pulled out of this service station skip are at least a sensible part of our evening meal.

The rest of the meal is a hotchpotch of disparate items that seemed like a good camping food at the time they were purchased. For our part, we have a tin of vegetable soup, or at least that's what we think it is. The picture looks like vegetable soup, but the writing is in French and we're not entirely sure. We also have some instant mash.

We've talked about this and neither of us is sure why we brought it with us. It's horrible stuff, but it'll pad out a meal and we really are hungry right now.

Our new Czech friends have got cheese and some sort of dried vegetable mix.

The end result certainly wouldn't get a glowing review in any restaurant guide, but although it's a culinary disaster, it's filling. There's no one here to judge it but us and we're all hungry enough not to care.

We sit up late into the night chatting about this and that, hitching stories and life experiences. Marek and Vaclav are heading back to Prague after a short hitching tour of Western Europe. They're understandably excited about the fall of the Iron

Curtain and how much it has opened up the world to them, and they're relieved to have lost the yoke of oppression that the USSR represented in their lives.

We all feel great optimism at the possibility of learning from each other's cultures and experiences and moving into an era of cooperation now that Europe is no longer divided. We're hopeful that the end of antagonism and belligerence between West and East will allow us to take the best from each system and disregard the worst.

Marek tells us that Prague is beautiful and encourages us to visit. He gives us his address and invites us to stay at his place if we do. We live in Ashford; we can't pretend it's beautiful, but we invite him to stay nevertheless.

For both Fred and me, it's our first time hitching in Europe. She's a really close friend and somehow we enjoy each other's company, even when we're sharing a tent for weeks on end.

We've been travelling around for a while and we've been to France, Belgium, Holland, Germany (where Fred's pen friend from when she was a child lives), and now we're back in France. We don't really have an itinerary and for my part I'm fairly easy about where we go.

When we'd looked at the pages in our hitch hikers guide which covered Czechoslovakia and Poland, although there was a certain forbidden mystique about them, they hadn't jumped out at us as ideal places to go on holiday. Neither of us really know why, but they just don't seem that appealing.

Fred is the first to vocalise where her views come from. She had a friend in school who was from Poland. She had come over to England as a refugee and spoke of Poland being grey and gloomy.

This image has obviously stuck with Fred. She doesn't have any specific thing in her mind which puts her off Eastern Europe, just a negative impression of it.

Discussing this reminds me of a short film about East Germany I saw as a child. We were taken to the 'Visual Aids Room'. I assume that 'visual aid' was some strange euphemism for a television, because that's what the room contained. They probably thought 'Television Room' would sound like far more fun than a child should have been having at school in the seventies.

We were told we were going to see how children in other countries lived. This sounded very interesting to me and I watched keenly.

I don't remember all that much detail, this happened a long time ago, but I do remember that the two boys in the film got up at 5am and washed in cold water before going on a long walk to school in the snow. It seemed they lived a much harsher life than me or any of my friends and you couldn't help but feel sorry for them.

I had hoped there would be a whole series of these short films showing life in different countries, but there was alas, only the one.

Recalling this now, it is plainly obvious to both myself and Fred that it was shown to us purely as propaganda; an attempt to show us how much worse life was on the other side of the Iron Curtain.

For both of us, the realisation that our image of Eastern Europe has been so affected by hearsay and propaganda is the trigger we need to visit and find out for ourselves.

Cabin Repairs

I wanted to write about the journey to the cabin, but I can't remember anything from leaving England, to walking up the hillside. (Autumn '96 to spring '97)

It's an absolutely gorgeous morning!

Every morning here is beautiful, even when it's pouring with rain, but today is a particularly beautiful sunny morning. The sound of birds fills the air and would drown out almost any noise, but there is no noise for it to compete with, apart from more bird song.

I've never been any good at recognising birds by their calls, but I imagine that even if I was, it would be hard to distinguish an individual bird in this orchestra of bird song.

As the dew warms in the golden morning sun, it raises a fragrance into the air of vegetation, flowers, warm soil and life itself. Looking out across the landscape, I see the most perfect view of mountains and rivers, primeval forests and lush green valleys.

Standing here with the sun on my back and the gentle breeze brushing my face, I feel lucky to be alive.

I'm waiting for the old woman who lives up the track to give me a lift. Soon I'll be on my way back to England. She's been giving me a lift to the shop and back every Thursday for months now.

When I first came here, I walked and hitched to the shop. It's five kilometres, so walkable, but hard work on the way back with a rucksack full of shopping. The first two kilometres going to the shop are down the hill to the main road, so the last two back are uphill and it's a steep climb.

It's possible to hitch once you're on the main road, and the locals were generous when it came to giving me lifts, but so far as I can tell, it's just me and the old lady who use the track up the hill.

The first time the old lady gave me a lift I was halfway up already. The first snow had fallen. It was only a light sprinkling, but it had made me think about the possibility of getting snowed-in as winter kicked in.

I realised that if I couldn't get to the shop, I'd have nothing to eat but apples. I picked them from the tree in the garden soon after I got here. They were large, green cooking apples. I found some slatted trays, which I think were originally intended for this purpose. They certainly work well.

I wrapped each apple in old newspaper, just as I had done as a child, first checking there were no bruises or imperfections. Then I placed the wrapped apples carefully in a tray and placed the trays in a cool dark corner of the barn. I put two pieces of wood under the bottom tray to raise it off the ground and allow a little airflow. I knew the apples would have a fair chance of lasting the winter that way.

To avoid risking a diet consisting purely of apple products, I'd decided to stock up on tinned and dried foods. I knew this was going to make my rucksack extremely heavy to carry up the hill, but it seemed worth the effort.

Having stocked up, I got halfway up and then, completely out of breath, I sat on the ground next to my rucksack, wondering if it would be best to leave half the shopping and come back for it, or to continue the gruelling walk with the full weight on my back.

That's when I heard the old lady's car coming towards me. I hadn't seen any vehicles or sign of them on the track until this point and thought I was probably alone on the hill.

I put my thumb out when the car came into view and was relieved to see it stop. Rarely have I been so pleased to get a lift. I tried to say in Czech where I wanted to go, but she just shrugged and made that dismissive sound that people make in the back of their throats, like the *ch* in *loch*.

As the gate that led to the cabin came into sight, I pointed and she dropped me off. I thanked her, but she just shrugged.

The next time the old lady gave me a lift was about two weeks later. It was a lovely crisp morning and I was about halfway down the hill on my way to the shop when I heard her car. I tried making conversation with my very limited Czech, but she met everything I said with the *ch* sound and a shrug.

When we got to the shop, we each did our shopping, I carried her shopping to the car and she gave me a lift back. I tried again to talk and was met with the same dismissive reaction.

When she dropped me off, she said in Czech 'Thursday, here, nine in the morning, every Thursday'.

To this day, that's the most she's ever said to me. Every Thursday since then I've got a lift with her to the shop, carried her bags to the car and been given a lift back to the cabin.

Today, instead of going to the shop, I'm leaving this little paradise in the hills and going back to England. I'm hoping I can thank her for all the lifts, but suspect that whatever I say will just be met with a dismissive *ch* and a shrug.

I came straight to the cabin from Fishhead's camp. I didn't want to impose myself on my friends in Ashford in the state of mind I found myself in. I sent a postcard from a service station in Belgium, which just said 'Hope you're all well. I've decided to take a break'.

That was five months ago now, when the autumn colours were just starting to show.

For the first three days I was here, I just sawed, split and stacked wood. I had no intention of sticking around to use the wood and there was plenty stacked up already. I didn't have any plans of how long I was going to stay, or indeed, any plans at all.

There was a tree which had fallen just by the cabin, and I just started to saw it up into logs and then split and stack them as something to do to occupy myself so that I didn't have to think.

I didn't even eat on the first day. I sawed, split and stacked wood until I was so knackered that all I could do was sleep.

When I woke up the next morning, I ate and then started on the wood again. That evening I sharpened the axe whilst waiting for my food to cook. I ate and then fell instantly asleep.

By the end of the third day, I had blisters on my hands and an impressively large stack of wood to show for it. It's a satisfying job, processing firewood like that. I started off with a fallen tree and by the time I'd finished, it was all converted into useable fuel.

There's something so meditative about splitting wood. You take a log and place in on the splitting block, paying attention to how the grain lies and noting any knots or twists. You look for a line through the log where the grain is as straight as possible so that when the sharpened edge of the axe hits the top of the log, it slips between two fibres, dividing fibre from fibre and splitting the wood along its length.

Having placed the log in just the right position on the splitting block, you pick up the axe and aim it at just that perfect spot. All of the force goes into the first part of the swing. This creates the momentum, which creates the centrifugal force, which causes the axe to arc through the air. Your grip on the handle controls the course of the arc, with near perfect accuracy.

When the axe makes contact with the log, you're using so little force that it feels like you could let go of the axe and it would fly through the log of its own volition.

You watch as the log neatly divides in half, with the two halves flying in opposite directions. The two halves separate so cleanly and easily it seems as if they were never attached at all, but just happened to be sat next to each other on the block.

You then pick up another log and place it on the splitting block, paying attention to how the grain lies and noting any knots or twists.

It's the constant repetition of this action again and again as you divide all of the logs which once made up a tree that makes it meditative. Each log requires enough concentration to prevent your mind from wandering, yet the whole process becomes close to subconscious through repetition.

When you come out of your meditative state, you are presented with a pile of firewood, where there was previously a pile of logs to split.

The cabin belongs to Marek's family. The first time I saw this place was with him and some other friends from Prague a few years ago. We came here to get out of the city and chill for the weekend.

It's a fairly basic cabin, with a wood-fired range as the only source of heating and cooking. It fits in beautifully with its woodland surroundings, being made from wood, which I assume came from these forests, complete with the raggedy edges that planks have if you don't straighten them up.

It's impossible to tell how long it has been here due to its rustic style and construction. Water comes from a spring and has to be carried into the house in buckets or bottles. There are electric lights which work off a home-made hydro setup, consisting of a car alternator and the propeller from an outboard motor, set up in a stream which runs down the hill. The lights are too dim to comfortably read by, but they provide just enough light for cooking and so that I don't bump into the furniture.

Marek said they used to come up here a lot as kids before his father died, but now it just sits empty except for when he comes here with his friends.

From what I've seen, nobody has been here since I last came. Marek said I could stay here whenever I wanted and I've taken him up on that offer twice.

The last time was two years ago during the summer. I'd been to a party. Then, when hitching back, I found myself not far from the cabin and decided to spend the night. That was before I got involved with road protest, when I was just dossing around, seeing what would occur next.

When I'd finished my woodpile, I started repairing things. There's a big barn behind the cabin; much bigger than the cabin itself. It's full of tools and materials which I imagine Marek's family must have brought up here. The roof had collapsed at one end and the rain had severely rusted all the tools in that area of the barn, so I started repairing the roof. It was made of wooden shingles, a number of which were rotted away, so I started making replacements. My first ones were terrible, but as time went on, I got my eye in and learnt to knock them out at a fair rate and with reasonable accuracy.

When the roof was watertight again, I started

sharpening and repairing tools. There was a whole collection of billhooks and axes and all sorts of chisels, draw-knives and other tools for cutting and shaping wood.

I cleaned each one up and sharpened it. I adjusted the teeth on the saws and oiled the moving parts on the hand drills. I cleaned out the boxes and drawers the tools were in and repaired them where they needed repairing.

There was a makeshift wood burner in the barn, made from an old oil drum. I swept up everything on the compacted earth floor and burnt what would burn to keep me warm as I worked.

It was getting into winter by the time the barn was shipshape again. I made repairs to the outside of the cabin where the cladding had gone and trimmed back the branches of the surrounding trees where they were brushing against it. I cleared the gutters and bodged a repair on the broken downpipe. There was some paint in the barn, which was old but still useable. I started painting the front of the cabin, but the paint ran out, so I couldn't paint the back or the sides.

Through the winter I repaired anything that needed repairing on the inside of the cabin. There were two bedrooms in the loft and a living room and kitchen downstairs. The cabin had only been intended as a summer getaway and I could only keep the kitchen warm, so I camped out there and only went into the other rooms to repair things. Where I was repairing movable items, I took them down to the kitchen to work on them and took them back when I had finished.

Throughout the winter, the range had to be fed twenty-four hours a day to keep the cabin to a liveable temperature. If it's turned right down it'll stay in for a few hours, but I still had to wake up at least a couple of times a night to feed it.

The range was the centre of my life during those winter months. It heated me and cooked my food. It supplied me all the hot water I've had through the use of a kettle and I'd sit in front of it for most of the day, fixing things and maintaining tools, writing poems and eating.

When the snow cleared and the first signs of spring arrived, I could work outside again. I repaired the fence besides the track and put the gate back on its hinges. I filled the potholes in the track with stones from the stream and cleared the ditch at the side to stop the water from flowing across it and eroding it further.

Eventually, I found enough peace in these tasks that I could just sit. For the whole time I'd been here, I'd busied myself, not because I had a task to perform, but because I was concerned what my thoughts would do if I didn't.

245

For a few weeks now, I've been spending a bit of time each day sitting in the garden, not doing anything, just watching the world. I sat out this morning, watching jays hoping around from branch to branch and listening to them screech at each other. Such beautiful birds and such terrible singers.

Occasionally, deer walk through the garden and early one morning I saw a wild boar followed by a group of boarlets snuffling around under the apple tree.

The garden is the remains of what was once a well-kept garden around the cabin. Someone had clearly put in a lot of effort. There are still stone paths and low walls separating areas which are at different levels, but it's now merged with the woods around it to the extent that it's hard to see where one meets the other, and the wildlife consider it all to be one and the same.

There's no radio or anything in the cabin, so I have had no communication with the outside world, except for shrugs and 'ch's from the old lady and brief interactions with the shopkeeper.

For the first month or so, I wasn't interested in or capable of communicating. After that, I opened a new notebook and started to write poetry in it.

The notebook tells an interesting tale. It starts with morose and angry poems about the world and politics and environmental damage.

It evolves over time into happier poems about the beauty of my immediate surroundings and then you can see the outside world creep back into my thoughts, represented by poems about the world which are at first full of melancholy, but move further and further into a determination to act and do something about what is wrong with society.

When I look back at the newly repaired cabin that I'm leaving, I know the act of repairing it repaired me as well.

I haven't seen Marek in ages and don't know if he'll ever come up here again. You could see all the work I've done here as a complete waste of energy, but I've gone to bed each night able to picture the achievements of the day.

That is what got me through the darkest of times and out the other side into this amazing day full of birdsong and beauty.

It really is an absolutely gorgeous morning!

Hills and Hares

Europe offered endless possibilities and endless opportunities to kill time and have adventures, but I still didn't have a clue what I wanted to do with my life. I think this was '91, but I'm not 100% sure.

This is a dream come true for me, something I have always wanted to do.

I'm in the passenger seat of an ancient-looking Hungarian lorry travelling through the Austrian countryside. The dream I am living out has nothing to do with lorries, although the lorry I'm currently in is reminiscent of the Tonka Trucks I used to play with as a child.

The important thing is what I can see from up here in the cab. When I was young, I had a copy of the Collins Guide to Mammals of Britain and Europe. I spent a lot of time out in nature and would sit quietly and see all sorts of animals.

I remember, one dewy morning, sitting on a fallen oak tree in a woodland glade, watching a fox eating blackberries. It got closer and closer to me, working its way along the bramble bushes. It was so engrossed in the blackberries that it was completely unaware of my presence.

Eventually, it was right at my feet. It looked up, saw me and froze. We both stayed entirely still, it looking at me and me looking at it. I was close enough to examine every detail of it. I could even smell it. It had a musty smell like an extreme version of the smell of a damp dog.

We remained completely still for a while, me not daring to move because I knew that as soon as I did, it would scarper off and it was seemingly waiting for me to make the first move.

Eventually, it gave up on me making the first move and took a step back very slowly and very carefully, watching me all the time. Then it took another step back and a third. Having got a bit of distance between me and it, although still not a lot, it turned and walked off at a brisk pace.

It didn't run, it just walked away. When it got to the edge of the clearing we were in, it looked back before disappearing out of sight.

I saw a lot of the mammals that were in my Collins guide, but of course in a book covering Britain and Europe, there were a number of mammals which I couldn't see in the Kent countryside. I used to love looking at all of the creatures in the book that were unfamiliar to me, from the spotted souslik, to larger and seemingly more exciting mammals like bears, wolves and elk. But the one mammal which really caught my imagination was the mountain hare. I don't have a clue why this particular animal struck such a cord with me, but it did.

Now I am sitting here from the vantage point of the cab of this truck, looking down at a field of rough grass. I see a small animal, which at first glance from this distance, could well be a large rabbit or a small hare, although it looks a little light in colour. Then I see another, which is lighter still and is displaying the white of it's underside.

Soon, there are fair-sized groups of them, some still have most of their white winter coats. There's no question I've finally seen the mountain hares which I so wanted to see as a child.

I'm so excited and really want to explain to the driver how important this moment is to me and why.

Unfortunately, we don't have a common language. So far as I can tell, he only speaks Hungarian. I don't speak any language well other than English and other than very basic phrases from my phrasebook, the only words I know in Hungarian are 'good dog' and 'sit'.

Our Hungarian neighbours, the Farkases, taught me dog commands so I could communicate with their dogs. My vocabulary in other languages is almost equally random.

One of the first words I learned in Czech was *svoboda*, which means Freedom. I'm not really sure why I learned that, but when Fred and I spent our first night in Prague, I did for some reason.

When we were in Germany, I wanted to learn enough German to hitch. Fred speaks fairly fluent German, so she was doing a lot of the talking, but I thought learning to ask for a lift would be useful, so I asked the Germans we were staying with what the German for *'Can I have a lift please?'* is.

It turns out that the German word for 'lift' is *mitfahrgelegenheit*. It's made up of the words *mit, fahr and gelegenheit*, which mean *with drive and opportunity*.

I was told that if I used the English 'lift' instead, people would understand, but I learnt to say *mitfahrgelegenheit* because it's such an amazing word. There's a certain Germanic poetry to it and it seems to sum up beautifully what it means to get a lift.

Reduced to not much more than gestures and a few words from a phrasebook, I struggle to explain to the driver how beautiful this moment is. He is patient and tries his hardest to understand what I'm saying.

It gets confusing and I realise that common sense would suggest the message is not worth the effort it takes to get across, but I persevere.

Eventually he gets it. He gets that I always wanted to see a mountain hare, ever since I was small and all these years later, much to my surprise, I have seen them due to having a lift in his truck and that seeing them has filled me with joy.

All of the effort was worth it and he gets what I mean. Then he laughs and indicates to me using gestures that they are everywhere here and then points down to the road, pointing at one after another flattened into two dimensions where vehicle after vehicle have run over them.

You can see they're mountain hares by the white patches which used to be their underside or indeed most of the bodies of those which have retained their winter coats. I can see now they are so common here that they are by far the most abundant form of roadkill on this stretch of road.

For the rest of the journey, my lift teaches me Hungarian and I teach him English. It is a very limited language lesson, which consists of pointing at items which happen to be in the cab of his lorry and a few we can see outside. I'm aware there may have been misunderstandings about what myself or my lift were pointing to, so I may have the wrong word for some of the stuff outside the lorry. I'm pretty confident about the stuff inside the lorry, which gives me a useful vocabulary, including the words for clipboard, air freshener and the windscreen scraper that you use to get ice off your windscreen.

In the early hours of the morning, we arrive in Hungary. My lift is trying to tell me all sorts of things about the country. I haven't slept and in my tired state, I don't get everything he is saying.

He points to a church, saying something about it. I don't understand at all.

A bit further down the road, he points at another church and says the same thing. I guess whatever he was saying will remain a mystery.

Something that is clearer is when he explains the reason he abides all the speed limits in Austria but completely ignored them in Hungary. He points to a police car and says 'money' in Hungarian.

I'm dropped off at a quiet little service station. There is only one building here, which functions as the shop, garage and cafe. There's a Czech lorry parked up and a car parked around the back of the building, which I assume belongs to the person who's running this place.

Sat in the window of the cafe area of the building is a man in blue overalls who is drinking a beer. I assume he's the driver of the lorry. It's early in the morning, but it's not unusual for Czech lorry drivers to start the day with a beer.

A car pulls in. It's a fairly well looked after, if old, Skoda.

I'm wondering if it's going my way. It doesn't

come over to the pumps to fill up but goes instead straight over to the inspection ramps.

A late middle-aged couple get out and he looks under the car while she stands at the side, handing him tools. Public inspection ramps seem to be quite a common thing in service stations here in Eastern Europe. I know the Polish driving test includes basic maintenance. It makes sense to have the ramps so people can repair their own cars.

I say it makes sense, but it would make no sense in a capitalist society. There's no profit in it for anyone. To make it pay, you would have to charge for it, which would either require it to be staffed, or to have some sort of automatic barrier. I see the ramps being used, but I don't think they are used enough to justify the cost of either. You could add it to the tasks of the person running the service station, but he already seems to have quite a few tasks on his hands. He isn't busy right now, but I imagine he must get busy at times.

I guess there are some things which are useful, but not profitable. As such, those of us living in a capitalist system don't have the benefit of them.

There are no other vehicles here, so I decide to get a coffee. I ask the Czech lorry driver if he's heading towards Budapest. He shakes his head and repeats the word '*ne*' , which means 'no' in Czech, many times.

I sip my coffee slowly, hoping that some promising-looking vehicle will come into the service station, but no such luck.

I watch the couple working on their car. The lorry driver leaves the building, gets in his lorry and drives off.

I've finished my coffee and take advantage of the facilities to get a wash in the hope it'll make me feel more awake.

As I walk back into the shop, I can hear someone speaking English in a London accent. 'Lighter,' he's saying, then he repeats it as if saying it more clearly will make the service station worker understand English.

I walk up to the counter and say 'Öngyújtó'.

The attendant nods, says something to me in Hungarian. and passes a lighter to the English bloke. I don't understand the attendants words, but by his intonation he seems to be thanking me for resolving the confusion.

I shrug and smile, feeling quite pleased to be able to use one of the words I've learnt today.

The English bloke pulls out a wallet from his jeans pocket, gives a note to the attendant and turns to me. 'You speak English?'

'Oh yes, I speak little else.'

'You get by in Hungarian alright.'

'A little,' I say. I don't explain how lucky it is

that he was asking for one of the few things I can ask for in Hungarian and I can see that to him it must look like I'm OK at the language.

'You're not going towards Budapest are you?' I ask hopefully.

'Yes, chap, but I've got to do a delivery first. How much of a rush are you in?' There's clearly no point in being in a rush right now, so I take the offer of a lift with a diversion. It certainly beats staying here and watching a car being fixed.

He hands me a map and asks me if I can navigate. The warehouse we're going to is marked on the map. Apparently, it's owned by a big western electronics company which uses it to store stuff to save tax.

The route looks fairly simple on the map. There's a side road off the road we're on which goes to the village that the warehouse is in.

When we turn onto the road in question, the village we're looking for is written on the signpost, so we know we're going in the right direction.

I tell the driver about the mountain hares, but we don't see any because we're a long way from any mountains now. I don't think he's really that interested anyway.

The road is fairly small. It's wide enough for two cars to pass, but if we meet anything in this lorry, we'll have to find a good passing place. The land around looks like a flood plain; it's marshy in places and flat for miles. In the distance, there are hills. Who knows, there may be mountain hares there.

The golden light of the sun gives a warm tinge to the morning mist. We see white birds which I think might be egrets in one of the marshier-looking bits.

We haven't seen any other vehicles, which is advantageous because there are very few suitable passing places.

Out of the blue, we come to a sign stating the road has a 3.5 tonne limit. We have two options and neither of them are great. We could reverse back to the last place where you could turn a lorry this size around; I think the last suitable place was over a mile back along the road.

Alternatively, we could risk it. I'm just a hitcher, so luckily this is not my decision to make. My lift decides he's going to risk it. He slows right down, but carries on. There doesn't seem to be any obvious reason for the weight limit. The road seems no less substantial than it did before the sign and we carry on for another mile or so without any issues.

Then we spot an issue. This issue is in the form of a police officer, stood next to his car.

'Can you translate?' my lift asks.

I try to explain that my Hungarian is very

limited. I'm thinking it would be fine if I was going to ask him for a clipboard or an air freshener, but my Hungarian certainly doesn't stretch to negotiating my way out of a traffic violation.

My lift is having none of this and in all fairness, I can see how he got the impression I can speak the language.

Before I can explain, we pull over and the police officer walks up to my side of the vehicle. I assume he hasn't noticed the steering wheel is on the wrong side.

He says something to me in Hungarian I don't understand.

I ask him, as well as I can in Hungarian, if he speaks English.

'Yes,' he says, much to my surprise.

As I said earlier, English is the only language I speak well, so communication is going to be much easier than I feared. We do still have the small problem that we are in a large lorry on a road with a 3.5 tonne weight limit.

Unsurprisingly, the police officer is not slow in pointing this out. I try to explain that by the time we saw the sign, we had come too far to go back.

I don't know if he doesn't understand what I'm saying, or he doesn't care. He doesn't look very impressed.

'Tell him I thought it said thirty five tonnes,'

says the driver.

I do and the police officer asks how heavy the lorry is.

'Forty two tons,' admits the driver.

I pass this on to the police officer, who now seems even less impressed.

'This is a big problem,' he says. 'I think you will be many hours at the police station and it will cost you a lot of money.'

I relay this back to my lift.

'Do you think he wants a bribe?' asks my lift.

If the driver wants to bribe him, I'd prefer not to be in the middle of it. If the Hungarian lorry driver I was with earlier was bribing the police officer, I could at least be confident that he knows the etiquette.

'Passport,' says the police officer.

I pass him mine and ask my lift for his. He passes it with 200 Deutsch Marks stuffed into it.

I can't really do anything else, so I just pass it over and hope I'm not spending the near future locked up in some Hungarian prison.

The police officer goes over to his car, looks like he's checking something and then returns with our passports. He hands them back to me, without the money, and tells us we should drive slowly because this road is not made for such a heavy vehicle.

When I hand the driver his passport he says,

'Ask him what I should do if I see another police officer.'

I relay this question.

'Give him fifty Deutsche Mark,' he says. 'Two hundred is a lot of money.'

As the police car drives away, my lift shrugs and says, 'You don't get corruption like that back home, do you? Back in Britain it's all smart suits, old school ties and off-shore investments, isn't it.'

Elephants And Giraffes

I was back in the UK and The Fugees were in the charts with Rumble in the Jungle. It was the spring of '97.

It's four o'clock in the morning and I'm walking into the arrivals hall at the docks.

From now until I leave the port, I'm going to be very deliberately thinking about my hitch from here to Ashford.

The reason for deliberately thinking about hitching is that it'll prevent me from inadvertently thinking about the blim of hash which is in my rucksack. It's that old thing that if you try not think about a pink elephant you will definitely think about a pink elephant. Not thinking about a pink elephant becomes much easier if you set yourself the task of thinking about a blue giraffe.

In this situation, I need to be thinking about something logical, fitting to the situation and based in the real world. Strolling through customs thinking

261

about giraffes would not be the best strategy.

Prof and I talked about this exact scenario when we were sitting around waiting for a digger to turn up on the protest in Kent. At the time it was purely theoretical, but here I am putting it into practice.

The theory is that we transfer our emotions to others that we meet through multiple means of communication, some of which we can control and others we can't, so to prevent detrimental emotions being transferred, you have to make yourself feel beneficial emotions.

Although customs officers are trained to spot certain signs, a lot of the time the decision of whether or not to search someone comes down to a hunch; an instinct or a feeling they have. These hunches, instincts, feelings or whatever you want to call them are triggered by subconscious cues and transfers of emotions.

If you're going through customs with some form of contraband, you're likely to feel anxious. If you try not to show the signs of your anxiety, you merely exaggerate them by becoming anxious about showing them. This exaggeration means you transfer the emotion to the customs officer more effectively. They pick up your emotion and feel anxious themselves.

Because you make them feel anxious, they search you. When the customs officer finds your contraband, they are praised by their colleagues, which triggers a dopamine response. This conditions them to repeat the behaviour of relying on these hunches.

Where instead of concentrating on the anxiety about contraband, you concentrate on the difficulty of your onward journey and how tired you are. If you transfer any emotion to the customs officer it will be that of lethargy instead of anxiety. A customs officer feeling lethargic will let you pass.

Rather than try to empty your mind of unhelpful thoughts, you fill it with useful thoughts.

That's the theory, anyway.

The doors to the customs area open and I consciously think about the cars coming off the boat. I watch them drive up to the customs booths.

I can see the first cars pulling up at the booths now. I'm noting in my mind that I've already missed those first cars. I'm also noting I'm going to miss quite a few more, because another group of foot passengers were let through in front of my group.

I know that if I miss the traffic off this boat, there isn't another boat for hours, so I'll be walking to a hitching spot. I've walked that route many times and I start to run through it in my mind.

I didn't sleep on the boat, so I've been up for nearly twenty-four hours now; I feel very tired already.

As I think about the walk, I can feel a frown forming on my face.

Suddenly, all of this beautifully-planned distractional thinking strategy is blown out of the water and my mind is not occupied by hitching or walking, elephants or giraffes.

Suddenly, my mind is fully occupied by the fact that standing behind the luggage scanner are Bon Jovi, Turnip, Tosser and a load of the other security guards from the protest. They're wearing exactly the same uniforms they wore on the protest, but now they're operating a baggage scanning machine rather than defending a digger.

Of all the scenarios I might be prepared for when walking through customs, people I know acting as the customs officers is not one of them.

I'm not prepared for it at all.

If I'd have known on the boat they were going to be here, I'd have ditched the blim, but it's a tad late for that now.

HMRC must have problems with numbers and must have just happened to bring in the very same security that were on the protest to fill in.

I know none of the security guards here would wish me any harm. I'm sure if they knew I was carrying they wouldn't want me to get caught, but they don't know I'm carrying and I'm not really in a position to tell them. I haven't seen any of them since the eviction at the Kent protest. I didn't get a chance to say goodbye then, due to being dragged away in handcuffs and put in the back of a meat wagon.

I'd love to go up to them and say hello, ask them how it's going and chat about old times, but any interaction between me and them which doesn't look like a normal part of their job is going to result in me being taken into one of the little rooms by the actual customs officers.

I have no plan B, so I can't see any option other than carrying on with plan A.

I'm looking out of the window, thinking about how many cars have gone through customs already. They're moving through at a reasonable speed. It seems highly likely I'll be walking to a hitching spot.

The lining is going in my left boot, which means the seam in the leather chafes against the back of my ankle. I deliberately concentrate on it and imagine how it will feel on the long walk. I concentrate on the weight of my rucksack on my shoulders.

I go through the walk in my head and the frown starts to form on my face again.

The person in front of me walks forward and the woman working at passport control asks me for my passport. I hand it over and she asks me where I've been.

I tell her I've been to the Czech Republic. I don't tell her I stopped off in Holland on my way back. I have plenty of stuff in my bag that shows I have been to the Czech Republic, including a bottle of Becherovka for Fred.

I have only one item which I picked up in Holland. I hope nobody finds it.

I start to concentrate on the chafing on the back of my ankle and I imagine how tired I will be by the time I reach my hitching spot. The cars have almost all gone now.

Ignoring the game of elephants and giraffes, I probably will miss the traffic off this boat.

The passport control officer passes me back my passport and I almost drop the hitching sign which is under my arm as I take it from her. I shuffle forward with everyone else, closer and closer to the luggage scanner.

I think about my route to Ashford. I could be lucky and get one lift from here to Ashford, but it's vastly more likely I'll get dropped off and have to get another lift.

Because it's so early, there won't be much traffic. I think about standing outside in this drizzly weather. My legs ache already, which helps me to imagine how they'll feel after a long walk and a long wait.

I shuffle forward to the part of the scanner where you put your luggage in, and I place my rucksack on the conveyor belt without looking at the people operating it. The strap flops to the side in a way that looks like it could get caught in the belt, so I push it onto the middle of the conveyor belt, before shuffling on.

Someone a few people in front of me gets pulled aside and taken into one of the little rooms by customs. They must have seen something suspicious in their luggage, or maybe on their face.

I think about that long walk. I think about the seam chafing my ankle. I grip the hitching sign in my hand and think about my chances of getting a lift at this time in the morning.

My rucksack comes out of the luggage scanner and is passed to me by Turnip. He passes it to me whilst hardly looking at me at all. There's no recognition on his face, just as there is none on mine.

I take it and continue to shuffle forward, thinking of my ankle, thinking of the walk and as I put it on my back, thinking of the weight of the rucksack. I continue walking forwards until I'm out of the building and I hear the clunk of the automatic doors closing behind me.

It's still near to pitch black outside as I step out onto the wet tarmac. It'll be a while before the sun rises. I know better than to think I'm home dry. I'm still in the port and customs officers could still be watching me. They could watch me after I leave the port, but certainly in the port it's better to be overly cautious.

I continue to frown as I walk with my head down towards the way out of the port. A car, which must have been delayed, drives out of the customs area. It drives out past the booth and heads towards me.

I hold up my sign and smile a tired smile. It drives past and I keep walking. The expanse of tarmac between the passenger terminal and the exit of the port seems enormous. Walking across it seems to take forever, but eventually I get there.

Finally, I'm out of the port. I allow my smile to grow and I allow my thoughts to move from my ankle to what just happened.

I can't believe what a strange and beautiful moment that was. All my old security friends all got what was going on. They all resisted the temptation to liven up an otherwise dull, early morning shift by giving me some grief. They all played along with the pretence that we didn't know each other.

They did what was necessary to ensure my day went smoothly, and I didn't spend it in a cell. It really is only a blim I have on me and it's not even for me. I haven't smoked anything since I started this protest malarkey. I haven't given up intoxicants until this capitalism issue is resolved like Prof has. I've just not felt like smoking, and I want my wits about me.

The blim is for Barry. It's his birthday tomorrow and seeing as I was going through Holland, I thought it would be a nice gesture.

I'm walking along with a smile on my face and a spring in my step when another car comes out through the customs point and drives towards me. This one's a battered old Ford Escort, with faded go-faster stripes and only one headlight working properly.

I hold up my sign and it pulls up next to me. The back of the car is absolutely stuffed with all sorts of bits and pieces thrown on top of each other, all higgledy-piggledy.

The driver shouts at me to shove it all over and put my rucksack in the back.

I do so and jump into the passenger seat.

Quite obviously, the reason this car has been delayed is because it got stopped by customs. Just as obvious are the reasons it got stopped. The dodgy headlight won't have helped, but I'm guessing it was the driver himself who was the main cause.

It's hard to tell his age with any level of accuracy, because he has an enormous, dishevelled, straggly beard. Poking out from behind this beard in all the places where it fails to entirely cover his face are an array of tattoos. They're not beautiful works of art; they're basic drawings and some writing. They all appear to have been done by someone who's either

269

never tried doing a tattoo before, or doesn't have the right equipment. This is not a great look for going through customs; arguably, it's not a great look for going through life.

'Sorry about the state of things,' he says, gesturing towards the back of the car. 'You'd think that if them bastards pulled you, took everything out of your car and didn't find anything, they'd put it all back neatly for you, but not a bit of it.'

There's a larger-than-life sound to his voice and feel to the way he holds himself, like he wants me to know he's not a man to be fucked with.

He's friendly, overly friendly if anything, but you can tell he's been through some stuff and isn't afraid to go through more.

We drive until we get to a petrol station where we pull in to fill up. He pulls up right behind a car which is already sat at the pumps. The bloke sitting in the car in front doesn't move at all. He isn't getting out to fill up. He isn't shuffling around like he's getting ready to drive off. He just sits there.

'Come on, mate,' says my lift in a slightly strained way.

We sit there for a few more seconds before he starts becoming noticeably agitated.

'Don't just fucking sit there,' he mutters.

He taps the steering wheel as if he's trying to hold himself back from doing something stupid. 'Oh come on,' he says. He's clearly not the most patient man in the world. 'Just fucking move!'

Up till now, everything he's said has been deliberately quiet, but this last plea was said at normal talking volume. It won't have been audible outside the car, but you can tell he's getting more and more wound up. He's had enough, winds down his window, sticks his head out as far as his neck will stretch and shouts at the top of his voice.

'Oi, you slag, move your fucking motor!'

The bloke in the car in front doesn't move or respond in any way. He just sits there.

I really wish I could show my hitching sign and at least give an indication that I have nothing more to do with this chap than happening to get a lift with him.

Unfortunately, my hitching sign is in the back under my rucksack. I sink a little lower in my seat. I don't really know what the point of this is.

The bloke in the car in front can still see me, I just look a little shorter. I'd happily slip down into the footwell and hide completely, like I did in Bon Jovi's car, but it would look a bit strange to my lift, so I just have to brave this situation out as well as I can.

Another bloke comes out of the shop, walks towards the car and gets into the left-hand seat. It's only when he drives off that we see the French number plates.

I'm really quite embarrassed by this. My lift just seems amused.

We fill up. My lift pays. He starts the car and the radio comes back on.

It's the news. It's the first time I've heard the news in English since sometime last year. Steven Norris is talking about road protest. My lift is saying something as well, but I completely miss what he's saying because of what's on the radio.

Steven Norris is saying that us road protestors were right to oppose Newbury and all the other roads, and that the government's thinking had failed to take into account the environmental damage. I know this is the truth of course, but I didn't expect to hear it come out of Steven Norris' mouth.

'Did you hear what he just said?' I ask my lift. I can't believe he's saying this now. All the time he was in post, he insisted the roads were all vital for the economic well-being of the nation. Now he's out of office and it's too late for his opinion to matter, he's suddenly on our side.

'Who the fuck is he?' my lift replies.

'He was the transport minister through all the road protests. Newbury Bypass and all that,' I say. 'That's Steven Norris.'

'What's this Newbury bypass when it's at home then?' asks my lift.

'It's that road with all the protestors,' I say. Surely everyone's heard of the Newbury Bypass. We certainly managed to make enough noise about it.

'I wouldn't know about any of that,' he says. 'I've been a bit out of the loop these last eight years. Banged up for armed robbery. All that stuff doesn't seem so relevant when you're inside. You know it's not likely to affect your day-to-day, so I never bothered listening to it. If it was a free country, you could go into a post office and walk out with the cash, but oh no! They throw the book at you for that sort of thing.'

Badgers And Brahms

People are complex creatures. ('92)

The service station where I've just been dropped off is relatively small, consisting of just four petrol pumps and a small kiosk-like shop.

It's entirely open, with no protection from the wind or any trees or bushes to block the view in any direction. It's as uninspiring as a service station can be and that really is quite uninspiring.

I've been dropped off at the pumps and, in other circumstances, I'd walk to the exit lane and hitch from there. Other circumstances would include, among other things, not having the police parked up on the exit lane, just where I'd stand if I was hitching.

The chances of someone pulling up next to the police car to pick me up are exceedingly slim.

I'm just wondering what to do about this when

a British car pulls up to one of the pumps. It's a Jaguar and it's a sort of metallic gold colour. It being British at least means I share a language with the driver.

I weigh up whether to go and ask for a lift. Looking over at the police car, which is showing no sign of vacating my preferred hitching spot, I decide to give it a go.

I approach the driver, a late middle-aged man in a blazer and striped tie. His hair is cropped short at the sides and only slightly longer on top.

In my best telephone voice, I ask, 'Excuse me, I don't suppose you're going to Essen, are you?'

'Oh hello,' he says in perfect received pronunciation, seemingly a little taken aback at being approached like this. 'Not actually to Essen, but I'm going past it on the Autobahn.' He then gives me a confused and slightly concerned look.

'Would you be able to give me a lift?' I ask.

At this point, he looks me up and down as if he's assessing my suitability as a passenger in his car.

'Well, why not?' he says with a smile. 'Wait here whilst I pay for the fuel. I will return shortly.' And he walks over to the the shop, leaving me standing by his car.

On his return, he gets into the car and signals for me to do the same.

The car is incredibly posh. The interior is all leather and there's a car-phone. I've seen them on the TV, but never in real life. It looks less brick-like than they look on TV. This is because it's seamlessly fitted into the car, making it look like an original part of the interior.

It would be great to phone someone on it. Imagine their surprise when I phoned up and told them I was in a car using a car-phone.

Obviously, I'm not going to ask to use it. I imagine it's very expensive to call out on. Would it even work in Germany? Who knows?

'So,' he says, followed by a long pause. 'Are you a student?'

'A student of life, I guess.' Why did I say that? What does it even mean? I felt a bit unbalanced by the question, because I'm neither a student nor working, so I didn't have a good answer and I came out with that meaningless drivel for some reason.

Now he definitely thinks I'm an idiot.

'I'm travelling around trying to see the world before settling down, I guess.' This is an improvement, hardly impressive, but definitely an improvement on the 'student of life' line.

'I was in the military at your age. Made me what I am today. Gave me direction and discipline. I based my whole career on it after leaving. You should consider it yourself.'

I'm absolutely not going to consider the military as an option, but I have to admit that what he is today does seem to have worked for him. Not everyone gets to drive a posh car like this with a car-phone and everything.

'What do you do now?' I ask, hoping to move the conversation on to him, not me.

'Well,' he says, leaving another one of those long pauses. 'I guess I'm a salesman of sorts.' He must know what he does and if he's a salesman or not.

'What do you sell?' I ask. Whatever it is, he's doing well out of it.

'Oh,' he says, 'it's all very hush hush.'

Well, that puts an end to that conversation.

We sit in silence for a minute or two before he asks me what I'm doing in Essen.

I explain I'm not going to Essen, but on to Prague. Essen just gets me to a better service station. I don't explain that by 'better' I mainly mean one with less police. A bigger service station would be better and so would a service station closer to Prague.

He tells me that he's staying on the A3 until just after Koln.

I look at the map and find a suitable service station.

The conversation is slow and slightly uncomfortable until he mentions that his house is surrounded by a woodland which he owns. Then we discuss woodlands and wildlife, topics which we are both enthusiastic about. His woodland is partly ancient deciduous woodland and partly a conifer plantation, which was planted up after the Second World War. He's thinning the conifers and slowly converting that part into a mix of conifer and deciduous. He tells me about his evenings spent in the woodland with his wife.

'We like to go out just after our evening meal,' he says wistfully. 'We pour ourselves a glass of wine each and walk down to the bottom of the garden to where it meets the woods, then on along a small track. We didn't make the track ourselves, and have never had to maintain it, other than removing the odd fallen branch. The deer use it and I think that they're quite effective at trimming the vegetation back and maintaining it in that respect.

'The track leads to a small area of holly which forms a natural looking hide. I mean, it's not actually natural at all. We've deliberately trimmed it and shaped it so that it conceals us perfectly. It gives us a fantastic view over the woodland valley and down into a clearing where there's a huge badger set. From the time that we leave the house, to the time we return, we don't speak at all. If we see something that the other one hasn't seen, we might indicate it by a tap on the shoulder and by pointing, but other than that we don't communicate. We're there just to observe and to take in the sublime beauty of the natural world.

'We've watched many generations of badgers grow up and go on to have cubs of their own. We've seen the set expand over the years. From time to time we see foxes or deer as they go about their business. We take great joy from listening to the strange eerie noises of the nightjars and the hoots of the tawny owls as they call from one end of the woods to the other. It sometimes seems like they intentionally go to opposite ends of the woods just to hoot at each other from a distance. It's an opportunity to escape from everything hectic. A chance to just sit with nature and observe.'

I tell him about the woods near the house where I lived as a child and how important they were to me. Just like his woods are for him, they were the place which allowed me to escape the world.

We exchange anecdotes about our experiences in nature and particularly our experiences of wildlife in woodlands, until the conversation falls away and we find ourselves sitting in silence. This is not the awkward silence of two people who are unable to find a common subject, but a peaceful serene and comfortable silence; a silence built on contemplation of the natural beauty of the world.

He leans forward and plays the CD in the car

stereo. The music he's playing has cellos in it. I think it may be Brahms. It's a hypnotic piece and seems fitting to the mood.

Our silence continues until we reach the service station where we are to part company.

This is a much better service station. It's bigger, so more traffic to get lifts off. It's also closer to Prague and, as far as I can see, there are no police around to deter people from giving me lifts.

He pulls into the carpark to drop me off. Right next to us is a Porsche. The driver, a man not much older than me, wearing jeans, a loose-fitting white shirt and large sunglasses, is just returning as I get out of the Jaguar.

I question whether I should ask for a lift, but whilst doing so, I inadvertently stare at him and he asks me something in German.

I don't catch what it is, so I attempt to ask him what he said.

He realises I'm English and asks me what I want. He has an American accent, but also sounds a little Eastern European.

I ask him for a lift and he says, 'Hey, why not?'

When I sit down in the passenger seat, I realise the seatbelt on my side doesn't work. He apologises for this and immediately pins me to the seat by accelerating out onto the autobahn at an incredible speed.

The car makes a horrible noise as if the bottom has scraped across something in the road, but the driver doesn't seem to mind and pulls out into the fast lane.

I know that if we crash, or he puts the brake on too fast, I'm going to hit the windscreen harder than I've ever hit anything in my life.

We're soon doing over two-hundred kilometres per hour. There's no speed limit, so legally, he can go as fast as he wants, but I'm aware enough of the laws of physics to know that if we crash at this speed, even with a seatbelt I'm probably going to die. Without one, I'm going to be a bloody mess somewhere a long distance from the remains of the car.

When we get to Frankfurt, there are roadworks and speed limit signs. The roadworks force him to slow down to a mere one-hundred-and-fifty kilometres per hour. The speed limit signs don't affect him at all.

We're accelerating away from a section of roadworks when a light flashes behind us. We both assume it's a speed camera.

'Hey, how fast was I going?' he asks. 'Did you see?'

'Two-hundred-and-thirty,' I respond. 'It could have been worse.'

He's still accelerating as there's a second flash

from behind us.

'What speed was I doing that time?' he asks.

'That was two-hundred-and-sixty,' I say. 'Are you not worried about the police?'

'Hey, these German traffic wardens,' he says. 'They're famously efficient and thorough, but I don't think they'll follow me down to Croatia and find me in a war zone. Do you?'

'You're from Croatia?'

'Hey yeah,' he says. 'I'm just in Germany to get the car lowered.'

'You had it lowered?' I say. This explains why it scraped the ground as we left the service station. It does leave me wondering why he didn't have the seatbelt fixed while he was there.

'It helps it grip the road at speed, however the roads in Croatia are not well-maintained enough to take it. When I go back I have to put it in a lockup and use another car, one which is better for the roads there.'

'So what do you do in Croatia?' I say.

'I'm a soldier,' comes the reply.

I had expected him to say he owned a business or had some high-flying career.

'It's a nice car for a soldier,' I remark.

'Hey, war,' he says, 'is a funny thing. Some people lose a lot of money, some people make a lot of money.'

The conversation is interrupted at this point by a BMW pulling out sharply in front of us, causing my lift to put his foot down hard on the brakes and I'm thrown up against the windscreen.

So far, this ride has just been frightening and uncomfortable, but I'm aware it could be a whole lot worse.

The BMW moves over to the right and we overtake it, accelerating fast until we're slowed down by traffic in front, at which point the BMW accelerates fast up behind us until it's only inches off the back of the Porsche.

The traffic in front clears and we accelerate away with the BMW chasing us. My lift pulls suddenly into the middle lane and jams the brakes on, sending me flying into the windscreen again.

I manage to push myself back into the seat. He pulls back into the fast lane behind the BMW. We're flying up towards it. He gets closer and closer to the back of the car. His front bumper touches their rear bumper. He puts his foot right down and pushes them along the autobahn at an unbelievably high speed.

I don't know exactly what speed we're doing, because I'm not looking at the speedo; I'm looking at the faces of the terrified passengers in the back of the BMW. They've turned their heads to face us, to plead with my lift to stop this insanity.

I'm fairly sure the noise I can hear the over the engine of the Porsche is the engine of their car as it revs higher than it was ever intended to.

I realise why he didn't get the seatbelt fixed. He doesn't care about my life, the lives of the men in the car in front of us, or probably even his own. I'm as frightened as the people in the car in front of us. Experience tells me that when a driver acts in such a demonstrably reckless manner as this, showing fear is only going to encourage them, so I remain silent.

My lift has a look of determination on his face, but shows no fear at all.

I don't know if it's the pleading of the passengers, some change of mind or whether the Croatian soldier who has chosen to be my driver today feels that he's made his point, but he takes his foot off the pedal and we slip back, away from the BMW.

As soon as there's space to do so, the driver of the BMW swerves his car straight across into the slow lane and disappears behind us. I feel the adrenaline drain from my body with the relief of coming out of that situation in one piece. I imagine that the driver and passengers in the BMW must feel just as relieved as I do.

It really is only down to luck that we're not all dead.

We pull into the service station where this

Croatian soldier is dropping me off.

Rarely have I been so pleased to get out of a car.

He wheel-spins away and I walk over to the petrol pumps, pleased to be walking on solid ground and just pleased not to be dead.

For a while, I sit on my rucksack, getting my head together, watching cars pull up to the pumps, fill up and drive away. Having got the last two lifts by asking directly rather than standing with a sign, I appreciate how much more effective this method is.

At the pump nearest me is some souped-up American car, with the engine sticking out through the bonnet. It's metallic blue with silver flames emblazoned along the side. The driver has jeans and a leather jacket and greasy-looking dark hair, which is slicked back.

He looks like he's copied his entire appearance off The Fonz.

At the next pump over, there's an old man who's just filled up his Peugeot estate. He's got a hanky out of his pocket and wrapped it around his forefinger. He's using it to rub some mark, or bit of dirt off the car.

I get up off my rucksack and go over to the old man to ask him for a lift.

House Of The Sea

Sometimes you need beautiful people in your life to remind you of the beauty in the world. This was shortly after I got back from the cabin.

It feels good to be back in Madcap's van. It feels like old times again; old times that weren't that long ago, but seem like a lifetime away.

When we pull in at the Uni, Prof is already there waiting.

Before long, we're heading up the M2. We're on our way to see some friends of Madcap and Prof's who've set up an intentional community in Scotland. They're doing up a semi-derelict farm, so keeping warm through the winter must have been a challenge. It certainly was for me in my cabin.

We're picking up two members of the community on the way. They've been down near Birmingham on some sort of action. I don't know any details, but it sounds quite full-on from the way it's being talked about.

We chat about what we've all been up to and swap news about mutual friends. Madcap and Prof have been spending a lot of time at the farm. They've also been helping out with a group who are doing street theatre actions in Bristol, mainly targeting the arms trade.

We're nearly at Birmingham by the time I tell them why I went to the Czech Republic. They don't seem surprised, which makes me wonder how well I was holding it together on the outside before my little crash.

Soon, we're driving down the High Street of some small town. A car pulls out right in front of us and Madcap jams the brakes on just in time.

'Are you fucking blind, you moron?' she yells at the driver, who is now well out of earshot, before pulling into the space he just vacated.

On the opposite side of the road is a chippy with a queue which stretches right around the corner. I can't believe there's such a long queue in such a small town. Practically everyone must be buying food at that chippy right now.

This is slightly unfortunate as we want food and this seems like our only option.

Prof jumps out and walks around the corner to find the back of the queue and get us some chips, leaving Madcap and me in the van.

'You know it doesn't end, don't you, Sketchy?'

Madcap says.

'What, the queue for the chippy?'

'No, the fight. The fight against injustice, the fight for a liveable world for everyone. The fight never stops. You can get involved and then you can step back, but it goes on. That's the thing, to be fair. You have to decide how much you want your life to be about fighting and how much rest and relaxation you need. What you're prepared to do and where your strengths and weaknesses are. I totally get going off to a cabin in the woods. We all need our respite. Prof and I have the farm. We go there and stay with Mary and Bill and live our lives concentrating on the everyday practicalities. It gives us the time out to stay sane, or at least as sane as we're capable of, to be fair. What I'm trying to say is that you have to find your own balance. You have to look after yourself, Jason. It's no good running head-on at the establishment again and again and destroying yourself in the process. You have to think carefully about what costs you are prepared to bear.'

Madcap looks me straight in the eye, like she's trying to check I'm really listening or taking in what she's saying. I am, but I'm not convinced this balance she's talking about is really achievable.

'I think, back in the day, Prof genuinely thought he could devote himself to dismantling capitalism, and within a few years that would be done and he could go back to partying. To be fair, to an extent, I did too. We were young and naive then. He was full of energy at first. We both were. We put everything we had into protesting and thought of nothing else.

'Then we both crashed. It could easily have been the end of us, the end of us as a couple and maybe the end altogether. Somehow, we managed to turn it round and make it work. Not everyone does. It's easy to go over the edge. You fight one battle with all your energy, just to find yourself in another, and another, and another, until something has to give. There's a lot of people battling on and on who really just want a quiet life where they can be a productive part of a community but can't step away from the fight.'

We talk at length about different ways of fighting the establishment and the toll they take on you. I know it's something I have to bear in mind.

Prof eventually appears from around the corner, and we're relived to see he's in the visible part of the queue.

The conversation moves on and by the time he has our chips and is back at the van, we're joking about how clearly no one in this town cooks their own food and how many people must die of starvation in the queue for the chippy each year.

This is nowhere near as funny as we make it in our heads and we have tears rolling down our cheeks that can't really be explained.

Madcap wipes the tears from her face and starts the van.

Soon we're out in the countryside and we pull off the road and reverse down a rough track. Madcap drives just far enough to be out of sight of the road and turns the lights off. We sit in the back of the van, in the dark, eating our chips.

We're waiting here for Madcap and Prof's friends. I'm intrigued to know what the action they're on involves. There doesn't appear to be anything around here except trees and darkness.

We finish our chips and sit there for what seems like an absolute age. We're sitting in silence so as not to be heard.

My eyes have adapted to the lack of light quite well now and I can make out the shapes of the trees better, but I still can't see anything other than trees and darkness. An owl flies down the track towards us. It screeches and flies up through the canopy of the trees above us.

In the distance, I see a shape moving up and down through the gloom. It's coming closer, bobbing up and down as it does so. It's white, but not white like the owl was; it's a duller white.

It looks like a hand.

It is a hand. There's a hand bobbing up and down and heading in our direction. I'm assuming there must be a person attached to it, but I can only see the hand.

It's carrying something large. As it gets closer, I can see the dark figure which is attached to it and then another dark figure behind.

Madcap jumps into the driver's seat and Prof opens the back doors. A man and a woman jump in. They're wearing black from head to toe, except the man is missing a glove. They both have heavy-looking bags on their backs which they take off and place on the floor.

The man is also carrying the largest pair of bolt croppers I've ever seen. They're well over a metre long. When he puts them down, I see they have the missing glove stuck to them.

Prof shuts the door and they sit down as Madcap drives onto the road and turns the lights on. The man is now struggling with the glove which is still on his other hand.

'I've only gone and superglued my glove on,' he says. He gives up trying to remove it and takes off his balaclava, exposing his almost clean-shaven head.

The woman already has her balaclava off. She has shoulder-length blonde hair and bright blue eyes. They both have massive grins on their faces.

'It went well then?' asks Prof.

'Oh aye!' they reply in unison.

'Graeme, Ali, this is Sketchy,' Prof says.

We nod at each other and say hi. Then they tell us all about the action.

It turns out that Prof and Madcap had little more information about what they were doing than I did. They've been to an isolated hotel where a mining company is holding a conference. Graeme explains the company in question has a terrible record of human rights abuses and environmental damage, even for a mining company.

The incident which inspired Graeme and Ali to do this action involved them poisoning the water supply to a village in Papua New Guinea, and then sending mercenaries in to forcibly remove the villagers when they complained.

'We thought we'd give them a little taste of their own medicine,' Ali said. 'They'll wake up tomorrow morning to find that the water supply to the hotel has been cut off, along with the lecky. It'll all work fine till seven o'clock, then both should go at once. When they go to reconnect them, they'll find it's a fair bit harder than it should be to get into the boiler room where the fuses are. By the time they get in, the whole room should be flooded.' She's speaking manically. The adrenaline is almost visible. 'We'd love to send mercenaries in as well to evict them,' she says, laughing. 'But we don't have the funds.'

They explain the device they rigged up, which

consists of an angle grinder, a timer and a clamp to hold it in place. It's simple but effective.

They didn't stop there though. They've also immobilised the cars in the visitors carpark to prevent them from going elsewhere for breakfast and changed the lock on the front gate. It is only a small taste of what happened to that village in Papua New Guinea, but it's an impressive action for two people to carry out alone.

We start talking about the advantages and disadvantages of actions like this, which are carried out by a small group. It's almost impossible for the police to gather intelligence on them, but they rarely make enough impact on their own to be newsworthy.

A much bigger impact could be made if a lot of these sorts of actions were coordinated. But if it's organised, there's more chance of a police infiltrator, or just someone with a loud mouth exposing the plans.

We all agree that all that needs to be coordinated is the date. If you could communicate a date effectively with enough people, everyone could organise their own actions within small affinity groups.

Like the way the critical mass of stall holders at a market gives all the stalls an advantage, the critical mass of protests on the same day helps to make the individual actions more effective.

We all think the first of May would be an appropriate day, as it's international workers' day. It's a good day to stand up to the establishment and make it clear that the minority who are at the top of the pyramid can be deposed by the many at the bottom.

It's the early hours of the morning and the motorway we're on is almost entirely empty. We're cruising along at seventy miles per hour and a car appears in the distance in front of us.

We start to catch up with it and it becomes clear that it's straddling the slow lane and the middle lane.

We get closer and it pulls into the slow lane, but as we are almost about to overtake, it starts to drift into the middle lane again.

'For fuck's sake,' says Madcap. 'Pick a lane, any fucking lane!' She beeps the horn and overtakes it in the fast lane. 'That thing in front of you, that's a steering wheel, you fucking moron!'

When Madcap announces she's tired and pulls into a service station to let Prof drive, I see that not only have Graeme and Ali been driven by Prof before, but they also are not as fearless as they first appeared.

As soon as Prof starts driving, which involves almost backing the vehicle into a ditch to the point where he drives out onto the motorway straight into the middle lane without intending to, they look terrified.

Like me, once they see that Prof has settled into the slow lane on this thankfully fairly empty motorway, they settle down and accept their fate.

As ever, Madcap seems completely unconcerned by Prof's terrible driving.

Graeme and her talk about the chip fat purifier she's going to set up for them so that they can run a generator at the commune on chip fat. Graeme says they've got a good contact for old chip oil who they met at the beach-tidy.

I ask what the beach-tidy is and he says that they get together once a month to tidy the beach.

I ask if it's something their community does, or if it's something they've joined in with which was already going on.

'Oh, we started it,' he says. 'A lot of the locals were convinced at first that we were doing it to be accepted and sure, it's cracking to be accepted, but that's not what the beach tidy is for at all. It's about being good anarchists. We can live fair happily without interacting with the local population, but that's not living up to our anarchic ideals. That's just being isolationist. It's fine to be isolationist and extremely understandable, but that's not what we're about. If we, as anarchists, want to live in a world without the formal structures the establishment relies on to keep everything going smoothly, we need to contribute to society. We need to do so freely and without reward. Some folk do that through protest and trying to make the world a better place that way. Almost everybody at the community has been heavily involved in protest at some point, some of us still are. Mainly everyone there just wants to live a quiet and productive life.'

I think that's fairly common.

Most people desire a quiet and productive life.

'The beach-tidy mornings are actually great fun,' Ali says. 'A number of the locals join in now and it's grown into something we never envisaged. To start with, we just tidied all the rubbish we found on the beach and tried to find uses for whatever we could. The stuff we can't find uses for gets recycled in some way, where that's possible. Unfortunately, most has to go to landfill. The bothy you'll be staying in has a multi coloured roof made from random bits of plastic we found on the beach. They've all been cut up into suitable sizes and nailed into place. It doesn't suit everyone's idea of aesthetics, but it's a practical solution to both the problem of the shite plastic and the problem of needing a roof for the bothy. We've got rolls and rolls of fishing line and we even got a container the size of an oil drum full of olives one time. That's a lot of olives. If we can't use what we find at Tigh na mara, it gets offered to anybody that can.

'We started taking the stuff we found back down to the beach for the next beach-tidy to see if anybody wanted it. The untangled and neatly rolled up reels of fishing wire are great, but there's only so many we can use, so we take them back after sorting them out and offer them to whoever turns up. The real change came last summer when we started to get gluts of stuff in the polytunnel and veg patch. We took a load of raspberries down first. Raspberries are great, but you can only eat so many. We'd made enough wine and jelly to last us a year or two, so we took them to see if anybody wanted to take them away. They all went, then the next month other folk turned up with their gluts of fruit and veg. They also gave them away.

'Slowly it grew. Now folk turn up with all sorts of stuff they don't need and give it away. Folk also bring along snacks and drinks for anybody doing the beach tidy. It's been quieter over the winter, but it was so busy by the end of last summer that tidying the beach hardly took any time at all. Mostly we were sitting around eating, drinking and chatting. Some people bring instruments. We even had a harpist to accompany the beach-tidy one time.'

'Do people take the piss? Do they just turn up, take stuff and leave without contributing?' I ask.

'Aye, it's rare, but it does happen,' says Graeme. 'We don't pure mind when they take stuff. It's all stuff that isn't needed by the folk giving it away. A few of them likely think we're idiots for giving it away, but that's because society hasn't equipped them to understand unconditional giving.'

'Quite deliberately' says Prof 'The establishment need us competing not cooperating. The people who can't understand unconditional giving, have been conditioned by capitalism to see all human interaction as transactional and competitive. They haven't been conditioned to see status as emanating from generosity or productivity, but quite the opposite, they've been conditioned to see status emanating from hoarding wealth and getting one over on people.'

'Absolutely,' says Graeme. 'Letting them have the free stuff without contributing and aye greeting them when they come to the beach the next month is the best tool we have to overcome that. It would be ridiculously optimistic to think we can get to the level of social evolution that a peaceful anarchic society requires in this or the next generation. Society doesn't even properly equip folk for democracy. For democracy to work and for the folk to effectively take power, they would have to understand the political structures and the consequences of policy decisions. Most folk don't have the first idea about any of that and have been taught it isn't their place to understand any of it. I don't understand the political structures that well myself. Few folk do.'

It's fascinating to hear how they're trying to gently ferment anarchy.

We chat all the way through the night and reach Tigh na Mara early in the morning.

Graeme and Ali show us the bothy I'll be staying in. The roof is a strange sight. Most of the plastic that it's made of is very faded, but there are a few bright orange sections and some parts have writing on them.

It's very neatly made, but it does look like a lot of old tat.

The interior has a completely different feel. It's beautifully done with lots of driftwood features and has a lovely warm feel. It has a mural of a sea scene at one end, which, when I look closer, I can see is made of pebbles and bits of glass which have been worn smooth by the sea.

There's a bookshelf which fills the wall at the other end made of huge beams of driftwood. There are hundreds of books on it and almost no space for the ones we've brought up. We were asked to bring a book each to leave in the bothy.

I've brought The Good Soldier Svejk. It's a book I absolutely love.

Prof is donating a copy of James Gleick's book, Chaos. No surprises there. He lends it to everyone. I know he has at least three copies.

When I borrowed it, I read one chapter a day so I had time to contemplate each chapter.

He lent a copy to Karen at the same time and there was one in Madcap's van.

Madcap has a book called A God of Small Things. It only came out last weekend. It looks interesting.

I might read it while I'm here if I have time.

Mustapha

Mustapha spoke seven languages and was incredibly quick-witted in his lucid moments. He could have really gone somewhere if he'd taken a different path. This was either '92 or '93.

It's a hot evening and it's been a hot day.

I'm not too surprised; this is summertime in Spain after all. I slept last night in my sleeping bag, out in the open on a beach in Tarragona. I went down to the beach late at night and lay there. I fell asleep watching the bats circling above my head and woke up this morning with pigeons in their place. It was only after I left the beach I realised how lucky I was not to be covered in guano.

It took me a while to get to a decent hitching spot and then not much longer for the sun to get too hot for me to stand out in it.

As a result, I've spent most of today lying in the shade of a tree, waiting for the day to cool down.

Eventually I did go out and hitch again. It was much cooler than it had been, but still uncomfortably warm for a ginger-haired, pale-skinned Northern European like me.

I probably wasn't helping myself much by looking so fatigued. Drivers want to pick up someone who'll be good company on their journey. My drained appearance as I slowly drifted into heatstroke was not a good look.

Luckily for me, the driver of a big black Mercedes took pity on me and picked me up.

The air conditioning in his car was turned right up so I went from dying of the heat straight into the fridge-like temperatures in his car. It was a real shock to the system, but the cold was a great improvement on being hot by the side of the road.

The driver, who's wearing a black suit which seems smart even as suits go, owns a business making coffins out of almond shells. He told me that as a child, he had played on the heaps of almond shells at his best friend's family business which was an almond processing plant. The shells were just unusable waste. His own family business was an undertakers. He went off to university and studied organic engineering or some similar discipline and managed to work out a way to make use of the almond shells.

When he found out where I live, he immediately asked me if I knew the band Caravan.

When I told him that the drummer was the

landlord of the pub I drink in in Ashford, his eyes nearly popped out of their sockets. He was clearly a massive fan and spent the rest of the journey waxing lyrical about how great they were back in the seventies.

Personally, although I like Caravan, I think that running The Castle is a much bigger contribution to society than being a drummer in the band. The Castle is the best pub in Ashford by a long way.

I'm sure some of the members of The Burlingford Club would disagree. Having a pub in the town centre whose clientele of bikers and assorted freaks and weirdos sprawl out onto the High Street probably isn't to everyone's taste, but it brings much-needed originality and life to an otherwise very average town.

He dropped me off at this service station near Barcelona about five minutes ago. I'm now walking down a line of parked up lorries asking for a lift to France.

I've heard a lot of different ways to say 'no', from the driver who rattled off a number of sentences very fast and aggressively in Spanish, of which I understood nothing, before winding his window up, to the driver who just laughed at me and turned his head so he could no longer see me.

I haven't heard a 'yes' yet, but then that's obvious, because if I had, I wouldn't be here any longer.

When I get to the end of the line of lorries, I start walking over to the petrol pumps to ask there.

Before I get to the pumps, I come across someone sat in their car. It's a tatty little Japanese sports car with Dutch number plates, which I expect was once someone's pride and joy. It now only looks vaguely roadworthy. The Dutch plates mean that the driver almost certainly speaks English and it's parked in my way, so I may as well ask.

I walk up to the window and say 'excuse me', but the driver, a man in a scruffy beige jacket who looks North African, is staring straight ahead and hasn't seen me. He scratches his head and pulls at a knot in his hair.

I tap on the window and, as I do so, two things happen; the driver jumps as if he's been shocked out of a trance and, at that same moment, water hits the back of my head like someone's thrown a glass of water at me.

I can't really react to the water because the driver's winding down his window now. I ask him if he could give me a lift and he looks at me like he doesn't understand what I'm saying.

I'm just about to ask him if he speaks English, having realised I had been somewhat presumptuous in not asking him in the first place, when he responds.

'Of course,' he says with a slight Dutch accent

and a suspicious tone, like it might be a trick question.

Another glassful of water hits me, and then another. The skies have opened up and I'm now in the heaviest rain I have ever known.

'Get in the car!' the driver says with some urgency.

I chuck my rucksack in the back and jump into the passenger seat.

As soon as I'm in the car, I realise there really wasn't any point in rushing; I'm drenched to the bone already and couldn't get any wetter.

The driver starts the engine and we're off.

We're crawling along at maybe five miles an hour, maybe not quite that fast. It seems he's forgotten where he's supposed to be driving and we're drifting out of our lane on to the verge.

He pulls the car up and sighs as if this is all too much for him.

'Can you drive?' he asks.

Well, this is an interesting question. I can drive, as in, I have driven a car before. I've even had some driving lessons, but not a test, so I can't legally drive. If I'm honest, I don't have the greatest natural driving abilities.

In normal conditions the answer would be no. In the current circumstances, the sensible thing to do would be to find another lift with a driver who can actually drive.

I don't take the sensible route.

'I'm not legal to drive here,' I say. This is of course the truth but leaves out the information that I am not legal to drive anywhere else either.

The driver doesn't seem to mind and we quickly run through the rain to swap seats. We're now both drenched to the bone.

My lift turns the heater right up to dry us off.

By the time we get out of the service station and onto the motorway, he's asleep. I'm a bit nervous, having never driven on this side of the road before and having never driven on a motorway, but it all seems to be going OK.

It's barely five minutes later when my lift wakes up, complaining it's too hot. He turns the heat right down.

He then becomes much more animated and starts chatting. He tells me his name is Mustapha, he's just got back from Morocco and the reason he was so incoherent when he picked me up was that he had just done some heroin.

It was apparently the last hit he had, from some I presume he brought back with him from Morocco. He's going to Holland, which is great as it'll get me close to Ostend where I'm heading, but he needs to stop at Clermont-Ferrand on the way.

Soon he's asleep again.

Not long later, he wakes up complaining it's

too cold and turns the heating right up.

He settles into a routine of falling asleep, waking up, complaining about the heat or the cold alternately, adjusting the dial and falling asleep again.

When we get near the French border, I pull over. Mustapha is going to have to drive for a bit. I've successfully driven so far without any issue, but the border police will want to see our paperwork and I don't have a driving licence.

We swap seats and Mustapha looks at the steering wheel like he's trying to remember how to drive.

Then he takes a small lump of something out of his pocket, and shows it to me, stating: 'This is my last piece of hash,' before putting it down in the cup holder between the two seats.

This doesn't seem to be the greatest hiding place, but now that I'm in the passenger seat I have the luxury of being the hitcher. If it gets found, I'm just hitching and therefore not responsible for anything found in the car.

I have my rucksack with me and there's nothing to worry about in there.

When we stop at the border, Mustapha is slouched in his seat, looking like he's going to fall asleep. The border guard asks him something in Spanish and he jumps a little like he's startled before responding in Spanish.

I don't know what was said, but the border guard looks distinctly unimpressed. He signals for Mustapha to pull the car over into a parking space where two more border guards are waiting.

They tell us to get out of the car. I don't understand the words, but the body language is pretty clear.

Mustapha seems to be trying to plead with them. Whatever he's saying isn't impressing them and they call over another guard with a dog.

It's pretty obvious the dog is going to find the hash.

I'm thinking this isn't such a bad spot to hitch from. The traffic has all had to stop for the border and there must be a decent lay-by for cars to pull up in.

I'll have to explain that I'm a hitcher, but once they look at my rucksack, they should accept my story. They'll probably be quite arsey, but I should be away soon.

The dog handler releases the dog into the car and sure enough it goes straight for the hash. It doesn't bark or point it's nose or indicate that it's found the hash in any way. It's clearly made the decision that there's not enough hash to share and it's just silently gulped it down in one movement.

It's now looking around the rest of the car, no

doubt hoping there's some more.

'Do you speak English?' Mustapha asks the border guards.

'Yes,' one of them replies.

'Italiano?'

Another border guard says, 'Sì.'

I don't know why he's asking this. He seems to speak perfectly passable Spanish.

'Deutsch?'

They all just shrug at him and he turns to me and says in German, 'That shit dog has just eaten my hash.'

It seems that he was looking for a language they didn't speak. My German is not great, but I get what he's saying. Anyway, I watched the dog eat his hash myself. I know what happened, Mustapha knows, and obviously the dogs knows.

It seems it's only the dog handler and the other customs officers who are unaware of this. I wonder how much hash the dog eats on an average work day.

When the dog has had a thorough search of the car and found nothing else to steal, the border guards start to empty all of our possessions onto the floor.

When they've done so, they give us permission to put it all back in the car and drive on.

We drive to the French part of the border

where we are stopped again by the border guards. The border guards talk to Mustapha and he replies in fluent French. He pulls over into a parking space and they send over another dog, but now there is nothing for it to find. They take everything out of the car and put it on the floor, including all the contents of my rucksack.

Then they kindly allow us to put it all back in the car and go on our way.

Mustapha pulls in at the next service station and takes some money from his wallet. He's concerned it's not enough to get him to Belgium where he can pay on his card.

I have a fifty franc note which I offer him and he puts in as much fuel as he can.

I get in the driver's seat and he gets into the back so he can lie down.

A few minutes later he wakes up and complains that the car is too hot. I turn the heat down and he falls back to sleep.

Soon enough he's awake and complaining it's too cold.

This time I try to turn the heat up to a middling sort of temperature, but he's having none of that.

'Turn it right up,' he says. 'I'm freezing.'

I'm quite pleased now that I had such a lazy day. It looks like I'm going to be driving through the night and the only company I presently have is the brief, but regular interjections from Mustapha about the temperature of the car being entirely wrong.

We're on the Route Nationale, so there's a bit more thinking involved than motorway driving, but for the most part I'm fairly comfortable that it's going OK.

When we get to Clermont-Ferrand, Mustapha's fast asleep. I pull over and try telling him to wake up, but this has no effect.

I get out and go around to the back of the car, open his door and try nudging him, but there is still no response, so I shake him by the shoulder and he wakes with a start, looks straight in my face and shouts something.

I think it's Arabic, but I'm not sure. He comes around properly and asks me indignantly why I'm waking him up.

I say that we're in Clermont-Ferrand and ask him where he wants me to go. He says he doesn't know. He's still half asleep and quite confused.

It's not very helpful really. He doesn't know where he wants to go, and neither do I.

He tells me to drive to the centre, but then sees another Arabic-looking bloke and tells me to stop so that he can talk to him.

He winds down his window and shouts 'Salaam', followed by something I don't understand. Then the two converse in Arabic. Mustapha seems to have some idea of where we're going now.

He gives me directions for a while but it soon becomes obvious we're lost.

Luckily the next person he speaks to manages to give him directions that he can translate for me which take us to where we're going.

Where we are going, it seems, is to a rough-looking housing estate and through a completely anonymous blue door at the bottom of a block of flats. It looks like it might be the outside of a fire door for a municipal building.

Inside is a room which has the feel of a village hall during a busy event. The tables are the sort of utilitarian fold-down type that you might find in a village hall, the chairs are those plastic moulded ones that such places use, and the drab but practical decor would fit right in at a village hall.

The main difference between this and most village halls I've been in is that everyone in here seems to be of North African descent. Certainly, I'm the only white person in the room.

We're immediately offered food. I can't understand what they are saying in what I assume is Arabic, with a smattering of French thrown in, but I can understand the gestures. Mustapha is saying we don't have time to eat, but he's too late; I've accepted their kind offer already and they bring me a plate with couscous and some sort of gently spiced lamb, or maybe it's mutton. There's some sort of dispute between Mustapha and the older men. It might be about him trying to leave before we ate, or it could be to do with whoever he's meeting here.

I hadn't really thought about why Mustapha wanted to come here, but I realise he probably wants to score more heroin.

Whoever he's asking after, they're probably not known as an upstanding pillar of the community.

Whatever's going on, the argument continues while I start my meal. Soon, two men in their mid-twenties appear and Mustapha goes off with them.

I've finished my meal and played a game of chess with one of the old men before they finally return.

We head out to the car, me trying to thank our hosts as much as possible despite the language barrier, Mustapha trying to speed up our exit despite hardly being in a fit state to walk.

One of the blokes he's with is carrying two plastic buckets with lids, which he puts in the boot of the car. Mustapha takes the lid off it to show me what's in it and explains that it's Bedouin food for when you're travelling in the desert.

He dips his finger in, tastes it and gestures to me to do the same. It tastes like a mix of muscovado sugar, spices and maybe nuts. It's very tasty and I can see why it would be good stuff to travel with.

He puts the lid back on. I close the boot and we get in the car. I get in the front. Mustapha gets in the back. He's asleep by the time we get out of the car park.

Although it would be useful to have someone helping with the navigation, I'm quite enjoying finding my way around the French road network.

So far it all seems to be going well. Mustapha is still waking up every now and again to complain that it's too hot or too cold, but other than that I'm on my own. It certainly makes a change from any hitching experience I've had up til now.

Soon I'll have to navigate around Paris and then I'm on the home run. I can drive up to Belgium and leave Mustapha to drive from there. By that point, he'll have had a night's sleep and he won't have far to go before he gets home.

Mustapha wakes up. The heating is turned fully up, so I go to turn it down to cold, but this time it's not the heat that's bothering him.

'We need to go into Paris,' he says.

If there's anything I don't need right now, it's to drive this car into Paris.

I've tried Paris as a pedestrian, and I have no intention of trying it as the unlicensed, uninsured driver of a car with some crazy heroin addict in tow.

It seems Mustapha only scored one hit of heroin in Clermont-Ferrand and now he's coming down badly. I try to reason with him.

He's told me he doesn't have any money, so I ask him how he's going to pay for the heroin. He says he'll come to a deal with them and that he has jewellery.

I know I could just pull into the next service station and leave him to it, but I don't. I tell him there's no way I'm driving in the city. He's going to have to take over the driving if he wants to go there.

He agrees to this like it's not an issue, but I've seen how much he struggled to drive for a few minutes through the Spanish-French border and I can't believe that he can cope with city traffic.

I'll try to get as close as possible to the city before changing places with him.

Coming into Paris, we're on a road with more lanes than I can count. I'm not a complete idiot, although my current situation might suggest that I am, and I can count as high as how ever many lanes there are, but I'm concentrating hard on being in the correct lane and not crashing.

The closer to the city we get, the less space the other cars are giving me. I'm now trapped in one of the centre lanes. I can't move left or right because the cars are blocking me in. There's also only a few inches between me and the cars in front and behind.

I can't think about directions because I'm concentrating too hard on staying alive.

By the time the lanes split off and I get a chance to pull over, we're in the city centre. Somehow, I managed not to crash; now we'll see how well Mustapha does.

I'm not sure which I prefer, Mustapha's driving or mine. His is definitely more dangerous than mine and we just nearly got hit by a truck, but at least I'm not responsible for it.

Again, I have the luxurious position of a hitcher. I am aware that any sane hitcher would get out and hitch, but we seem to have passed that point. Mustapha hasn't told me where he's going and I'm not really sure that he knows.

I'm not going to distract him by asking. I think it's better that he concentrates on the road.

We're in the far-left lane of a five-lane road when Mustapha shouts, 'There!'.

I don't know what he's seen and I don't really get a chance to think about it before the lights change and he accelerates as fast as the car will go to get in front of the traffic.

He screeches across all five lanes in one go, pulling up by the side of the road on the furthest lane to the right. He's completely oblivious to the traffic behind us.

The cars behind are jamming their brakes on and swerving across lanes to avoid him and horns are blasting out all over the place.

Now that he's pulled up in the right-hand lane, he's forced all the traffic to move to the left, causing absolute chaos. Mustapha is a man on a mission so he's completely oblivious to all this.

He jumps out of the car, nearly getting run over and runs down the steps of a Metro station. I'm left sat in the car with almost every other vehicle on the road sounding their horns at me as they deal with the chaos that Mustapha has left in his wake.

I'm sitting here wondering whether the police will turn up before or after a vehicle hits the car. It's only a matter of time for one or the other to happen.

Mustapha emerges from the Metro accompanied by two enormous blokes shaking their heads as they walk towards the car.

As they get in the back, the suspension goes right down under their weight and they have to squeeze in to close the door of the car. They entirely fill the back seats with no room to spare.

Mustapha is speaking to them in French, so I can catch bits of the conversation, but not much. They're black and Mustapha is trying to persuade them to trust him with a line that goes something like: 'You're African, I'm African, we're brothers.'

They are not in any way persuaded by this or anything else that Mustapha has to say.

When we pull up at the entrance to a block of flats on a rough-looking estate, Mustapha hands them his wedding ring as a sign that he trusts them and promises them money when they return with the heroin.

They walk into the block of flats and I get out of the car. I was up for a certain amount of risk, but this is stupid.

'What are you doing?' says Mustapha, who seems completely shocked that I don't want to stick around to see how this pans out.

'I'm going.' Although this means walking out of a rough-looking housing estate and finding a way out of the city so I can hitch, it's clearly the only sensible option.

I'm kicking myself for getting into this situation.

'Why are you going?' His comment and his tone of voice makes me realise how much Mustapha is relying on me and how vulnerable he is right now.

'Look,' I say. 'Those men have just taken your ring and you'll probably never see them again, but there's the possibility they will return with the heroin and want money that you don't have.' I figure that the least I can do is explain the situation to him.

'I can give them more rings,' he replies. He's entirely blinded by his cravings and hasn't even considered that this could go wrong.

'You've told them you have money,' I say. 'What if they return with guns?'

'Get in the car, we'll go,' he says. He looks really

concerned now, like he's woken up from a dream and discovered that reality is much worse than he could have imagined.

The fact is they wouldn't have needed guns. They're both huge. I'm not a fighter and Mustapha is in such a bad state, he'd lose a fight with an injured sloth.

Partly because it saves me the hassle and danger of walking through what is clearly not the safest area and partly because I'm aware that Mustapha is entirely reliant on me, I get back into the car.

Mustapha tries to find his way out of the city. He's concerned we might not have enough fuel to get us to Belgium where his bank card will work.

His answer to this is to drive randomly around Paris while he thinks up a solution.

I've seen how good he is at thinking and don't trust this strategy.

Somehow I persuade him to head north and work it out on our way out of the city.

He doesn't work anything out and nor do I, but we do leave Paris and I take over the driving again. Soon he's asleep. He's in the passenger seat now, not laid out across the back seat, but he doesn't wake up to complain about the heat or for any other reason.

He sleeps soundly, sitting up. Even when his head flops around as we turn corners, he remains fast asleep. He's clearly exhausted himself with his little adventure in Paris.

The road is fairly empty. It's the early hours of the morning and I cruise along at a steady speed, trying to preserve the fuel as much as possible. There are roadworks with signs in French which I can't read, but there's very little traffic on the road, so I have time to work out where I'm supposed to be.

We're directed onto a newly-built stretch of road for a bit, which is lovely and smooth, then back onto the old road. It looks like they're replacing the road, which is no bad thing. The old road is just patch upon patch, broken up with the occasional pothole.

I'm quite liking Mustapha being fast asleep. I don't want him waking up because we hit a pothole and starting to complain about the temperature of the car again.

There's a new road running alongside it for miles as we drive. There's a roundabout, which is displaying more road signs than could possibly be required. Some make sense, some really don't.

We exit onto the new road and drive along it for quite a long stretch, sometimes in sight of the remains of the old road. We rejoin another section of the old road, the car vibrates and makes a loud rumbling sound going over the bumpy surface.

I look over at Mustapha. So far he's still fast

asleep.

We change between the two a number of times. There's a roundabout where I get confused, but I work it out again and I'm back on the nice smooth road.

I'm trying to keep the acceleration and braking to a minimum to preserve fuel. With no other traffic around, I'm cruising along at 100kmph on a smooth, flat road, making good time and not using too much fuel.

Suddenly the road surface disappears from under me. The smooth top surface has run out and I'm now driving on a lower layer of the road, which makes a louder rumbling noise and makes the car vibrate more than the old road did by a long way.

I can see now why this road is quite so empty. I can see that it is in fact because I took the wrong turning at that roundabout.

I slow right down, expecting the lower surface to disappear and the road to run out entirely, but instead we get to another roundabout. I have to move some bollards to get back on the correct road.

I get back in the car, drive forwards and see another car behind me. I'm relieved to see it. It's a French car. The driver should understand the road signs and it's unlikely that we're both on the wrong road.

Mustapha is still sleeping like a baby.

We're coming up to the border with Belgium, so I wake Mustapha.

I pull over and we swap places. He can hardly walk and to get from one side of the car to the other he has to lean on the bonnet to prevent himself from falling over.

He makes it though and slumps heavily into the driver's seat. At first, he just sits there in a trance.

After a while, I remind him he's supposed to be driving and he starts the engine and sits there, staring forward with the engine going.

'Mustapha,' I say.

'Yeah, yeah, yeah,' he says in an aggravated tone and starts driving, slowly at first and then he gets up to a reasonable driving speed.

I'm aware that if the border guards speak to Mustapha they're almost certainly going to realise he's in no fit state to be driving.

If they get him to get out of the vehicle, there's no question they'll realise.

He slows down for the border and they wave us through, hardly looking at us at all. He drives until we're out of sight and pulls over.

I get back in the driver's seat and he climbs into the back, exhausted, like that bit of driving took his last ounce of energy.

Almost as soon as I start driving, I see the second border hut.

I hadn't thought this through at all. Of course, there are two border huts. One French and one Belgian.

If I stop now, in sight of the border hut, we'll definitely get grief. If I get pulled driving through the border, I'm in no end of grief.

Forgive me if this isn't the greatest bit of decision making; I've been driving all night after all. I continue driving and hope for the best.

I am luckier than you could imagine. There is no one at the Belgian border hut and I drive straight through.

Ostend, where I'm heading, is not far from the border and still in a fairly straight line to Holland. We haven't talked about where Mustapha is going to drop me off, or as it turns out, I'm going to drop me off, but having driven him from Barcelona to Belgium, I don't think it's too cheeky to drive to Ostend.

I pull up at the roundabout on the edge of town which I usually walk to when I'm hitching out of Ostend. It's only a short walk to the port from here and it seems like a safer place for Mustapha to remember how to drive than the town centre.

I wake him up and he's as confused as I expect him to be. I explain where he is and which direction it is to get him home.

'Head to Ghent, then on to Antwerp.' I can see

he isn't taking this in, so I point to the sign saying Ghent. 'That way,' I say.

'Hey, I can speak English, you know,' he says in a curt tone. Then in a softer manner he continues, 'You will come and see me in Holland, won't you?'

'I will,' I lie and start walking off towards the port.

'Stop, stop,' he shouts after me. 'You don't have my address.'

I walk back, get out my notebook and start looking for a pen.

He picks up my hitching sign marker and scrawls his address in my notebook.

'You will come, won't you?' he says.

'Yes, I will,' I lie again.

Damn Protestors

Early morning on the 1ˢᵗ of May 1997. Cyril was an interesting chap.

'Capitalism is, by its very nature, the most efficient and effective method of allocating resources to where they are needed.

'To oppose it is absolute madness. I have no idea what these protestors think they're going to achieve. The fact is that we live in a democracy and if you want to change something, there are ways and means of making that happen.

'If these protestors are not happy with how things are being done, why don't they just stand for parliament? If their ideas really are worthwhile, surely that is the way to get them implemented, but oh no, they want to disrupt everyone's lives. This lot aren't interested in positive change. They just want to get in the way and get on the television.

'No protest has ever achieved anything positive.

Just look at the mess South Africa is in now. The ANC have absolutely destroyed the country, with the encouragement of the bleeding-heart lefties. They're terrorists and the left has always fully supported their terrorism. Everyone from the BBC to the idiots in the Labour Party seem to think this Mandela chap is the best thing since sliced bread.

'The fact is he's a terrorist and they should have hung him while they had the chance. Now that he's president, the country is going to the dogs. You mark my words, they'll be begging the white people to take the country over soon, once they realise how unqualified they are to run it.'

This monologue has been going on for over an hour now and his argument is as convincing as his greasy comb-over. I could, of course, counter every point he makes, but I have more important things on my mind and I'm trying not to look like a protestor right now.

'If these idiots who are intent on causing disruption today did get their way, they'd bankrupt the country. It would be like the USSR all over again, but this time it would be our freedoms that would be destroyed.

'We've seen what communism looks like and it looks like a bloody mess. Apparently, they're saying capitalism is causing global warming. What absolute rubbish. Does anyone really believe that the planet is getting warmer? Are these people's memories so short they don't remember that just last year we had an extremely cold winter? I can tell you, it didn't feel much like global warming then. We have a lake, you know, and it froze solid. It froze more than it has at any time since we bought our house. We've lived there for over ten years and I can tell you that it's getting colder.

'Regardless, even if it did warm up a little, I fail to see why that would be any sort of problem. I have a holiday home in the South of France. It's lovely down there and you know what's lovely about it? It's warm. If the planet warmed by a few degrees and Britain became like the South of France, who could possibly complain about that?

'I mean these damn protestors can always no doubt find something to complain about, but how could they complain about the weather getting better? It's nonsense.

'You wait. It'll start cooling down at some point, then all these worriers will become hysterical over the fear we're going into an ice age. When will people come to their senses and realise that the weather is changeable, always has been, always will be and we have no effect on it? The weather, I'm afraid, is something you just have to live with and accept.

'The real trouble here isn't capitalism, or global

warming, or whatever else this lot gets its knickers in a twist about. It's a lack of discipline and order. When I was a child, I knew not to step out of line or I'd be beaten. I don't mean a little slap on the wrist or a gentle telling off. I was properly beaten, so I knew right from wrong.

'Then of course, we had national service back then. It made a man of you, the army did. These protestors, they've all grown up without any real discipline. I can tell you, if you put them in the army, the whole lot of them, they'd soon learn some sense.'

Partly this is my own fault. He never would have picked me up if I hadn't made myself look so respectable. I've lost my dready hair. It was never dreads as such, more a matted mess, but it's now a very short and remarkably tidy looking haircut. I thought it would end up looking like a short bobbly mess, but I reckon I could work in an office with this haircut and not seem out of place. 'You're not allowed to say that these days though, are you? It's not bloody politically correct enough. They're censoring everything we say just in case we offend one group or another. I'm probably not even allowed to say that. Next thing you know, they'll have police recording your every word, just in case you say something that offends the blacks or the gays or some bloody lesbian socialist whatever.

'This country is going to the dogs. It's probably

already gone to the dogs, but no one is allowed to point it out because that would be offensive to dogs or something.

'They're even banning nursery rhymes. I mean, seriously, what sort of state have things got to where you're not even allowed to recite a nursery rhyme to your own child? If someone heard you starting to say "Eeny, Meeny, Miny, Mo", the political correctness police would be on you like a flash.

'If these protestors want to protest about something, why don't they protest about our freedom of speech? Surely that's important to them. More important than some nonsense about stopping capitalism.

'It's just jealousy, I tell you. They're too lazy to get off their arses and make something of their lives, so they complain about everyone who has done so and is enjoying the benefits. Why shouldn't I live in a nice house and why shouldn't I have a nice holiday home? I work hard for it. I'm not even in my nice house for most of the week, I'm in my London flat, which is really quite modest, so that I can work and pay the bills.

'If these damn protestors had my work ethic, they wouldn't have time to be out there getting in everyone's way, they'd be too busy working.'

I'm wearing my smartest clothes. They

probably still look like a poor person's work clothes to my lift, but they're smart for me. I borrowed some trade plates. I needed to get to London but didn't want to look like I was going to the protest, so I'm doing all I can to look respectable.

Carrying trade plates and looking like I'd been delivering a vehicle seemed like the best way of doing that. Mr Bloody-protestors-it's-not-like-my-day certainly seems to have been fooled by it. I'm fairly sure he'd burst a blood-vessel if he realised he was giving me a lift into Central London so that I could join the protest.

Forgiving the violent criminals and those who are clearly suffering from a mental health disorder is relatively easy compared to forgiving the people who have been handed everything on a plate, see their privilege as their birthright and truly believe they've worked hard for all they have.

This bloke told me earlier that he was given his first rental properties by his parents. He said this in a completely unabashed attempt to convince me that he had made his own way in life by taking the advantages given to him and working hard to make the most of them.

He probably can't imagine a world in which he wasn't born with those advantages. I certainly know that he thinks his genes are better than the working class's, which is why his family is so successful. He told me as much a while back, just before he started lecturing me about how the suffragettes should have just waited a while and they would have got the vote anyway, because that was the direction things were going in.

I don't want to listen to anything he has to say and am only tolerating him because I really need to get into London. In all fairness, he has given me a lift, even if it is only because he sees me as a straight, white man who is hitching for what he perceives to be a good reason. I wish him no harm and don't want to punish him, but for others to get their fair share he will have to learn to live with less.

As that bloke on the radio said, 'On the road to equality, the over-privileged will have to lose some privilege'.

As soon as I'm out of the car, I head to the library. Libraries are a great place to lie low. You can hang out all day without spending money, sitting around reading books and it doesn't look suspicious at all.

The timing today is crucial as the police are going to be doing all they can to disrupt our actions. I have no clue how many actions other than ours will happen today. From the fuss they've been making about it all on the news, they must expect some major drama.

Even though we put flyers out to try to

encourage others to take part, we worked on the basis that it might well just be our action on its own.

I've heard snippets of information about other groups and what they're doing. The police scuppered some of them with early morning raids this morning, but I don't think they got any of our friends.

It's impossible to say how many people know about it. We printed off five thousand flyers, but I've seen badly photocopied versions of those, which shows there are more out there.

I heard as well that someone advertised it on the world wide web. I don't know if that will get to many people. I don't really know how that all works, but we certainly seem to have got the press, the police and the establishment in general worried and that's what today is all about.

Felix

A lot of people who gave me lifts told me that they wished they'd travelled more. No one ever said that they wished they'd travelled less and settled down earlier. ('93)

I'm standing by the side of the road with a sign.

This is how a lot of hitching stories start. The road is somewhere near Koln, and the sign says 'KO'. There are many things I like about Germany and one of them is that you can make very short hitching signs. On registration plates, 'KO' means the car is registered in Koblenz, and enough German people seem to know these initials that they work on hitching signs.

I'm not actually going to Koblenz at all, I'm off to Prague, but the first step is to get to a better hitching spot. There's a service station between here and Koblenz which is much better for hitching than this junction, where most of the traffic is local.

I've only been stood at the side of this road for a few minutes. It's a lovely warm summer's day, so

I'm not having to work hard to keep smiling yet. If I'm still here after a few hours, I'll have to check my smile to make sure it's not turning into a grimace.

I'm making eye contact with the drivers as they approach me. The driver of a blue BMW returns my smile and pulls up to give me a lift. He's probably in his mid-forties and has an air of confidence and a relaxed manner. He's wearing a shirt and tie and his suit jacket is hanging in the back of the car.

As soon as he hears my attempt at speaking German, he switches to English and introduces himself as Felix. It's surprising how often you can get lifts which last for hours and get into deep, fascinating conversations and never know the driver's name. If there are just two of you in the car, names are entirely unnecessary.

Felix asks where in Koblenz I want to go. I ask him to drop me at the services before the city, so I can hitch on to Prague.

He's going to a meeting in Nuremberg and offers to take me to a service station there. This sounds great and I settle in for a long lift.

When he asks why I'm going to Prague, I don't have a decent answer. I really am just bumming around. I'm going to see friends, but I don't know which friends I'll bump into, so that seems less than convincing in my head.

I'm not really doing anything with my life at

the moment. There's no educational path that really excites me. I can live happily on very little money, so don't really see the point in busting a gut working in an attempt to become rich.

I have a feeling there's something fun or important to do with my life if I can just suss out what it is, but I haven't sussed it out yet. Based solely on the fact that he's going all the way to Nuremberg for a meeting, Felix clearly has much more direction than me.

My slightly self-conscious and rambling explanation is taken far more positively than I expected.

'Back in the sixties I did the same for a while,' Felix says. 'I went on holiday to Turkey with my friend Max. It was cheaper than we thought, so we extended it. Turkey was great, but we were told that Iran was more of an adventure, so we hitched there.'

This does sound like an adventure. I'd love to see more of the world, but I have to admit, I find the idea of hitching in Iran quite daunting.

'Iran is culturally so different from Germany, much more so than Turkey. Hitching from Ankara and then around Iran made the world feel much smaller and less scary to us. Regardless of the differences between the people we met and ourselves, we realised there was far more that was the same. We got lifts from people we had no common language with and communicated with gestures and facial expressions. We sat in rickety trucks transporting goods, and in flashy cars with rich businessmen. We were always made to feel welcome.

'On our first night in Iran, we slept on the roof of a house. A man picked us up and insisted we meet his family and eat a meal. This then turned into an invitation to stay over. We laid on the roof of his house with full bellies and watched the most star-filled sky we had ever seen. Of course, the great thing about hitching is that it is generally only the nicest people who pick you up.'

Felix is entirely right here. When hitching, you spend a lot of time with people driving past you until someone who is on average much nicer than those people picks you up. We're not far into the journey, but I'd be happy to put money on Felix himself being a genuinely sound bloke.

'One lift was followed by another and people suggested places we should see. The road into Iran lead out on the other side and into Afghanistan. Months later, we found ourselves in a town which was little more than a shop, a hotel and a small collection of houses.

'We decided to stay for the night. We had slept in many precarious places, but there was nowhere to sleep other than the hotel. A man called Kamal, who was working in the hotel, spoke some English.

He was keen to practice and show this off. He asked what we thought of Afghanistan, if we were going to India, where we were from and why we had chosen to come to this particular town. He asked these questions one after the other and left little or no time for us to answer them before asking the next one. He asked us if we smoke hashish. We told him that we have smoked it a few times. He said that his cousin had a cannabis farm in the hills and asked us if we would like to see it. We both thought that this sounded like a great adventure.'

I'm with Felix here. This sounds like just my sort of adventure. I would be nervous about it, just like I would be about hitching in Iran, but I guess adventures happen when you leave your comfort zone.

'The next morning, Kamal gave us a lift to the farm on his motorbike and side car. We left town and went up into the hills and then down into a lush green valley. Kamal was riding far too fast for the rough dirt road we were on and the bike was bouncing around all over the place.'

I'm on the edge of my seat at this point.

Obviously, I'm not actually on the edge of my seat. I'm actually sat entirely normally in my seat. I'm desperate to know where this story goes next, but Felix pulls in to a service station to get fuel.

As it's a hot day, the air is full of flying insects,

so while he's filling the car, I clean the windscreen.

Felix comes back and offers me a can of fizzy drink. I don't know what flavour it's pretending to be, but it's cool and I appreciate it.

We start moving again and I'm asking him to tell me what happened in Afghanistan.

Felix says they travelled through fields of what looked like "wheat or corn or big grass". I don't know if Felix wasn't sure what crop it was at the time, or isn't sure now what the correct English word is.

'Then,' he continues, 'we realised we had arrived. There was marijuana growing everywhere. At the speed we were going you could mistake it for another crop by the look, but it was smelly. Very smelly. The air was thick with the smell, and it seemed to be having a calming effect, like we were stoned just being around that much dope.

'Along the track, a car in front of us stopped, blocking our way and two guys got out. One of them looked very angry and the other one, looked absolutely livid. He was shouting abuse at Kamal from the moment he got out of the car. What made this situation worse is that they both had guns. The shouting one was waving his gun around frantically as he shouted at Kamal. He was not pointing it at anyone like he was intending to use it. He was manically gesturing with it to express his anger. Sometimes he was pointing it at Kamal or at Max or me, but only like an angry person might point a finger if they didn't happen to have a gun in their hand.'

Felix's eyes widen in fear and he pushes his head back into the headrest as if he's trying to back away from the moment he's reliving. His expression changes to one which looks convincingly like the expression of someone with a gun pointed in their face.

'This argument was not in a language I could identify. I could not understand them, but it was clear from the gestures and tone that we were in big trouble. Kamal was apologetic and concerned, but not as concerned or apologetic as I think he needed to be. Max looked just as scared as I was. The two men with guns returned to their car and drove off.

'Max and I looked at each other with relief. Whatever had just happened was over and we had not been shot, hurt in any way or even had anything stolen. Then Kamal turned around and said "don't worry, this is my cousin. We go to the farm". Without any further discussion, he started the bike and followed his cousin's car. We had no time to consider this, let alone object.

'Somehow, with the shouting and the guns and the terrible powerless position that we found ourselves in, the joy had been taken out of the whole adventure. My only thought then, and I think also

Max's, was about how we get out of the situation alive, and the fact was that at that moment, we had no way of influencing anything.'

Yeah, I get this. Nothing takes the joy out of a situation like angry men with guns do.

'The car stopped, and Kamal pulled up behind it. We were next to a high wall with an enormous door in it. The door was made of wood, reinforced with a metal lattice and it had a big metal ring as a door handle. There was a keyhole large enough to put your fingers through.'

As Felix explains this, he puts his hand out with his fingers straight like he's going to slap someone and stares at his hand.

Momentarily I'm concerned that he's not concentrating on driving as he tries to remember if the keyhole really was that large.

'The shouting man takes us through the door into a compound. Kamal was still sitting on the bike. The door was stiff and Shouting Man had to shove it hard with his shoulder to open it. Inside were three small stone buildings. They were square houses with no glass in the windows and curtains instead of doors. Max and me were led into one of the buildings which contained nothing other than a small wood stove and a sort of thin mattress. The second man the slightly less angry one, followed us in. He had a mattress from one of the other buildings and he put it on the floor. Then we heard Kamal drive off on his bike. We could see we were staying there whether we liked it or not.'

'He just left you there?' I'm quite pleased to just be hearing about this adventure, rather than actually being there myself.

'Yes. We did not know what was happening. The second man left and came back with a container of water, a kettle, a teapot and a few other bits and pieces. It was the sort of kettle you put on a cooker and the teapot is this beautiful ornamental teapot, made of a brassy metal with blue and black designs on it, like in a museum. Shouting Man was not so angry looking now. He seemed to have accepted whatever was happening. He certainly was not happy, but at least he was not shouting. He put his gun down, lit the stove and started to make tea.'

'They made you tea?' This is an unexpected twist on a kidnapping story.

'Yes, that is the point I realised he was not going to kill us. He would not waste his time making us tea if we were about to die.'

There's a certain amount of logic to that statement. I guess sometimes you have to find comfort wherever you can.

'I was still very scared, but not as scared as before this. So, there we were, drinking sweet black tea in a little stone hut on a dope farm somewhere in Afghanistan with two men who we share no language with and whose intentions were a total mystery. When this strange little tea ceremony was over, our reluctant hosts stand up to leave.

'Just before leaving, Shouting Man turned to us and said "hashish?". Neither of us know how to react to this, but he did not wait too long before he threw a huge lump of hashish to Max. Max caught it and just stared at it in his hand without thanking the man for it or saying anything.

'The two men left. They closed the compound door behind them and from the house we could hear a key the size of my hand being turned in the lock.'

His hand moves as he talks about the key again. He seems to be imagining himself turning this massive key.

'So, I know we should keep our heads clear in such a situation, but, the situation is so out of our control, that we really have no choice. We have to go along with it. We had a pipe we had bought in a market in Kabul. We filled it up and had a smoke. It seemed like the best hashish I had ever had,' says Felix. 'But it might have just been that it was the first time I had smoked so soon after thinking I was going to die. For whatever reason, the high was amazing!'

I don't know about this; not smoking seems like the sensible option here, but I guess the really sensible option was ultimately to stay in Germany and not have these risky adventures. If he'd have done that, my journey wouldn't be nearly so entertaining.

'Later we hear a key turning in the compound lock again and two men came in. They were younger than Shouting Man and his friend. One was carrying a gun and looking stern. The other one was carrying a basket and looking like he knew he had drawn the short straw. The basket was not very heavy, but it was large and cumbersome.

'The man with the gun only opened the heavy compound door as wide as he needed to squeeze in. He stood in front of the door, posing with the gun. This meant that the man with the basket had to slalom around him. We did not want to upset him, but we could not help thinking this looks funny. The way that he posed with the gun was really quite desperate. He could not see how much the other bloke was struggling behind him.

'Luckily, even though we had been smoking, we managed not to laugh. The man carrying the basket gave a small but friendly smile as he lay it at the door of our little house. Both men left without saying any words. 'When we looked, the basket had in it food and a backgammon board. We ate, smoked, drank tea and played backgammon. We did not know how long we would be there or what would happen to us.'

Nice of his captors to think about supplying them with a backgammon board, but this does sound like they weren't going to be let out anytime soon.

'That evening, a hot meal was delivered in a series of metal containers with lids, stacked on top of each other and tied together with a leather strap. It was a real feast, better than anything we had eaten since leaving Germany. We had been careful with money and maybe had not eaten as well as we should have on our travels. The next morning, another basket arrived, containing more food. The man carrying the basket signalled to us to return the containers.

'This was our daily routine. In the morning, a basket of food arrived and the metal containers we left outside were taken away. In the evening, a hot meal was delivered. Each day the man with the gun tried to look more manly and threatening than he did the day before, and the man carrying the basket smiled a smile which got friendlier each day.

'Each day, we thanked him and did a small bow of the head so that he understood the meaning if not the words themselves. We spent our days in the cool shade of the building and after their evening meal we took our mattresses up onto the roof and lay back, watching the stars.'

This is a strange form of captivity and must

have been terrifying, despite the tea, food and dope. He clearly got out alive though, otherwise he wouldn't be here.

'So we counted the days and on what I had counted as the fifteenth day, although Max insisted it was the sixteenth, we were escorted from our hut, out of the compound. The view outside had changed completely. The marijuana had all been harvested and we could see across the valley. It is a low wide valley, with rocky areas around the edges. The stumps of harvested plants stretch out in front of us for hundreds of metres.

'The sightseeing did not last for long. We were told to get in the back of a small wooden truck. It was incredibly hot inside. With bad suspension and terrible roads the ride was as unbearably bumpy as it was hot. Sitting on our rucksacks helped, but every now and again a sharp turn or a particularly bumpy bit of road caused the rucksacks to fly out from under us and we landed on the hard floor of the truck. There were large wooden crates in the back with us which slid around as the truck accelerated, braked or took sharp turns. There was a little knot in the wood which we could look through to see out, but we could not really see anything helpful.'

I've had some fairly uncomfortable rides myself, although nothing anywhere near the concerning context of the ride that Felix was describing. He's painting a picture which is so realistic I can almost feel myself rattling around in the back of that truck with them. This just highlights to me how comfortable my present ride is, both physically and mentally. Felix is great company and as if telling the story is making him yearn for even more comfort, he's turning the air conditioning up a notch, cooling the car down just a little.

'We rattled around in the back of the truck until the sun went down. Then we pulled up in a rocky valley. I was so relieved not to be moving anymore! The sides of the valley were steep and the stream that ran through it was just a small trickle of water. There was nothing growing other than a few stunted trees which looked like they had tried their hardest to cling on to life. We sat on the hard ground, drinking tea and eating kebabs that we cooked over a fire, followed by sweet pastries and cakes.

'Then suddenly I had this thought, 'What are they fattening us up for?' I wondered if there is maybe, a market for white slaves but decided that two pampered western boys like us were not likely to have a lot of value as slaves; probably fattening us up was only reducing our value.

'Soon the break stopped and we were back on the road. I had no time for fear then because I was concentrating on holding onto the luggage again whilst being thrown around the back of the truck. It was morning when the door was opened, we were ordered out and our luggage was thrown out after us.'

'Where were you?' I'm hoping he isn't about to describe an Afghan slave market to me.

'We had no idea, or what to do next and we just stood silently as the truck drove off. We were on our own, with no explanation of why we had been held. We were on a small single-track road. We did not know what was in either direction. The sun was rising, so we could see that the road goes roughly east to west, but this is really no help.

'A car came from the east. We tried to wave it down, but it just drove past. A pickup truck appeared from the other direction. We crossed the road to try to wave it down. It pulled up on the wrong side of the road and a man shouted at us in English to get in the back.

'Almost as soon as it started moving, we were again fearing for our lives. A car drove towards the truck we were in from the other direction. The road was wide enough for two vehicles to pass without any problem, but instead of moving over to the right to give space for the car to get past, the truck swerved over to the left. The car was then forced to swerve to its left to avoid us. We were so relieved there is no crash. It was only when we joined a larger road that we realised all the traffic was driving on the left, as it does in Pakistan. This was not the dangerous situation we thought it was, but it really was frightening at the time.'

As Felix relives this, you can see his fear and then the relief on his face. He tells me that Max and himself had become quite comfortable with their lack of any plan or direction, but after being dropped off in Peschawar, they knew they had to make some sort of decision.

'So, we decided to head to Lahore and then just over the border to India before heading back. We had done well at not spending any money and our two weeks of being well fed in captivity has helped with that. With over half of our holiday money still left, we felt we could afford to go a little further before heading back.

'Just like that "one last drink" before heading home, a small diversion can lead to another and so on. This is how we came to find ourselves some time later, and over a year since we left Germany, on a beach in Kerala, relaxing during the day and partying at night. We felt we had discovered the secret to life itself. We had very little but there was nothing more that we needed.'

This beach in Kerala sounds good. I quite fancy partying on a beach for a bit.

'We knew that although we are having fun, our situation was not economically sustainable. We worked out that for five thousand Deutsche Marks we could set ourselves up in India permanently. We decided to head back to Germany, do whatever it takes to get the money together and get back to India as fast as possible. Along with this plan came a realisation. Although the world had become a smaller place to us, not just through our experiences in Iran, but through all of our travels after that, when you turn around to head back overland from India, it's a very long way. The return journey was very different to the journey out. We were no longer kids straight out of school; we were seasoned travellers, who had learned, not just from our own experiences, but from the tales told by all the other travellers we had met. We also had direction, somewhere to go and a reason to go there.'

Felix's voice is different when he tells this bit of the story. He's no longer talking in the excited, fast paced way he was through the fun bits, or even through the scarier bits of his story. He now has a weariness to his voice and a slower tempo.

'So after a long journey, when we returned to our hometown, I no longer felt I belonged there and I think Max felt the same. People we knew were sitting at the same bar stools as when we left; the shops were the same; the food was the same and even the conversations seemed to be the same. It was like watching a film you've seen a thousand times, where you know exactly what is going to happen next, but the characters are entirely unaware. It was like that except we were supposed to relate to the characters because this was not a film; it was real life. This all made us more determined to get the money together and leave.

'We both quickly found jobs, but we both knew it is going to take a long time to get the money together. These were not high-paid jobs. We also both hated having a boss. After leaving school and having a taste of freedom, we both preferred to suffer from our own bad decisions than to live with someone else's. We decided we had to work for ourselves and set up a business.'

I completely relate to Felix here. I hate having a boss; I hate the whole concept of having other people making decisions about my life. I've never understood how your school days can be the best days of your life.

Surely when you take control of your life, unless you are extraordinarily bad at making decisions, that has to be an improvement.

'You know how much profit our business made last year?' Felix asks.

Of course, I don't have a clue. Felix hasn't even told me what the business is, but he leaves me a long enough pause that I could make a guess if I felt so inclined.

I don't, so he tells me.

'Three million Deutsche Marks,' he says. The pride in his voice is blended with a tone that indicates an element of disappointment that he lost his way. 'I should be on a beach in Kerala watching beautiful sunsets and eating the super-ripe mangoes you get there which are literally dripping with flavour,' he says. 'But by the time the business was worth enough that we could have cashed it all in and raised the five thousand DM, we thought it would be good to get a bit more money together and live in India with more luxuries.'

Of course, the more luxuries you can afford, the more you desire. He'd settled in Germany, met his partner and had children. He had responsibilities to his family and to their employees. The dream of moving out to India was just that; an old dream which never came to fruition.

We're pulling into the service station where we will part company. I've hardly said a word for these last four hours as Felix has told his story as if he was offloading it on me.

I still don't know what his business is or what his plan was if he had returned to India with his five thousand DM. He's clearly happy with his life, but like all lives it could have taken any one of an infinite number of different paths.

I wonder how often he thinks about how the

path that took him back to India would have panned out.

He drops me off and I take a few steps before seeing a car with Czech number plates.

I ask the driver if he speaks English, which he does.

Seconds later I am sitting in his car, heading to Plzeň.

Today is a good day.

Follow The Elephant

Around lunchtime on the 1ˢᵗ of May 1997

I'm going to make sure I enjoy this lift, because I'm fairly sure my next lift will be in a police van and after that, my travelling is going to be severely curtailed for quite a while.

Here I am in Central London, riding on the back of an elephant. I'm sitting on its neck and my harness is attached to the end of its trunk to prevent me from falling.

It's not a real elephant, of course. I wouldn't clip a karabiner to the end of a real elephant's trunk.

It's actually a concrete lorry dressed up to look like an elephant. There's a frame attached to the top of the cab in the shape of an elephant's head. The head is designed to be strong enough to hold my weight, whilst being light enough that we could lift it into place to attach it to the cab.

Attached to the head, stretching over the top of the whole lorry is another frame of carbon fibre tent poles supporting an elephant costume. This has been stitched together out of lightweight grey fabric. But the sheer size of it makes it extremely heavy and cumbersome to get into place.

It took seven of us to dress the concrete lorry up for this stunt.

All seven of us expect to spend some time in prison for what we're doing today. We are, of course, not the only people involved. Friends and friends of friends have played roles in getting us to where we are. Most of these people knew few details of the action. It had to be on a need-to-know basis. You never know who's an undercover cop and who's being watched. The people who helped did so because they trusted our judgement on the details of this action. Between them, they've put in an extraordinary amount of work.

I hope they're pleased with the result.

Annie from Fred's camp made the elephant costume. She hired out the village hall and got some other local supporters of their protest to help stitch it. They didn't know what the costume was for at all, just that we needed it for an environmental protest.

Thomas, a lorry driver from our protest back in Kent, was supposed to be taking the concrete lorry to the construction site of a skyscraper. Hundreds of lorry loads of concrete are being poured into the ground there to build a building, the purpose of which is to make money for people who are already rich. It's owned via a tax haven. We have no concerns about costing them money.

He drove the lorry to where we were waiting and handed it over to us. We're concerned about Thomas. He says it's fine. A friend of his who's a cleaner where he works has tidied away all traces of him from the personnel and transport records. No one really notices cleaners and they have access to all areas of a business. I hope she's done a thorough job.

The costs, the material for the costume, the banners and travel money were funded through a donation by a friend, who supports us but doesn't have the time to join in herself. And no, it's not Linda McCartney, just in case there's any confusion.

I could have used some of the travel money myself and taken a train up here, but I quite like hitching. With hindsight, maybe the train would have been a more enjoyable option just this once.

We're on our way to the headquarters of one of the worlds largest oil companies. We pass a BBC outside-broadcast van, which is sat at the side of the road. The ones with a big extending aerial out of the top.

As we go past it, we accelerate, creating a

gap behind us. The van pulls out into the gap and follows us.

Over the sounds of the traffic, I can hear No Leaders For The Free by P.A.I.N. playing on a sound system somewhere in the distance.

Everyone is staring at us, no doubt wondering what this giant elephant is doing in Central London. Children are waving at me and I'm waving back at them. They must think this is some sort of free circus. In a way, I guess it is.

Prof is on the pavement, just outside the building we're targetting, talking to a police officer. I can't hear what he's saying from here, but the police officer is looking at him, almost like he's staring straight through him. He's nodding along like one of those nodding dogs you get in cars. He looks like he's trying to follow what Prof says, but the glazed look in his eyes shows that he's completely lost.

Whatever Prof's saying, it's working. His role right now is to distract the police, and that police officer is definitely distracted.

Fred is halfway up a lamppost on the other side of the road. She drops a length of string to Fishhead, who runs across the road and hands it to Monk. As soon as Monk has the string, he starts climbing and within no time at all, he's at the top of his lamppost.

The police officer is still lost in whatever world Prof has created for him.

We come to a halt right next to the pair of them and slowly turn to the right to block both lanes and the entrance to the oil company's car park.

I pull the cord which releases the elephant costume, allowing it to drop to the floor. Until now, it's been held off the ground like a woman in the olden days might hold up her skirt when curtsying. The engine begins to rev noisily and I can hear the concrete pouring out of the back of the lorry under the elephant costume and slopping onto the ground.

The chute has been adapted so that the concrete pours mainly between the rear wheels of the lorry. If we can stay here long enough for the concrete to start setting, this lorry is going to become very difficult to move. In places, the concrete is starting to push against the bottom of the costume, causing it to bulge.

The engine stops and I can hear Prof still talking to the police officer, who's entirely oblivious to what's happening around him. Prof's voice is warm and calming and there's a dull monotony to the rhythm of his words.

'This decimal system needs investigating.

If you divide one by three,

you get nought point three three three recurring.

If you then multiply nought point three three three recurring by three,

you get nought point nine nine nine recurring.
Where has the other part gone?
It is an infinitesimally small quantity,
	but it disappears every time someone divides
one by three
	and that must happen a lot.
If you add all up those infinitesimally small
amounts,
	the sum is still infinitesimally small,
	but that's not really the point.
The point is that it's missing
	and no one seems to be investigating where it's
gone.'

The police officer has stopped nodding now and is just standing there, staring through Prof with a completely blank expression on his face.

Madcap gets out of the cab of the lorry and locks the door. I throw down a rope and she climbs up to join me. I've sat on many diggers with Madcap, but this is the first time we've shared a view of Central London like this.

I take a flask of tea out of my bag and pour us each a cup.

Fred and Monk are nearly at the top of their lampposts. Monk did well to climb at that speed with a heavy rucksack on his back, but then climbing is what he's best at. If he wasn't trying to save the world, he could be some sort of Olympic climber,

I reckon. I don't know if they have climbing in the Olympics, but if they did, I'd put my money on Monk.

The police officer is still staring blankly while absorbed in Prof's never ending spiel.

'... If we had the duo-decimal system, we wouldn't have this problem.

You can divide twelve by two, three and four without any issue.

It's not as neat for a fifth as the decimal system is,

but it doesn't lose any along the way,
and we wouldn't use fifths as much anyway
if we were counting in twelves.
When you get back to the station,
you should talk to your superiors
and establish an ongoing investigation
into the missing quantity,
however small it is.'

The outside broadcast van has raised its ariel and a woman with a TV camera is standing next to it, filming the elephant, Madcap and me.

A police car has pulled up on the end of the road. It can't get any nearer to us because there's a great big elephant blocking the traffic and the traffic is blocking their way.

The police run towards us. It's quite a long way to run wearing a uniform and carrying all the tat they have hanging off their belts.

Meanwhile, Fred and Monk are beginning the process of unfurling their banner above my head. First Fred pulls the string which Monk has now attached a rope to. When Fred has the rope, she uses that to pull the banner which is in Monk's rucksack until she has one end of it. Then they release the bottom of the banner at both ends.

It's almost as long as the road is wide and reads 'Climate Change is the Elephant in the Room'.

One of the police officers running towards us has almost reached the elephant when Prof turns towards him, turns back to the police officer he's been speaking to all this time and shouts 'Impersonating a police officer!'

The police officer Prof has been speaking to then comes instantly out of his trance, turns to the approaching police officer and confronts him. When the rest of the police arrive, slightly out of breath, they find two police officers in some unexplained dispute, being filmed for the TV.

For a moment, they just stand there, trying to work out what to do, then they physically intervene.

Prof has quietly stepped aside and is now over talking to the BBC reporter. I don't know the reporter's name. I rarely watch TV these days, but I've seen him on the news.

It's no coincidence they followed us onto

the bridge. Madcap met them when Monk was pretending to hang himself. They were just told where to wait and to "follow the elephant". Prof didn't meet them when Madcap did, because like me he was getting a lift in the police van by the time they turned up.

Now, by the way the film crew are standing around listening to him, it looks like he's telling them a story. I can't hear what he's saying over the noise of the police who all seem to be shouting at each other at the same time.

I'm fully aware of the irony of all this. This action will cause more environmental impact than I normally cause in a year. The concrete has an impact, the congestion we're causing has an impact, the damage to the lorry has an impact and the clear up will also have an impact.

We discussed this at length when we were deciding whether to do this and how to carry it out. We lost one member of the team who thought the environmental impact was too high to justify and decided not to continue.

I'm under no illusion that we'll be seen as heroes. We'll be pilloried in the press. They'll highlight the environmental impact of this action and use it to belittle us, but in doing so, they'll talk about the issues we're trying to highlight.

This action will inconvenience ordinary

people, but that inconvenience is nothing compared with the inconvenience of climate change when the effects start to be seen. Some will say they support the cause but we're going about it the wrong way. They said this about the suffragettes and people who fought fascism in the 1930s.

They'll say it about us, but the only reason they'll discuss these issues is because of people like us who are doing what we can to highlight them. We'll be given airtime, if only so that they can ridicule us.

Hopefully some of our message will get out in the process.

I'd love to believe that we can solve the crisis we're facing by signing petitions and writing to our MPs, but that would be entirely ineffectual. My local MP is often at dinners sponsored by oil companies. A letter would receive a bland generic response and then be ignored.

I have a vote, but even if I didn't live in a safe Tory seat, neither of the main parties are proposing the dramatic changes we need to ensure the world remains habitable. The establishment has clearly recognised the power of the Labour party and assimilated it. It'll do nothing to challenge the status quo under the current leadership, who seem to take their instructions from Rupert Murdoch.

If a party did propose the dramatic changes

that are required, they would be going up against the whole of the establishment to implement them.

This action will not in itself bring about major change, but as part of a growing movement it will help to chip away at the system which controls us and is destroying the planet we live on.

Hopefully, it will inspire people to take action in a way that suits their skills and their circumstances. I'm single and have no dependents or responsibilities. As much as the prospect terrifies me, I can afford to spend some time in prison. Some people are marching today, others are doing sit-ins in various strategic places. There's a black fax campaign against The Sun newspaper. By faxing black sheets to them, you can clog up their fax machines with ink so that subsequent faxes are unreadable. Attacking their communication technology is an effective way to disarm those who act against the interests of the people and the planet.

That meteorologist had a point, not just in relation to climate change, but in relation to most of the issues the human race faces; the tools are there to solve these problems, but they are in the hands of people who are not interested in solving them.

We need the people of the world to rise up against the establishment and demand change. We need the powers that be to know they have no choice but to get out of the way and accept that change.

Public support alone is not enough. In the same way that we have made it more expensive to build roads through prime habitat by sitting on diggers and camping in the trees, we need to go much further and make every action that destroys the earth too expensive to be profitable.

The only way we can do that is to make it clear that the structures which prevent change will be completely and utterly destroyed. They will keep making laws like the Criminal Justice Act as an attempt to stifle protest, but we must not let them stop us.

They need to see we're desperate and will take desperate action. Whatever the costs of acting, we must bear in mind that the costs of not acting are far greater.

The police seem to be getting themselves together now. Soon, they'll start the process of working out how to remove Madcap and me from the elephant and remove the elephant from the bridge. This will now become a race between them and the setting concrete.

It looks like the TV crew are preparing to broadcast. The reporter has got hold of the microphone and the woman with the camera seems to be getting ready to film him with the elephant and us in the background. Another member of the crew, I don't know what his job is, is doing something with technical-looking equipment of some sort.

Prof is still chatting with them. The person whose been doing stuff with equipment hands the microphone to Prof, who's standing in front of the camera with his back to me. The reporter moves over to stand next to the camera and lifts one hand in the air, with his forefinger pointing to the sky.

Looking straight at Prof, he counts down. 'Five, four, three.'

Prof lifts the microphone to his mouth.

'Two, one.' The reporter brings his pointing finger down as if he was conducting an orchestra.

Prof speaks straight into the camera.

Final Thoughts

I often think about that little boy carrying milk back from the farm down the road.

I've got a lot of time for thinking these days.

There's only so much to observe here. I know the number of bricks in each wall of my cell and I can recognise the screws by the sound of their footsteps as they walk up and down the landing, with their keys jangling in time with their stride.

With so little stimulation, your mind wanders back through your life and you're bound to think through all the possibilities, paths you didn't walk down, opportunities you didn't take, decisions you made and people you met.

What would have happened if I hadn't had that lift?

What would have happened if I hadn't listened

to that person?

Other people seem to go through life unconcerned by the issues society faces.

I don't know if I should ask why I care so much, or why they care so little.

In a strange way, the world is brought into clear focus in here. The drab interior of the cell contrasts with the vivid colours in my memory.

As I recall my previous experiences, they are brighter and more real than they've ever been. When I think about the countryside I grew up in, I can hear the voices of our neighbours as clearly as if they were speaking to me now.

Recalling my first lift with Madcap and Prof, I can taste the stew Mary fed us.

When I think about riding back from that party on Blaze's bike, I can feel the cool, wet mist on my face.

I can see the woman in the poll tax riot, with her head cracked open. I can see the blood running down her face. I can see the blood soaked baby in her arms.

I wish I couldn't, but I can. I think about that baby sometimes.

When I get out, I'm going to savour every moment. I'm going to eat great food, party through the night into the early morning and watch the sunrise with a rekindled love for life and freedom.

I know, however that the feasting and partying will only take me so far.

It doesn't matter if I'm optimistic or pessimistic.

I have to act for my own sanity whether or not it will make a difference. I have to act to make the world a better place, so I can sleep at night, knowing my day has been worthwhile and that I am worthwhile.

Whilst I immerse myself in the pleasures of each day, I will do what I can to sow the seeds for a better tomorrow.